A NOVEL

-•THE•-

GNOME
EXCHANGE
PROGRAM

NORTH POLE RESCUE

A NOVEL

THE

GNOME EXCHANGE PROGRAM

NORTH POLE RESCUE

MATT CALIRI

SWEETWATER
BOOKS

An imprint of Cedar Fort, Inc.
Springville, Utah

ISBN 13: 978-1-4621-2012-3

Published by Sweetwater Books, an imprint of Cedar Fort, Inc.,
2373 W. 700 S., Springville, UT 84663
Distributed by Cedar Fort, Inc. www.cedarfort.com

Names: Caliri, Matt, 1979- author.
Title: The gnome exchange program : North Pole rescue / Matt Caliri.
Description: Springville, Utah : Sweetwater Books, an Imprint of Cedar Fort,
   Inc., [2017] | Summary: Santa asks Geronimo, a gnome, to help save
   Christmas from his evil brother Krampus.
Identifiers: LCCN 2017018879 (print) | LCCN 2017026710 (ebook) | ISBN
   9781462127719 (epub and moby) | ISBN 9781462120123 (perfect bound : alk.
   paper)
Subjects: | CYAC: Gnomes--Fiction. | Santa Claus--Fiction. |
   Christmas--Fiction. | LCGFT: Christmas fiction. | Novels.
Classification: LCC PZ7.1.C313 (ebook) | LCC PZ7.1.C313 Gn 2017 (print) | DDC
   [Fic]--dc23
LC record available at https://lccn.loc.gov/2017018879

Cover design by Priscilla Chaves
Back cover design by Katie Payne
Cover design © 2017 by Cedar Fort, Inc.
Edited and typeset by Erica Myers

Printed in the United States of America

10 9 8 7 6 5 4 3 2 1

Printed on acid-free paper

To my parents, the real Mr. and Mrs. Claus

"Be soft. Do not let the world make you hard. Do not let pain make you hate. Do not let the bitterness steal your sweetness. Take pride that even though the rest of the world may disagree, you still believe it to be a beautiful place."

⤳ Kurt Vonnegut ↢

⬱PROLOGUE⬱

Long ago in the dark, early hours of the morning, two odd-looking figures crept down a knoll and into a sleeping village. Shrouded in mist, they moved undetected in the morning darkness. The larger figure was round and towering with a big, brown beard. The smaller figure was shiny, slimy, and skeleton-thin. The larger one laid his heavy sack down while the smaller one slipped an apple barrel off his back. The two travelers plopped down on the soft night grass. Krampus turned to his half brother, Nicholas, and said, "It's too early for this. I don't understand why we can't do this in the daytime, after lunch."

"Krampus, everybody would see us," said Nicholas. "It would ruin it."

"Ruin what?" asked Krampus.

"The mystery . . . the magic . . ." Nicholas's eyes twinkled as he looked over the small village below. "People don't always want reasons for how things got there, or why it's there. They're just happy to have it."

"Joy makes me nauseous," said Krampus. "Let's get this over with." The two figures sauntered down the hill toward the first

1

hut. Krampus pushed gently on the door. As the door opened, the moonlight shone on a mouse scurrying across the floorboards. The room was vacant.

"Anything?" Nicholas asked. He towered over the door and had to bend his mammoth frame in order to peer over Krampus's shoulder.

"Not a sound I hear. Except for a mouse," said Krampus. He stepped inside and swiveled around to face Nicholas. He stuck his scrawny, ash-colored arm out and said, "Nicholas, you're not gonna fit through this doorway. Give me the bag of junk."

"You watch your tongue, Krampus," Nicholas boomed. "My little friends worked hard to make these toys. But you're right," Nicholas continued, "I'm gonna have to find another way to spread joy without anyone finding out about it." Nicholas's gaze found the roof of the hut and lingered there.

"That's how crazy people talk," said Krampus as he took the bag from Nicholas. Krampus then crept deeper into the room, leaving the door open. He walked up to a tiny spruce that stood against a small frosty window. Kneeling down, he rifled through the big brown sack. "What did this one want?" he muttered to himself. "The horse? Drum set? Book of fairy tales?"

Nicholas answered but not to the question Krampus asked. "The roof!" Nicholas shouted. "I should arrive on the roof! Go down the chimney or something."

Krampus sat cross-legged surrounded by mounds of toys. "Chimney? How're you going to get down a chimney if you can't get through a door?"

"I don't know, but it sure makes the whole thing a lot more interesting." Compelled by inspiration, Nicholas walked outside to examine the roof.

"Nicholas," Krampus said, not realizing Nicholas had walked off out of earshot. "Forget about the roof for two seconds, and tell me which one of these worthless pieces of trash is staying in this particular hut."

"The penguin," said a tiny voice in the corner of the room.

Six-year-old Nancy, dressed in red and green striped pajamas, stepped out of the far shadows of the room and into the moonlight that beamed through the window.

"What are you doing walking around in the middle of the night, Nancy?" asked Krampus.

"How do you know my name?" asked Nancy.

Krampus finally stepped out of the pool of shadows that seemed to have cloaked him since entering the village. He was now completely visible to the girl as he crept toward her. Nancy's jaw dropped at the sight of his scaly skin, his elongated jaw, his red, veiny eyes, and the birch branches that sprouted out of his head, twisted and gnarled. Her eyes welled with tears as Krampus approached her. She was frozen with fear. When he was just a few feet from Nancy, Krampus rolled his tongue out of his snout. The length of it nearly reached the floor.

"We know all about you, Nancy," said Krampus. He stopped his advance a few inches from her nose. "We know how good you've been, how bad you've been." He leaned into her ear and hissed, "We made a lissssssst." Krampus's tongue flickered against her ear. She finally let loose a horrible wail.

Outside, Nicholas heard the child's scream while ice-sculpting the bust of a reindeer. Nicholas sucked in the icy air in a panic. He ran back to the house, but it was too late. By the time Nicholas got to the door, the inside of the hut was illuminated with people holding candles and moving about in search of Nancy. The whole family was up, bustling about in confusion. Two toddlers, a boy and a girl, started looking under beds and inside hampers. Nancy's mother was yelling her daughter's name in the backyard over and over and over. Nancy's father swept through the hut in a mad search. Nancy and Krampus were nowhere to be seen.

"Ho, there!" belted Nicholas. Nancy's mother, father, and younger brother froze in their spots and turned toward the door. What they saw was the largest man they had ever seen. He had big brown boots the size of fruit baskets, and his tree-trunk legs lead to a potbelly that jiggled and swayed as he stammered before them. He had rosy cheeks and a thick brown beard that framed his mouth's horrified expression. His eyes, while an icy blue, were warm, tender, and somehow life-affirming. The family slowly drew near him like a beacon of light. They held each other as they looked up at the fantastic human specimen.

"I'll get your daughter back," was all Nicholas could think to say. "This is all my fault, and I'm deeply sorry." After a moment, Nicholas continued, "On a related note, do you know where I could find any reindeer around here?"

PART 1

1

ALL GNOMES LOVE TREES

Moonlight flickered through the swaying leaves of the Great Oak Diner. The leaves appeared to wave goodbye to the gnomes as their little bodies crawled down branches and headed for home. It was past 9:30, late for any gnome, but especially trying for Geronimo. He couldn't stand these tree-house restaurants. He was very much against the idea of hanging out in a tree while trying to eat. Trying to enjoy inchworm tacos while food from other patrons rain down on you from higher branches, no thank you. His parents, on the other hand, loved eating in trees, as did any other self-respecting gnome. Geronimo just didn't have the heart to tell them how he really felt. And keeping this secret was hard for him, since he hated keeping secrets. He rarely ever lied, and when he did, it was usually out of sheer panic. He was positive the truth would horrify his parents. *All gnomes love trees*, they would say. *What exactly is your problem?*

Geronimo scanned what was left of the Saturday night dinner crowd—nothing but half-empty bowls of grasshopper salad being pecked on by Hermit Thrush and Whip-poor-wills. Busboys would collect the dishes and then zip line them to the kitchen in a far-off tree. The restaurant was closing down around them. His rotating gaze of the dinner crowd finally fell on his parents sitting snug beside him on the same branch, beaming back at him.

All he wanted was to go home and have his birthday dinner be over. This was not just a birthday dinner, after all. This was a going-away dinner. His parents were shipping him off to the North Pole. They sat grinning from pointy ear to pointy ear, as if this was the best thing that could've ever happened to their son. Geronimo loved his parents, Harold and Penelope, but at the moment, he could not stand looking at their faces. He tried a new tactic and slowly let his eyelids drop, pretending to fall asleep in front of them.

"Geronimo?" hushed his dad. Geronimo kept his eyes closed. He was winning. Suddenly, he felt cold water splash against his face. He gasped, eyes popping open.

"Bdahh! What was that for?" Geronimo exclaimed.

"Listen, sweetie," his mom said, "we know you're not crazy about this exchange program, but we wouldn't push so hard if we didn't think it was for the best."

"And let's be honest, kiddo," said his dad, "you don't have many friends."

"Harold," said Penelope, "You can't just say something like that. Geronimo has plenty of friends."

"Whether you're aware of it or not, Penny," said Harold, "our son is a bit of a loner."

Penelope glared at Harold.

"It's true, Mom," said Geronimo. "I am a bit of a loner. All told I have two-and-a-half friends." He took a pencil out of his shirt pocket and started to scribble on a crumpled napkin. His parents watched him in silence for a few moments until his dad said, "Momo, you're not drawing those silly unicorns again, are you?"

"They're not silly," he replied, his face reddening as he put his pencil back in his shirt. He gazed at the drawing before putting it back in the pocket of his shorts. It was a picture of him riding a unicorn in outer space.

"That's why this would be such a great opportunity for you," said his father. "It will get you out of your head. This is a chance to go on a real adventure, not just one of your dreamed-up ones on a napkin. You'll meet all walks of life, experiencing things you could only dream of. You'll be thanking us in the end, champ. Trust me. Heck, I wish I could go!"

"Why don't you?" asked Geronimo.

"I can't," said his dad.

"I just can't believe you're sending me away on my birthday," said Geronimo. With big sad eyes, he looked up at the stars through the flitting leaves. "For my birthday I get the gift of exile."

"Don't be so dramatic," said his mother. "Give it a chance. If you don't like it, you can come back."

"You know what I would like is to get off this tree and go to sleep," Geronimo finally confessed. His parents nodded their heads in silent consent. They all stood and walked toward the trunk for their long, slow descent to the ground below.

"Did you say goodbye to Eleanor?" his mother asked as they scaled the trunk together. "I would hope so since you leave tomorrow."

"Of course I did," Geronimo lied.

2
TOO CHANCY, DON'T DO IT

Geronimo sat studiously over the unassembled toy rocket, glaring down at countless bits and pieces of gray and red plastic. He had been in the North Pole for a week now and had yet to complete the assembly of a single toy. To give you an idea of how bad this was, a first-year toymaker averaged twelve assembled toys a day. Geronimo knew this because it was brought up to him every day at lunchtime by a seemingly new elf. His incompetency left him feeling isolated and miserable. With his head bowed, his pointy green hat sloped down his face and slid over his nose, causing him to sneeze. The force of the sneeze spread the toy pieces clear off his workbench. The noise was so disruptive that all four hundred elves in the Great Hall stopped their work to scowl at him.

At the behest of his parents, Geronimo had filled out an application last year to switch places with one of Santa's elves for a Christmas season. An elf that wanted to try something different, like holding guard in front of a house, would be exchanged with a gnome who was feeling equally out of sorts and wanted to try his luck working for Santa. So far, Geronimo had experienced no luck. He was clearly not cut out for this toy-making business.

"Hey, Geronimo," said Clarence, the Floor Manager, shaking Geronimo from his thoughts, "The boss wants to see you."

"In his office?" Geronimo asked.

"No, in his sled," quipped Clarence. The entire hall erupted with elfin laughter, a silvery sharp, machine-gun tempo. Geronimo blushed. "Yes," Clarence replied, "in his office."

Geronimo walked down the assembly line. Shiny metals and squeaky plastics moved through the hall on multi-level belts that never stopped moving. Countless elfin hands turned, twisted, and screwed parts together that rolled their way. All through the work the elves looked mirthful, even grateful. There seemed to be something in their genetic make-up that was missing in Geronimo's DNA. Maybe Santa could give him a pill or something.

Walking into Santa's office, Geronimo saw the walls painted in candy cane stripes with maroons and grays, giving it an earthy, toned-down Christmas feeling. A fire snapped and crackled in the corner of the room as the big man sat comfortably behind his plastic foldout table. Santa was wearing a plain white undershirt and shorts that could pass as boxers. With just a small rolodex and a few manila folders laid out in front of him, he resembled more of a car salesman than a mythic hero.

Geronimo appeared in the doorway.

"You look tired," Santa said in a rich baritone voice. "Feel free to lie down if you like." He pointed toward the green, velvet couch.

Santa grabbed two glasses from the cabinet. "Eggnog?" he asked, gesturing toward the rows of holiday-themed drinks behind the glass doors of Santa's jumbo-sized mini fridge.

"No thanks. I can't stand the stuff," Geronimo replied.

"I know how you feel. Between you and me, I haven't had a glass of nog since Christmas '93. The year Dasher left . . ." Santa averted his eyes and fell silent. A silver tear rolled down his rosy right cheek. Santa's tears were the color of tinsel. Geronimo would have been more amazed at this rare sighting if it wasn't for the even stronger feeling of guilt he now felt over making Santa cry.

"I'm sorry, Santa."

"Don't give it another thought," said the big man, wiping the tear from his cheek. Santa walked to the window behind his desk, switching the subject as he switched his location. Outside, the Antarctic sun was setting over a white, frosty horizon. "Anyhow," he began, "it's no secret on the floor that making toys isn't your cup of peppermint tea."

"So you're sending me back?" said Geronimo.

"No," Santa replied, "no, we don't do that here, unless you want to go back. We don't return toys and we don't return workers. Don't care if they're elf, gnome, or butterfly."

"You hire butterflies?"

"Not yet. But I'm open to it. My question to you is do you want to keep going?"

"Yes," Geronimo said, shocked at his own answer. "But I don't want to make toys anymore. There has to be something else I can do around here. Do you need someone to watch movies?"

Santa shook his head while gently swirling his cider.

Have you ever heard of the PBA?" asked Santa.

"I can't say I have. Are they a hip-hop group?"

"The Polar Bear Alliance," said Santa. He then stood up from his chair and pulled a screen down from behind his desk.

Geronimo thought he was looking at some sort of war zone. On the screen were military schematics sprawled over what looked like large territories of land. It reminded him of the board game

11

Risk, which he had been working on in the shop earlier that week. The project was reassigned after they discovered Geronimo was renaming the board game boxes to *TOO CHANCEY, DON'T DO IT.*

Tacked on Santa's war map were photos of polar bears, elves gone AWOL, rabid reindeers, and giant electric turtles. There was another photo placed high up on the map and separate from the others. To Geronimo, the figure in the photo resembled a baby gargoyle. The baby gargoyle photo was connected to the other photos with a red marker.

"This may look like a harmonious, freely operating enterprise," said Santa, "but whatever autonomy we have created for ourselves has only been earned by fighting those who seek to destroy us. I am speaking, of course, of the Polar Bear's Alliance with my half brother, Krampus.'

"Mr. Claus," said Geronimo, "I'm afraid you lost me at 'autonomy.'"

"Please let me finish," said Santa, "The Polar Bear Alliance has been gaining power with their new allegiance, Krampus."

"He's your half -brother?"

"Yes, it's a long story. I'm sorry if this seems like a lot to digest, but we have very little time to work with. For the past five hundred years, pulling off Christmas has literally been a miracle."

"I didn't sign up to be a part of a military operation, sir," said Geronimo.

"Please, call me Santa," said Santa.

"I didn't sign up to be part of any military operation, Santa," repeated Geronimo.

"Geronimo, I respect any thoughts or decisions you may have on the matter. But first let me ask you one question: do you want to keep trying to make a toy on the assembly line, or do you want to help save Christmas for at least one more year? There's a war on joy out there, kid," said Santa, "it's time to pick your side."

I should be standing on the front lawn of 618 Black Cherry Ln, Geronimo thought. *I should be guarding that chunk of grass in front of the purple house. I miss going on walks with Eleanor. I miss watching her through the window from the garden, eating breakfast with her mom and dad, and laughing.*

"I know about your gnomic blood, Geronimo," Santa broke in, opening up a manila folder lying on his desk with "Geronimo" scribbled on it in green crayon. "Historically, your people are seven times stronger than men, can run at speeds of thirty-five miles per hour, and possess better eyesight than a hawk," said Santa. He leaned in and added, "You are the right gnome for the job. You could be my little secret weapon."

"First off, all the super skills you mentioned? That's, like, our best guys," said Geronimo. "And you have to be a full-grown gnome to pull most of that stuff off."

There was a quiet knock at the door. "Come on in, Clarence," said Santa. Clarence opened the door. "Sorry to interrupt, but there's been an assembly crash with the pelican vacuum cleaners," said Clarence.

"I'll be right there," Santa replied. Clarence retreated back onto the floor.

"I need an answer, Geronimo."

"What would I be doing?"

"We'll sneak you into the Polar Bear Country Club where they have a map to Krampus's castle. Find the map and then use it to locate and apprehend my brother. Then bring him to me unharmed."

"Oh, is that all?"

"For now."

"How come you don't just go get him yourself? Don't you know where your own brother lives?"

"No, I don't. To be honest, we've sort of drifted apart these last 1,700 years or so."

"Wow," replied Geronimo. "That's a lot of drifting. Listen, can I just tell it to you plain, Santa?"

Santa nodded.

"This whole thing feels like a far-fetched action movie. I am just not gonna be able to *do* all that. I got worn out just hearing you talk about it. And what's the deal with Krampus, anyway?"

Santa rolled up his war map. He folded his arms, his eyes squinting at Geronimo, "He has a long, creepy tongue, birch branches sprouting from his head, and a nasty attitude. He'll probably try and eat you."

"Okay," said Geronimo, "so you're sending me on a pretty much impossible mission full of demons and bears that want to eat me. What do I get if I succeed?"

"Nothing," said Santa, "it's just something you might find meaningful."

"I'm not buying it," said Geronimo.

"Okay then, we're done here," said Santa. He got out of his chair and walked toward the door, visibly annoyed. "I'll have to find someone else," he said. "Please excuse me, I must see to these pelican vacuum cleaners. We'll discuss your future at another time." Did he just tell off Santa? Who did he think he was?

"Wait!" cried Geronimo. Santa casually stopped in his tracks with his hand on the red ornament-shaped doorknob. What's the one thing that could sweeten the deal? The one thing in life he's desired more than anything else? *That's easy*, he thought.

"Any chance I get to ride a unicorn?"

Santa sighed and stared back at him. "Doubtful," he said. "They're out of season."

"Okay," said Geronimo, "I'll do it."

3

HERE COMES PEANUT BUTTER

P er Santa's instructions, Geronimo stood under a full moon beside a sled full of miniature spruce trees. He was waiting for a creature named T.C. "Basically a slightly smaller version of a centaur," Santa told him. Geronimo had not been waiting long when T.C. trotted out of the shadows. Above the waist, T.C. wore a red-and-white-checkered-shirt, had pointy elf ears, a brown, burly moustache, and reindeer antlers. Below the waist, he was all reindeer: four strong, sturdy legs and a coat of brown that matched his moustache.

"Hello, Geronimo," T.C. began, "my name is Tony. Tony Curtis. Most people call me T.C."

"Oh," said Geronimo, feigning interest.

"'Oh' is right. I'll also accept, 'Ho ho ho.'"

Geronimo stared back at him, his arms folded as if he were waiting in an elevator.

"No sense of humor, check," said T.C., turning his rump to the gnome.

"I get it," said Geronimo. He scurried over to face T.C., eager not to tick off another member of Santa's community. "Like Santa, 'Ho ho ho . . .'"

T.C. blinked back at him a few times. "So here's the story," he said, "you're gonna hide in this wagon full of mini Christmas trees we're selling to the PBCC. Are you familiar with the PBCC?"

"Prune-Based Catholic Charities?"

"No. It stands for the Polar Bear Country Club, where they keep the map to Krampus's castle. Donner and Schnitzel will help fly us over there and then I'll sneak you into the joint."

"There's a reindeer named Schnitzel?" asked Geronimo.

"Yes. He's German stock. Listen, we're sneaking you into the country club via their order of teeny tiny Christmas trees. They love tiny things, the polar bears. It's a genuine curiosity. Wait till you see how small their walls are." Geronimo listened to T.C. with a dull and confused expression.

"Anyway," T.C. continued, "once inside the club, make sure you read the detailed instructions Santa wrote for you and folded up and placed near the bottom of the wagon. The instructions will give you ideas where the map might be. Just make sure the polar bears don't find out about you or your plans, unless you want to be beaten into bite-sized wafers."

"I don't like this mission anymore. I want out," said Geronimo. "No one's even trying to sell it. It's just pure danger."

"Trust me, this plan will work. You're four times smarter and quicker than those big, furry oafs. And if by chance you're discovered, just tell them gnome meat is poisonous. It works every time."

Geronimo shook his head as he climbed inside the cart. "This isn't an exchange program," Geronimo said as he shimmied his body into the prickly needles, "this is an ex-gnome program. A suicide mission if I've ever seen one." Geronimo quickly sank below the branches and out of sight.

"Can you breathe?" asked T.C.

"Barely," Geronimo muffled.

"Perfect." said T.C. He picked up the sled handles and trotted into the long shadows of the forest. Waves of sleepiness rolled over the gnome, and before long he was out like a light.

When he finally came to, he twitched and jerked his body completely out of the cart and onto pebbled ground. He was now wide-awake, and in pain.

"Whoa there, gnome," said T.C. in a tense whisper. "That's a heck of a way to get yourself going in the morning."

Geronimo got up. His knees shook from inactivity. He looked around him and saw what looked like the entrance to a fancy country club, one that you might see in Hawaii. Sunshine glinted over palm trees, waterfalls, and grassy hills. Shining gloriously above the large stone atrium ten yards from where they stood were the gold letters "PBCC." The grounds of the country club were dotted with cabins, suites, and ranches. Sports facilities were splayed out evenly throughout a grid of streets that comprised the club property. The property line was in the shape of a circle, designated by a three-foot wall made of marble and mounted with cannons. The wall was built so small that most polar bears could actually step over it.

"Where are we?" Geronimo asked. "How long have I been sleeping?"

"I'm sorry, Geronimo," said T.C. "Santa was right. I should have put in more sleepy-time powder in the trees. We're four hundred light-years from Earth via the wormhole we went through back there. Trust me, when you want to get from point A to point Z without all the letters in between, wormholes are the way to go."

Geronimo staggered backward, shocked. "What?" he yelled.

T.C. walked toward the gnome with his fingers at his lips. "Shhh," he whispered, sidling up to Geronimo. They both turned their gazes to the compound entrance.

"We have to keep our voices down. We're uninvited guests."

"I thought we were delivering trees."

"Yes, but it's what you would call a 'surprise delivery.'"

"Great," said Geronimo with an eye-roll, "I'm sure this will go over well." He buried himself back into the cart.

"What's all the racket out there?" bellowed a voice from inside the compound.

T.C. froze for an instant, paralyzed with fear. Snapping out of it, he rolled the cart toward the atrium. A drawbridge lowered in front of them as they got closer, allowing them to cross over a deep ravine in the ground a few feet from the wall. As the drawbridge touched down at the foot of the wall, the giant front door of a building labeled "Business and Registration" crept open. T.C. broke into a slow trot across the drawbridge.

"Peanut butter's coming out," whispered T.C.

"Peanut butter?" whispered back Geronimo.

"Code for 'polar bears,'" said T.C.

The polar bear walking toward them looked like he was on vacation. It wore Bermuda shorts, dark sunglasses, and a Phoenix Suns basketball jersey. Nestled within the pines, Geronimo was once again falling asleep. He could barely make out their initial exchange before he was completely out.

"Hot enough for you, tree peddler?" asked the polar bear.

"Some like it hot, I suppose," said T.C.

4

MR. SCRATCH AND
MISS PRISCILLA

Back on planet Earth, an elf named Murdock had finally arrived at the front lawn of 618 Black Cherry Ln. Murdock was the exchange elf in the Gnome Exchange Program, and he was currently staring at a garden hose in Eleanor's backyard, stock-still and frozen with fear.

"What are you doing in my yard?" shouted eleven-year-old Eleanor from the screen door of the back patio. She slid open the screen door and slammed it behind her with a noise so loud it brought a shudder down the elf's tiny spine. She stomped across the patio and down onto the grass. When she came to a halt, she widened her stance into a defensive posture. She wore jeans caked in dirt and a G.I. Joe T-shirt. Her hands were on her waist. "Where is Geronimo?" she asked Murdock.

"He didn't tell you?" Murdock asked. His eyes were still on the garden hose. He spoke with a crisp, clear tone of voice that can only naturally develop at the high altitudes of the North Pole. "There's been an exchange," said Murdock, "me and your gnome friend are part of the Gnome Exchange Program. I'm not surprised he failed to tell you all this. I hear gnomes are horrible with good-byes. Nevertheless, my name is Murdock. I'm an elf."

Eleanor broke into tears. "How could he? How could he leave without saying good-bye?" she cried.

Murdock broke his glare from the garden hose and finally looked at Eleanor. "I'm sorry, Francine. He should've done the right thing and told you he was leaving."

"My name is not Francine, it's Eleanor!" exclaimed Eleanor.

Murdock took a scrap of paper from the pocket of his white vest. He briefly examined it and then put it back in his pocket. His cheeks blushed. "Sorry, you're right. It is Eleanor," he said.

"Of course it's Eleanor!" she yelled, angry that her name appeared still up for debate.

"It's funny because my mother's name was Francine," said Murdock, his face slack and thoughtful.

"Where is Geronimo? And when are you leaving?" asked Eleanor.

"I'll tell you everything you want to know as soon as you remove that snake from your property." Murdock pointed to the hose with his eyes bugging out.

Eleanor looked at Murdock, and then the garden hose, then back at Murdock. She exploded with laughter. Murdock looked perplexed and embarrassed. "Well, not *your* property, of course. I meant your parents' property." Eleanor rolled on the grass in delight. "It's not that funny," said Murdock. She got up and ran to the hose and threw the loose end at Murdock.

Murdock screamed a horrible shrill, then leapt as if the object in flight was a grenade. He wound up in a clump five feet from where he had been standing. Eleanor was laughing so hard she could barely stand back up. "I see now it's a hose!" Murdock shouted in order to be heard over Eleanor's hysterics. "You don't suppose we could go inside and I could have a teensy cup of tea with a dash of nutmeg and clove? I can explain things much better when sitting in front of a nice cup of tea."

Exhausted now, Eleanor sat upright in the grass. She nodded slowly, considering the proposition. She then jabbed her finger toward Murdock like it was a switchblade and said, "If I catch you stealing anything, I'll throw you right out the window."

"Oh my," said Murdock.

"And I won't even bother to open the window first, either. You'll smash through all the glass."

"Oh, what a horrible thought. I wouldn't dream of stealing anything."

"Good," said Eleanor, "follow me."

Eleanor and Murdock sat at a small table in a child-sized parlor room. Sitting to the left of Murdock was Scratch the teddy bear. To the right of him was Priscilla the porcelain doll. Murdock looked around the table as he took a sip from his tiny teacup. "I didn't realize it would be a party."

"This is Mr. Scratch and Miss Priscilla," said Eleanor, "unfortunately they're not very interested in anything you have to say."

"Mmm."

"What's your name again?"

"Murdock. You can call me Murdock." Murdock turned his head to Scratch and muttered, "Have you been here long?"

"Don't bother," said Eleanor, "they're not interested. Mr. Murdock, all we're interested in knowing is where Geronimo is and when he'll be returning."

"I don't know where Geronimo is right now, but I received recent news from Santa himself that he's sent Geronimo on a secret mission of great importance."

"Santa Claus?" Eleanor repeated, thrown aback.

"Santa Claus," said Murdock.

Eleanor quickly recovered from this news as she furrowed her brow and looked out the window. "I have absolutely no respect for that man," she said.

"Are you trying to be funny?" gasped Murdock.

"Never. When is Geronimo coming back?" Eleanor repeated.

"Who knows?" said Murdock. "He might fail his mission. I might fail my mission. He may never come back. I may never come back! Some of it's up to you. Some of it isn't." This strange loop of questioning brought Eleanor to tears. "Oh, don't cry, Eleanor. Perhaps I was too blunt about the whole matter. Where *is* the babysitter, by the way?"

"She's upstairs on the phone."

"How old are you, Eleanor? It's not in your dossier."

"Eleven. How old are you?"

"Forty-two."

"You're older than my dad but smaller than his boots," said Eleanor.

Murdock moved his teeny cup to the side and leaned in. "I'm here, Eleanor, to turn you into a well-mannered young lady. And if that doesn't happen in time, you will be visited by a not very nice thing, which is already on the hunt for you. My mission is to simply keep you safe from his bloodthirsty plans. And the word floating around HQ is that if I succeed at my mission before Geronimo does, I get a vacation in the Poconos."

"Go poke your own nose," said Eleanor.

"It's a place, not a thing to do."

"Whatever. What is the 'not very nice thing' anyway? Some sort of big, mean dog?" asked Eleanor.

"I can't tell you," said Murdock, "because then you'll try and look it up and you'll get terribly, terribly frightened."

"What does Geronimo have to do?"

"He has to capture that not very nice thing and bring it back to Santa—alive."

"And what do you have to do?" asked Eleanor.

"I have to prevent the not very nice thing from finding you."

"What's his gripe against me?" asked Eleanor as she poured Miss Priscilla more pretend tea.

"Believe it or not," said Murdock as he added a dash of pretend cream to Mr. Scratch's cup, "you're near the top of his naughty list this year. You'd be a big catch for him."

"I'd like to see him try," said Eleanor. With that, she unveiled an orange Gatorade from somewhere under the table. She unscrewed the cap and started chugging the orange liquid with great vigor, all the while keeping a leery eye on Murdock. When she was finally done she gasped for air, screwed the cap back on, and placed the Gatorade back down on the ground.

"Geronimo's mission sounds harder," she said.

"It's hard to say at this juncture," said Murdock. He took his last sip of pretend tea with his eyes on Eleanor just over the lip of the cup. A silence fell over the tea party. Distant teenage phone chatter could be heard upstairs.

"I don't like your stupid, fancy words," said Eleanor. "And you smell like goat cheese. I hate goat cheese."

5

MIDNIGHT SNACKS

Geronimo awoke to the distinct raucous of a bouncing basketball on a gym floor. He lifted his head out of the trees. He was still in the sled, parked in a dark, empty locker room. He jumped out of the sled, and as he did so, Santa's folded instructions flittered out of the wagon and onto the floor. He grabbed the paper from the ground and then heard "boom, boom, boom." He was sure someone was coming, so he ran recklessly through the first doors he found.

He staggered into a well-lit gymnasium. The ball suddenly stopped dribbling. Just like that he had completely blown his cover. Geronimo turned his head toward the polar bear with the basketball. It was the same bear that was wearing the Phoenix Suns jersey on the drawbridge right before he passed out for the second time. Standing at the three-point line, the polar bear stared back at the gnome, dribbling with a dumbfounded expression on his face. After a long and intense stare-down by the polar bear, he made a herky-jerky motion as he spun away from Geronimo toward the goal and threw up a hook shot. The ball sailed far right and high above the backboard. The shot's outcome somehow made Geronimo feel a little better about his current predicament. The polar bear shook his head and sauntered up to the gnome. He sat down cross-legged across from him. "Dan Majerle was my hero," said the polar bear.

Geronimo tried not to respond, but he couldn't help himself.

"Who-what? Dan who?" asked Geronimo.

"The man, Dan the Man, taught me everything I know about three-pointers."

"Except how to make them," muttered Geronimo. The comment came out so fast Geronimo could barely believe what happened. The polar bear's ears bristled, his snout twitched, and his lips curled up, showing his outrageous fangs.

"Don't you realize this is a private club?" asked the polar bear.

"I do, and I'm sorry," said Geronimo. "I was just dropping trees off and got lost. Sorry to disturb you. I'll be on my way now." Geronimo started to walk away as if politely leaving a dinner party.

"What is that paper in your hand?" The polar bear reached for the instructions while also inadvertently grabbing the gnome's hat as he questioned. Geronimo completely forgot he was holding Santa's instructions. With the gnome's hat bunched up in one paw, the polar bear unfolded the paper and looked it over. Geronimo watched the bear's eyes fall upon every word, sketch, and diagram that Santa had intended for Geronimo. The animal suddenly laughed a riotous bellied "bwaaah!" that faded into tears of delirium. He sniffed a few times in a subdued merriment before shredding the paper to pieces, along with the gnome's hat. He then gathered up all the bits of paper and hat and held them in a ball above Geronimo's head, letting the pieces fall like snow over the gnome.

"I will give you one chance to leave here alive, Mr. Gnome," The polar bear said. "If you beat me at the game of Horse, I shall grant you pardon. If I beat you, I make you my midnight snack!"

"You can't eat gnome," said Geronimo.

"Sure you can," said the polar bear.

"No you can't, silly bear, we're poisonous."

The pole bear narrowed his eyes at Geronimo. "I'm checking with Snopes to see if that's true. If not, you're one dead gnome!" The polar bear walked toward the exit.

"Aren't you worried I'm gonna escape?" asked Geronimo. The polar bear paused in his tracks.

"It's *impossible* to escape the country club," replied the polar bear, releasing another belly laugh as he left the gym.

6
BURNED AND SHOT

Krampus was staring at himself through a darkened mirror late into the night. It was three in the morning and, as usual, he couldn't sleep. "What if I told you you were the kindest man alive?" he asked his reflection. His white lips broadened into a wide smile. Already tired of this exercise, he slowly retracted his smile until his lips were small and shy-looking. He sniffed the icy air just before belting out, "What if I told you everyone *hates* you!" Outside, the moon peaked around a massive, slow-moving cloud. The light of the moon poked through the mud-caked windows and shot threads of light between Krampus and the mirror. Looking himself directly in the eye, he said, "We are who we decide to be." With a satisfied sigh and a deep yawn, he turned his back to the mirror, took two steps into pitch-blackness, and then tripped and crashed violently to the floor. He screamed in agony, whimpered, and then fell asleep.

Krampus awoke five hours later to a harsh morning light. White, burning sunlight slashed his face. The quick footsteps of an elf hurried into the room. "Grrgg!" said Krampus as he twitched his head up from the stone floor.

"Pardon me, Your Majesty," said the elf. The elf swiped the plate off the ground and left a cup of tea near Krampus's head. Just as the elf was about to close the door behind him, Krampus perked up.

"Why did you leave that plate on the ground?" he shouted. "Last night I tripped on it in the dark. You could've killed the king! You should be burned and shot!"

"In that order?" asked the elf. His voice was calm and neutral, as if he were assisting the mentally ill.

"Whatever. Guards!" Krampus bellowed, scrambling up from the ground. "Guards!" he repeated as he marched past the elf and into the dark, cavernous stone hallway. His voice echoed through the narrow, twisting walkways of the castle.

"Your Highness, the guards are all gone," said the elf in the same tone of voice a nurse might use with a patient.

"Krampus walked back into the bedroom and grabbed a black robe off a telescope. "What do you mean the guards are gone?" he asked. He wrapped the robe around his lean, scaly body. "Where have they gone to?"

"They left early this morning," said the elf.

"Ingrates!" Krampus hollered. He grabbed a vase from a shelf on the wall and threw it across the room. The vase shattered upon impact, with the bits of vase falling into a large mound of previously thrown and smashed vases.

"You have only four vases left, Your Majesty," the elf said, eyeing the four remaining vases on the long shelf wall.

"Now I only have three!" said Krampus as he grabbed another vase and threw this one errantly at his telescope by the window.

He gasped. "Not my super-powered telescope!" He ran over to look through the eyehole. "Whew, no damage." He removed his eye from the telescope and shifted his attention to his castle property. "I'd like to check out the boneyard today," said Krampus, changing the subject. "Pencil Thelma in for 1:30."

The elf stared back at Krampus. "Excuse me for asking, Your Highness, but what is there to actually 'check out' at the boneyard? It's just a bunch of bones."

"There's maintenance to be done," said Krampus, leaning over and grabbing long rolls of paper from the ground. He reached for his slim spectacles on the windowsill and put them on. He half unfurled one of the rolls of paper in his hands and held it up for inspection. "Plus," he continued, "Christmas is in three weeks. The boneyard has to look presentable for the fresh arrivals." Krampus rapidly scanned through the list of names on the large parchment. "Naughty boys and girls galore," he said gleefully. "What a sea of sinful little creatures. If only we had a bigger net." Krampus handed the scrolls back to the elf. "File this for me," he said as he turned back toward the window, closing his eyes as the breeze hit his face. After a moment, he opened them again and, misty-eyed, said, "If I had someone like me stealing away nasty children and gobbling them up when I was a child, I would've been spared this wretched life long ago." Silver streaks ran down his gaunt, scaly cheeks.

"You're glittering again, Your Excellency," said the elf.

Krampus wiped the glitter from his face, which only served to spread the sparkle even more. The morning sun was just breaking out of the clouds, and he was now shining gloriously against the sunlight pouring through the window and onto his face.

"Better?" asked Krampus. He turned toward his elf servant in shimmering, golden glory.

31

Astonished at the sight, the elf confessed, "You're like a shining star in the morning sky, Your Majesty!"

Krampus glared at the elf with a look of complete disgust. "Bring me my tea," he said. The elf dutifully picked the cup up from the ground and handed it to him. He sniffed the tea. "Besides the boneyard business," said Krampus, "I'll also be strolling the perimeter of the compound. I sense my dear brother is making a move on me."

"What makes you so sure?" asked the elf.

"We're half brothers," said Krampus, "There are times when I swear I can sense his next move. Make sure Thelma is saddled."

"Of course, Your Excellency," said the elf.

"Oh, and I'll need all my sabers," added Krampus.

"You have two," said the elf. "Two sabers, Oh Great One."

"Yes."

"That's all you have."

"I know," said Krampus, "that's why I asked for all of them." He sniffed his tea for the last time. "Did you poison this tea?" asked Krampus.

"Of course not, Your Highness. Why do you ask?"

"I don't know," said Krampus as he tipped the cup toward his mouth. "Everything else seems to be vanishing around here."

⟋7⟍
FORTY-SEVEN YEARS

The polar bear, who preferred to refer to himself as Dan, busted through the big oak doors of the Smoking Lounge. He shattered the silent peace of cigar smoke, leather chairs, and old books. He whirled around with schoolboy excitement, making slight eye contact with each member of the Great Eleven.

The Great Eleven was a counsel of eleven polar bears that ruled with supreme authority over all other polar bears. They were considered the oldest, wisest, and toughest. Their names were Fort, Smick, Wolan, Bruck, Joost, Sneed, Ringo, Blufus, Ferny, Cocoa, and Snopes. Snopes was the leader. He sat in a cushy, black leather chair behind the desk near the far wall of the lounge.

"What is it this time, Dirf?" asked Snopes. He twirled his tiny glass of brandy as he waited for Dirf's repsonse.

"Let me guess," said Sneed, "you saw Larry Bird stuck out in the snow." The others chuckled.

"I told you my name is not Dirf, it's Dan," replied Dan. "There's been a security breach." They all stopped laughing and waited for his next words.

"There is a gnome in the building."

Snopes drew silent, gravely nodding his head. "I'll alert the media," he said. His massive paw reached for the maple-colored phone on his desk. Everyone laughed.

"He was sent by Santa," Dan yelled over the laughter. The laughter subsided with the speed of breaking glass.

"How do you know he was sent by Santa?" asked Snopes.

"He had instructions from Santa to invade our country club and steal the map to Krampus's Castle. Santa wants his brother taken back to the North Pole."

"By a gnome?" said Smick in the corner, playing pool. This was followed by jeers. Snopes was stroking his furry chin with his right front paw, his eyes squinting. "He's taking the offensive. He's trying to sever the allegiance we have with his brother."

"Well, what should we do?" asked Dan.

"Keep him down below," replied Snopes. "Where is the little vermin now?"

"I made him wait in the gym," replied Dan.

"You made him what?" said Snopes.

After Dan left, Geronimo went in search of an escape route. First, he went back to the locker room where he had woken up. He searched the walls of the locker room and found no doors and no windows. Defeated, he walked back to his sled and dropped to his knees. According to gnome tradition, you must bend down and kiss the ground when you find yourself in a state of ultimate despair. Geronimo was not sure why he chose to make his ceremonial smooch underneath the sled, but he was glad he did. When his lips made contact with the floor, he could feel a gap in the wood. It was a long, straight line on the floor. *Not a crack*, Geronimo thought, *but a door*. He quickly pushed the sled forward. A perfect rectangle was carved into the floor with a latch fastened to one end. Geronimo pulled at the latch and heaved the hidden door upward. The opening revealed a long, dark staircase. It seemed to descend into nowhere. Geronimo closed the trap door behind him using metal rungs that ran down the bottom side of the door. Once closed, it became impossibly dark. He heard dripping noises, and the air was damp. It wasn't an easy life, being a foot tall. He hugged one side of the ladder as he went down, and his wooden clogs barely caught each step below him. When he finally reached the last rung, his legs hung freely, and beyond his shoes was a pool of darkness. Just as he was about to cry out in panic, he heard a voice not far below him say, "You can drop if you want. It's not a big deal."

Feeling stupid, Geronimo let go of the last rung and fell a short drop onto the stone floor.

"Where am I?" Geronimo asked.

"You're in a dungeon," said the low, scratchy voice somewhere in the darkness.

"Where is the light? Is there a light?" Geronimo waved his arms around in the darkness.

"No. Not in the dungeon, I'm afraid," said the voice. "In fact, we haven't had light in the dungeon in forty-five years."

"Don't tell me you've been in here for forty-five years."

"I have not been in here for forty-five years. I've been in here for forty-seven years," replied the voice. "Congratulations to me, I guess."

Geronimo was horrified. "Is the ladder the only way out?" he asked.

"I don't know. I was put in this cell in the corner, behind metal bars. I've never been beyond this 5 x 5 cubic space."

Suddenly, the trap door above them opened. From the dim light of the locker room above, Geronimo could see the outline of a big, white, furry head.

"Oh good," said Dan. "This is where we were going to dump you for now, anyway. Nighty-night, little gnome." With that, Dan closed the trap door. A clunky metal sound was heard and then the sound of Dan's giant feet stomping off into the distance. Geronimo fell silent. The few moments of silence was quickly shattered by the chuckling of the jailed prisoner.

"For now," said the prisoner. "That's just what they told me. My name is Ned. What's yours?"

"Geronimo."

"It's nice to meet you, Geronimo."

"How did you wind up here?"

"I was on a very important mission from Santa Claus," said Ned. "I know it sounds ridiculous, but it's true."

Geronimo closed his eyes, knelt down, and kissed the floor.

～8～
A BASKET FULL OF KNIVES

Back at 618 Dark Cherry Ln, Murdock and Eleanor were taking a not-so-quiet stroll around the neighborhood. Murdock was very anxious throughout the walk, though it had nothing to do with being seen. Being exposed, studied, and manipulated by humans was not a concern simply because the vast majority of human beings, particularly adults, don't believe in elves, therefore they're unable to see them. Children, on the other hand, who are able to suspend belief in fantastical creatures, see elves simply because they believe in them. The true source of Murdock's anxiety and frustration was with Eleanor herself. In the first ten minutes of the walk, Murdock had witnessed Eleanor spit at several parked cars, hiss at a baby in a stroller, and then dump a full pitcher of lemonade from Ricky's lemonade stand into the sewage drain. Ricky, a neighborhood kid who was exactly half Eleanor's age and size, could only watch with his arms folded and hot tears rolling down his face. "Sorry, Ricky," Eleanor said, "Lemons are out of season. That lemonade was rotten. You could've killed someone."

At that moment, a patrol car crept up to the intersection in front of them. The expressions of the policemen as they slowed to a stop changed from carefree amusement to light concern at the sight of Ricky's fresh tears. The policeman closest to the children, in the passenger seat, stuck his broad, grinning face out of the window. He wore big, bulbous, black shades. Ricky's level of indignation went up a few more notches with his newfound belief that swift and mighty justice would be done on the matter. With her hands folded, Eleanor stared coldly at the police officer.

"Why are you crying, bud?" asked the officer.

"Eleanor dumped all my lemonade out again!" shouted Ricky, "I can't *take* it anymore!" Ricky emotionally doubled down into a full-on wail. He pressed his lemony fists against his ruddy eyes and stung himself unintentionally, releasing unspeakable pain. His mouth went slack with drool. Eleanor was silent and frozen in her spot. She kept her head askance toward the trees as she awaited her verdict. The policeman tucked his head back into the car to discuss something with his partner behind the wheel. From the children's perspective, the private conversation inside the police car seemed to be whether the police should bother actually getting out of the car or not.

Inside the car, Officer Kelly sipped at his heavily creamed coffee. "Bullies are a hot-button issue these days," he said, staring off into the distance from behind the wheel.

"I think it would be bad karma if we simply drove off, leaving this," said Officer Cooper. He looked back over his shoulder at the sobbing Ricky with lemon juice in his eyes and an obstinate Eleanor standing next to him.

"All right," said Officer Kelly as he unbuckled his seatbelt. "Let's turn some frowns upside down." The officers got out of the car and joined the kids on the sidewalk. Ricky started in right away. "You should arrest her and her little elf and put them in jail," said Ricky, pointing at Eleanor.

"Her little elf?" repeated Officer Kelly.

"They can't see or hear me, Ricky, because they don't believe in me," said Murdock. He then turned to Eleanor. "I suggest we hurry back to the house, Eleanor, before your babysitter discovers your absence."

"I hope she does discover my absence," Eleanor replied.

"Who are you talking to?" asked Officer Cooper.

"She's talking to the elf," responded Ricky, now pointing to where Murdock stood.

Both officers stared at the spot where Murdock was standing and saw nothing but sidewalk. Officer Kelly asked what he hoped to be his final departing question. "Where are your parents?"

"Mine are inside," said Ricky, thumbing toward the house in front of them.

"Mine are in southern France," said Eleanor.

"Well, son, go on in and get cleaned up," said Officer Kelly. "Tell your mom and dad everything is all right. We'll take it from here." Ricky gave the policeman a serious nod, then put a closed sign over his stand and sprinted toward his house. Officer Cooper then whispered something to his fellow officer.

"Who is taking care of you while your parents are out of town?" Officer Kelly asked Eleanor.

"Tell the nice policeman that you have a babysitter waiting at home for you and that you were just on your way back now," instructed Murdock.

"No one," replied Eleanor. "No one's watching me. I was left in a basket." At this, Murdock sat cross-legged on the sidewalk, his small head buried in his tiny hands. "Full of knives," Eleanor added.

"Did she just say a 'basket of knives'?" Officer Cooper whispered to Officer Kelly.

"She did," said Officer Kelly. "Listen, Eleanor, it is Eleanor, right?"

"Yes," she replied.

"Well, listen, Eleanor," continued Officer Kelly, "I know you like to make up stories. But we need to know you're with an adult before we can leave you. Do you know your address?"

"Yeah," replied Eleanor, "123 Basket Street."

This last remark snapped whatever patience Officer Kelly had left. He bent down to eye level with Eleanor. "If we can't find someone who is in charge of you, Eleanor, then we'll have to bring you to the station until we do. Now do you understand how important and serious this is?"

Eleanor looked away from the officer's face. Her expression was dull and detached. "Go ahead. Put me behind bars. I'm ready for it." Officer Kelly sighed and looked up at the sky as he brought his walkie-talkie to his mouth. "Sorry, Eleanor, the cells are all full. You'll have to sit on a chair in the lobby."

Officer Cooper crawled back inside the passenger seat, while Officer Kelly opened the back seat door for Eleanor, motioning for her to get inside as he reported back to the station. "Yeah, we have a possible but unlikely 837, ten- to twelve-year-old child will not identify her legal guardian, taking her in to make some calls. Roger that," said Officer Kelly into his walkie. Eleanor and Murdock hopped into the back seat of the patrol car. "Really?" Officer Cooper whispered to Officer Kelly as he climbed back behind the wheel.

"We have to take it seriously," said Officer Kelly, "especially with the rash of missing kids we get this time of year."

"This actually might be a good thing," said Murdock, nestled up against Eleanor's mud-encrusted jeans. "Where's a safer place to avoid a kidnapping than a police station?"

"Kidnapping?" Eleanor exclaimed.

Officer Cooper swiveled his head back toward Eleanor in alarm. "You're not getting kidnapped, sweetie, we're bringing you to the police station so we can find out who your guardians are, since you won't tell us."

The engine started and the car began to roll forward. "Try and control your outbursts. Someone is trying to kidnap you," said Murdock. "It's my job to stop that from happening. I thought we covered this already."

"I thought you were trying to turn me into a well-behaved girl so something terrible wouldn't happen to me," said Eleanor.

"We do want you to be a well-behaved girl," replied Officer Kelly, "because girls who misbehave get into trouble." He leaned over to his partner and asked, "What is she talking about?" His partner shrugged his shoulders in response and kept his eyes locked on the road.

"Yes, it's true," replied Murdock to Eleanor, "but if I run out of time and fail to instill any redeemable qualities whatsoever, I still have to protect you—even if you're rotten to the core."

"Do you think I'm rotten to the core?" Eleanor asked in a quiet, shaky voice. Her eyes welled up. Murdock, Officer Kelly, and Officer Cooper all looked back at Eleanor in the backseat. "Oh no, no, no, not at all, not at all," they all simultaneously reassured her.

"The assignment given to me by Santa was to keep you safe," said Murdock, "that is my only purpose in this mission."

"What if I don't want to be saved?" Eleanor replied. This brought silence over the entire car. No one said another word until they arrived at the station.

41

9
BLACK FALLS

A late-morning fog rolled in and shrouded the hillside that lay between Krampus's castle and Troll River. "I'm not sure where we are anymore, Thelma," Krampus said to the shadow donkey he rode upon. "Guide us back to the castle," he ordered. Lost in his own woods, he'd been roaming for hours through endless thickets. Since Thelma was not visible to the naked eye, Krampus had to put fake reindeer antlers on her to keep track of her movements. Anytime Thelma was successful in taking off the antlers tied tightly around her invisible donkey neck, it could take as long as a month for Krampus to find her again.

Thelma grunted as she spun around in place, once, twice, her hooves slipping on the rocky incline of the wet, moss-covered hill. She didn't know which way to go either. She finally picked a direction, which just happened to be the opposite direction of the castle, toward Troll River. On the other side of the river were miles and miles of featureless terrain, called Pointless. On Pointless, it's as if nature itself protested against Krampus by withdrawing any signs of life: trees, plants, animals, and even water. It was clearly and precisely pointless.

Krampus was sound asleep atop Thelma by the time they got to the river's edge. Thelma had caught scent of the river's fresh flowing current and thirstily ambled over for a drink. She bowed her head and took in great gulps of the cool water. With her body sloped downward, Krampus slowly slid toward the river. He snorted as he passed her ears and then his frail, withered body quietly *splooshed* below the surface.

It was a fast-moving current. Thelma was already ten yards out, happily gulping down water by the time Krampus bobbed his head above the surface. He flailed wildly for twigs, branches, anything he could grab onto. Troll River ended at Black Falls.

As a child, Krampus once asked a local merchant in his home village about Black Falls. The merchant told him to think of the most frightening thing you could possibly imagine, and then quadruple that. That's Black Falls. Krampus imagined the water as blood, the fall ten thousand feet, and the bottom swarming with saber tooth sharks and giant electric turtles.

After a period of continual underwater somersaults, Krampus finally started using his frog-like limbs to stroke his way toward one side of the river. As his body rushed forward, he was able to creep diagonally toward the Pointless side of the land. Krampus was just starting to feel hopeful about his newfound progress when he noticed the color of the water change from light brown to dark, murky rouge. *It's just as I imagined*, he thought. Black Falls was near. He pushed as hard as he could through the water, swimming for his life. The sound of the falls was now thunderous. Krampus's long, brittle fingernails scraped the rocks on the Pointless side of the river in search of something to grip. He turned his head to the side as he struggled sideways. He was now twenty feet from the drop, and the force of the current made it impossible for him to snag anything. Suddenly, he felt something grab the loose, gray skin from the back of his neck, lift his body out of the water, and hurl him onto the Pointless side of Troll River. The act was so swift and shocking that Krampus's initial reaction was anger and humiliation. Dust had billowed into his eyes and mouth while he rolled on the sand. Coughing up orange dust, he sat up and yelled, "Who dares toss the king out of rivers?" Krampus could hear hooves trot up to him, but his still-blurry vision didn't allow him to see who or what it was.

Then a voice said, "My name is T.C., and you're welcome."

This encounter was actually a bit of dumb luck for T.C., who had been utterly lost in the featureless expanse of Pointless for the past two days. After dropping the cart of trees off with Geronimo, he left the PBCC and disembarked on his interstellar return trip. However, shortly after taking flight, his route was disrupted by a slight change in the magnetic alignment of the planets and stars he traversed through. As a result, he had accidentally wound up exactly where Geronimo's mission was supposed to send the gnome, at the footsteps of Krampus's castle.

"Welcome? Welcome for what?" asked Krampus as he marched over to T.C. "The only thing I would welcome is your departure." With his eyes free of dust, Krampus could clearly see the elf-reindeer-centaur before him.

"What an adorable abomination you are," said Krampus, looking him up and down. "You work for Nicky, don't you?"

"We don't call him that, but yes, I do," said T.C.

"Don't you know who I am?" Krampus asked as he crept closer to T.C., flicking his tongue out. "Aren't you going to try and apprehend me?"

T.C. thought about this and decided to choose the action that would most infuriate Krampus. His actual motive was to find the caged children first, then deal with Krampus afterwards. Until then, he would pretend his business was with the Krampus's servant elf.

"I'm not here to see you, Krampus. I'm here to see a rogue elf. Good day to you." T.C. slowly trotted off back across the river, smirking to himself. Krampus spat on the ground in response. He stood there, disgusted, as he watched T.C. cross the river. It now dawned on him that he had no way of getting safely across the river back to his castle, unless he wanted to spend the three weeks of travel it would take to walk around Troll River. T.C. was his only ride.

"Hey, dog boy!" Krampus shouted, "if you give me a lift back to the castle, I'll let you dine with me." T.C. was already making his way back to Krampus, knowing he was stuck. He knew he may need Krampus to find all the abducted children.

Trotting back toward the river with Krampus now astride the centaur, T.C. asked, "What were you doing in the river, anyway?"

"I fell asleep on my shadow donkey," said Krampus. "When I woke up, I was in the river."

"Sounds like you live a pretty exciting life."

"Mr. Excitement, that's me."

10
TEA-SIDE CHATS

Santa's monstrous frame, donned in his favorite candy-cane-print pajamas, was slumped over his desk as he worked late into the frosty, winter night. A pool of light shone over his head from the small desk lamp above. His cuckoo clock showed 2:15 in the morning. The industrial-sized workshop beyond the glass wall of his office was pitch-black and soundless. Santa's eyes grew droopy as he leafed through a mound of papers. Losing the battle against sleep, his head sagged downward and his eyes closed with finality.

At the sound of his first snore, a red buzzing light went off on the war map behind him. He opened his eyes and swiveled his chair around to face the map. His jaw dropped at what he saw, his expression somewhere between concern and bewilderment.

"What's the news?" asked Clarence, appearing at the opened door out of nowhere. Clarence was the Floor Manager of the Great Hall, who had earlier poked fun at Geronimo while summoning him to Santa's office. "I heard the buzzing." Clarence, dressed in a pointy nightcap, blue pajamas, and slippers, didn't need to wait for an invite. He pattered into the office and plopped down on the green velvet couch. "Is Geronimo near the castle?" he asked.

"No, he's not. It's T.C.," replied Santa.

"T.C.? I don't get it. How—"

"I don't know, I don't know," replied Santa, rubbing his eyes. "We got T.C.'s signal that he's near the castle."

"So what's our next move? Have T.C. try and bring Krampus back?"

"No," said Santa, "that would be a slap in the face to Geronimo. This is his mission, even if he is, at the moment, stuck in a dungeon."

"How do you know that?" asked Clarence.

"I got someone inside their country club working with me. Won't tell you who, though, so please don't ask."

"Who is it?"

"It's a bear named Fort," said Santa, "me and him go way back. He thinks Snopes is losing it. Fudgesicles, why am I so bad at keeping secrets?"

"Why didn't you just get Fort to find the map to Krampus's castle?" Clarence asked.

"He doesn't know where it is either. He said it's been simply misplaced and none of the bears can find it."

At that moment, Mrs. Claus walked into the doorway in her mint-chocolate-cookie-patterned pajamas. She was carrying a tray with two tea cups of chamomile tea, one much larger than the other. She gave Santa a disapproving look and did not acknowledge Clarence, who sat adjacent to her on the couch. She rested the tray on the coffee table in front of the couch.

"Oh, you're so thoughtful, Rose," said Santa. "Do you mind bringing my cup to me?"

"Yes, I do," said Rose. "You can get it yourself. You and your little slumber-party buddy. I brought this tea in order to put you to sleep, not to encourage this behavior."

"Why you gotta be like dat?" Santa replied in half-sleep articulation.

"You're talking to me with your eyes closed, Nicky," said Rose. "You need to get to bed. These late nights have been going on for way too long."

"I can't help it, baby!" exclaimed Santa. "The stakes are higher than they've ever been! There's already a bunch of missing children cases—all tonight." Santa raised his arm and shook the documents enclosed in his fist. "This is hot off the wire," he said. "Krampus's son is moving on us. Tonight!"

"You mean Gromp?" exclaimed Clarence. "But Gromp hates Krampus."

"I know," said Santa, vigorously nodding his head back at Clarence. "I think his old man cut him a deal. Everyone can be bought. Especially during Christmastime."

"If you're not in bed next to me in fifteen minutes, you can kiss breakfast good-bye," said Rose.

"You wouldn't," said Santa.

"I will," said Rose as she turned back to the door with quiet footsteps and walked out of the office without looking back.

"I better call it a night," Santa grunted. He shook his head and looked over at a sound-asleep Clarence. Santa opened the bottom drawer of his desk and took out a big green blanket. He walked over to the couch, put the blanket over Clarence, and turned the lights out.

With his chamomile in hand, Santa schlepped into his bedroom to find his wife sitting upright in bed. He crawled into the covers beside his wife and gave her a peck on the cheek. "Why are you still up?" he asked.

"Because I nearly forgot there's something else I didn't tell you," said Rose. "And since you made the right decision to come to bed, I will give you the gift of information as a reward."

"Oh goody," said Santa.

"Tomorrow is Krampus's birthday," said Rose.

"So what? He hates birthdays, especially his own."

"I never told you this, but, he has called me on his birthday every year for the last, well, fifty-two years."

"Why have you never told me this?" asked Santa, baffled by the news.

"Well, there's not much to say about it. He just hangs up every time. As soon as I say 'hello' he says, 'It's my birthday,' and then hangs up immediately."

"That's so him," said Santa.

"And I worried that telling you about it would scare him away from even that amount of reaching out."

"So why are you telling me now?"

"Well," said Rose, "things have gotten so bad this year with the high volume of kidnappings, that maybe when he calls tomorrow you can answer the phone instead of me."

"It's worth a shot," said Santa. "I haven't spoken a word to him since that first Christmas."

11
ABDUCTION

This was Eleanor's first time in a police station. It was harshly lit and filled with moving bodies. It smelled like coffee and sweat. She walked into the building with Murdock on her left and Officer Kelly on her right holding her hand. Officer Kelly spotted Captain Monahan whisking by the front desk with a cheese danish in hand and his head buried in the sports section of the newspaper.

"Captain Monahan," Officer Kelly said. The grisly Captain Monahan stopped his quick stride and painfully unlocked his eyes from the newspaper. The captain's gaze shifted from Officer Kelly to Eleanor. "Looks like you caught an eighty-pounder," said Monahan. "Nice work!"

"She won't tell me her address or her phone number," said Officer Kelly. "What do I do with her?"

The captain shook his head and replied, "Have her wait on the wall." He motioned with his eyes to a line of people sitting against the far wall. "Tell Angela to talk to her," he added. Captain Monahan looked down at Eleanor and said with a gentle tone, "Maybe she's just scared of big, fat, scary policeman."

"Look who's talking, hamburger with legs," Eleanor blurted out. Captain Monahan laughed, charmed at the remark.

"Ask him to put you in a cell," Murdock told Eleanor.

"Put me in a cell," demanded Eleanor.

"The jail cells are for very bad people," the captain replied with less patience in his voice, "they're not for playing." Captain Monahan pointed to an empty seat on the bench. "So you're going to sit over there, and a nice lady named Angela will come out and talk to you about how important it is to give information to the police. Information allows us to keep you safe." The captain nodded to Officer Kelly.

"All right, little missy, let's get you seated over here," said Officer Kelly as he nudged her toward the row of chairs past the Captain Monahan's desk. Murdock spun in front of her, walking backward as he talked. "Tell them a very scary man is hunting you down and the safest place for you to be right now is a jail cell."

Eleanor stopped walking. With tightened lips and squinted eyes she asked the elf, "Are you asking me to lie? Geronimo would never ask me to lie."

"I'm not lying," said Murdock. The elf's eyes grew big at what was happening behind Eleanor near the front entrance.

"*Everyone down on the floor!*" screamed a man wearing a trench coat and a sombrero that shielded his face from view. "I'm loaded with dynamite," said the man, "and I'm going to blow this whole building to kingdom come if you don't all get down on the ground—*now!*"

The man opened his coat to reveal rows of orange sticks and multicolored wires attached to his chest. He spun in place to the sound of shrieks and horrors. "Get on the ground, now!" the man repeated. This time, everyone inside the station dropped to the ground except for Eleanor and Murdock.

Eleanor was still facing Murdock. She was too afraid to turn around. Her knee-jerk impulse to be noncompliant was so strong that her body would not physically obey the command of "get down." Terrified of the man behind her, she started to cry.

"You!" said the man in the trench coat. The "you" gave Eleanor chills. When she turned around to face the man, he was pointing right at her. He then put his palm up and curled his index finger. "Come here, Eleanor," the man said in a pleasant, neighborly tone.

Eleanor's legs wobbled. Her heart raced. Murdock slid his tiny hand into hers and looked up at her. "I will not let anyone hurt you," said Murdock, "it is my sworn oath to protect you. That said, listen to the man. Go with him. I'll be right by your side the whole time." Eleanor squeezed his hand, still unable to speak. Murdock took the first step forward, and Eleanor followed.

ᘒ*12*ᘏ
POINTLESS

The sticks of dynamite strapped to the man in the sombrero were not explosives at all. They were tubes filled with charged quantum fluid, which powered the person wearing it to the nearest wormhole. His trench coat was actually a type of spaceship called a Space Bubbler. With the bubbler, one is able to travel swiftly and gracefully in an oxygenated bubble that could fit up to five people.

In this case, the nearest wormhole led to the closest dump-off point to the captor's destination: that vast, featureless desert of Pointless.

The three figures sifted quietly through the dunes, figuring it pointless to talk. Everything felt pointless. Even Eleanor's shock and disorientation due to space travel paled in comparison to how immensely pointless everything suddenly felt. One just couldn't help it. Due to his elfin temperament, however, Murdock was a little less susceptible to the mysterious despair that clung to most other life-forms attempting travel through Pointless. Instead of feeling woeful over their current state, he was able to put his mental acuity to work.

"Where are you taking us?" asked Murdock.

"The doll house," Gromp responded without looking back.

"Why?" asked Murdock.

Gromp hadn't turned around yet. Murdock and Eleanor had not gotten a good look at his face, until now. The man in the sombrero stopped in his tracks. The other two instinctively stopped as well. Murdock and Eleanor could feel the big reveal at hand. Gromp swiveled around and threw off his sombrero. What they saw was an astonishingly handsome face: blue eyes, long eyelashes, shock-white hair, and a small, tense mouth. Eleanor was momentarily ripped out of Pointless's spell.

"Gorgeous!" she belted.

"Shut up," said Gromp.

Even Murdock couldn't help himself. He knew about Gromp's existence but had never seen him before. "And how it is that the son of a hideous demon winds up looking like Prince Charming?"

"My mom was pretty. So I heard, anyway." Gromp gazed wistfully into the distance while putting his sombrero back on. "Vamanos!" he said while turning his back on them to continue on. They all resumed their march through the dunes.

"Why are you taking us to the doll house?" Murdock tried again.

"Eleanor's been a naughty girl and that's where naughty girls go—to the doll house. Besides, it's pointless to bring it up now."

"No, but *why* are you doing this?" asked Murdock. "You hate your father. Why would you ever do him favors?"

"We actually get along just fine now," said Gromp in a tone that sounded practiced.

"I don't believe you."

"If you don't stop with this pointless chatter, I will gag the both of you!" said Gromp, clenching and raising a white rag above his head. The elf turned his head forward and resumed walking. Gromp joined his stride as all three fell into a communal silence. Murdock slowed his walking pace so that he was side-by-side and in stride with Eleanor. He locked his gaze on her. She faced forward, oblivious.

"Eleanor," said a whisper inside her mind that sounded a lot like Murdock. "It's me, Murdock. Stop feeling so pointless. It's stupid." Eleanor spun her head at Murdock, who was staring intensely at her. "I'm reaching you through a special elfin telepathy. I can send you messages, but I can't hear yours. I'd have told you about this earlier but I wanted to wait until you were more acclimated so you wouldn't blow my cover. Anyway, Gromp has a weakness. Bring his father up as much as possible. He hates it—"

"You're talking too fast and too loud!" screamed Eleanor. All three stopped walking. Gromp stared at Eleanor in disbelief. "What is wrong with you two?" Gromp wrapped rags around both their mouths, staying true to his warning. He talked like a mother strapping her kids into their car seats. "Listen," he said as he knotted the rags behind their heads, "we're very close to the boatman. Things won't feel as pointless once we get to Troll River. But it's pointless to discuss anything at this point."

With that, they all resumed their pace in silence, walking without words or rest into the evening. The silence wasn't broken until a lighthouse became visible on Troll River's rocky shore just a few hundred yards away.

~ 13 ~
THE ELEVEN MYSTERIES

Twop, went the sack of baked potatoes onto the dungeon floor. Geronimo's eyes startled open. The trapdoor high above slammed shut, the lock clicking. Heavy footsteps drifted out of earshot. "What number bag is that?" Geronimo asked. His throat felt dry and hoarse.

"Ten," Ned replied.

"And—we get one bag of potatoes per day?"

"We get one bag every two days," said Ned.

"So I've been here for twenty days?" asked Geronimo.

"Twenty days," confirmed Ned. "But if you travel through my mind, it will allow you to exist in two different places at the same time. So while one Geronimo will be asleep in this dungeon, the other will be continuing his mission at the mouth of the Great Gorge."

"Travel through your mind . . ." repeated Geronimo. *This man has lost his mind down here*, thought Geronimo.

"You want to know why I'm in here, young gnome?" asked Ned.

"Not really," said Geronimo.

"I was thrown into this dungeon because of my wizardry," said Ned. "I'm a wizard. My bloodline traces back to Merlin. Perhaps you've heard of him?" Geronimo had no immediate response to any of this. Ned frowned, disappointed.

"I don't believe in wizards," said Geronimo.

"Oh, that's a shame," said Ned, sounding genuinely hurt by this news. "In that case you won't be able to enter my mind, plunge into the Great Gorge, and learn the Eleven Mysteries that will set you free from this dungeon. Too bad."

More silence from Geronimo.

"May I ask," Ned continued, "why it is you don't believe I'm a wizard?"

"I think if you were a wizard, you would have found a way out by now," said Geronimo.

"What if I told you I choose to be here?"

"Then you're just nuts."

"I am a wizard, and a wizard has his weasons," said Ned.

"Did you just say 'weasons'?"

"Close your eyes, gnome!" Ned commanded with a voice that was deep and resounding and unlike any tone he had taken prior with Geronimo. The change was so startling to Geronimo he instantly closed his eyes.

The second his eyes were closed he found himself outside. It was late in the afternoon, and he was clinging to a rock wall that overlooked an immense gorge. When he opened his eyes again, the gorge was still there. He shut his eyes again, and this time saw darkness. He opened them again, and there again was the gorge. In front of him and almost pressing against his face was the jagged, slippery, and very vertical wall of rock. Waves crashed violently far below him. The wind whipped across the surface of the rock face, yanking his tiny fingers from their trembling grip. One slip of his finger could send his miniscule frame hurdling deep into the vast gorge below. Had the wizard somehow transported him? Or was he under a spell, and his body still stuck in the prison? One thing was for sure: Geronimo now believed in wizards.

Geronimo turned his head as much as he could to look behind him. What he saw was a scowling sea, dark and wild. Geronimo could not imagine a more uninviting body of water. As if to force this invitation, the wind suddenly picked up with great force, upper-cutting him in the chin. His fingers slipped from the rocks like loose, little feathers as his body repelled with wild urgency from the rock wall.

Geronimo thought he had shattered through a sheet of ice as he broke the surface of the water. His head bobbed up and down to the erratic rhythm of the waves. He tried relaxing his body, and the water naturally pushed him to the surface of the water. As he floated on his back, the current slowed and he drifted farther out into the vast green sea. Oddly enough, this quickly turned into the most pleasant part of Geronimo's adventure so far. Keeping his body afloat felt effortless. The sun was setting on the horizon. The air tasted salty sweet as he started to doze off.

When he awoke, he found himself beached under a full moon.

"Greetings," a voice spoke above his head further up the beach. Geronimo sat up and turned his body to face the voice. What he found was a tall, white man dressed vaguely as a pirate. He wore khaki shorts and a white blousy shirt.

"Is this your beach?" Geronimo asked, too bewildered to make any sort of sense with his questions. He wasn't sure at all himself why he felt the need to know the owner of the beach, if there even was one.

"Oh, no, not me," said the man. "But I am the owner of that boat over there." He pointed toward a sailboat lying against a mess of green foliage behind him up the beach. Geronimo turned to where he pointed and saw the sailboat nestled in the shadows of the brush. "I could give you a lift if you like," offered the boatman. "I'm actually shoving off in a bit, so this is good timing."

Geronimo stood up and yawned, stretching his legs. With his eyes fixed on the horizon, he said, "I need to go to the Great Gorge so I can learn the Eleven Mysteries, so I can break out of a dungeon, so I can capture Krampus, bring him to Santa, and ultimately save Christmas. Now, can you take me to the Great Gorge?"

"What's Christmas?" asked the boatman.

Geronimo was lost for words.

"Forget it. I can take you *near* the Great Gorge," the boatman said as he walked up the beach to his sailboat. Geronimo followed. "But I can't take you into the Great Gorge. It's too dangerous. I'm just going to drop you off on a flyby. Also, I'll be picking up a few other passengers along the way."

"Others? Are you like a water taxi?" asked Geronimo as he followed the footsteps of the boatman, who quickly swiveled around with a sour expression on his face. "I am no taxi, gnome. I am the boatman. The boatman provides passage between different lands, different worlds, and different realities."

"Far out," said the gnome. "You're not going to ask me to close my eyes, are you?"

"I'll ask nothing of you other than you follow three simple rules while on my boat. If you break any of them, even slightly, I'll have to push you overboard. I'm sorry, I don't like it, but I have to do it. Rule number 1, do not speak on my boat unless what you have to say is the most interesting thing imaginable. Number 2, no roughhousing. And number 3 is the most important. Once we are in the boat, whatever you do, don't look back. Can you obey these rules, young gnome?"

"Geronimo," said Geronimo. "My name is Geronimo."

"Can you obey these rules, Geronimo?" repeated the boatman.

"I shall do my best, boatman."

"Great. We're off!" said the boatman. He headed to the back of the boat while Geronimo shuffled to the front. They hopped into the gently lurching boat and drifted softly through the gray water. With the boatman's eyes behind the boat, toward the horizon, the first thing Geronimo did when he settled into his seat was look back.

⟨14⟩
THE DOLLHOUSE

Thelma! Thelma! Thelma!" Krampus had been yelling for his invisible donkey for the past two minutes. Bits of sausage spat from his mouth with every shout. T.C. stood across from Krampus at the other end of a long and narrow dining table. He couldn't see his host due to the mounds of food piled high in front of him. Krampus held two giant dried sausages in his hands as if they were utensils.

"I don't think Thelma is coming," said T.C.

"Silence!" shouted Krampus as he shot even larger bits of chewed meat out of his mouth. "Show some manners. You're a guest, for crying out loud."

"Of course, forgive me," said T.C., careful not to set off Krampus until he had found the children.

At that moment an elf walked in. Standing exactly halfway between Krampus and T.C, he decided to address the centaur first.

"Your feet and face look tired, toymaker," said the elf. "Tell me, what is your name?"

"T.C. And yours?"

"I lost memory of my name years ago due to a tragic accident. I prefer to be unnamed," said the unnamed elf. "I do, on the other hand, have full knowledge of my gender and age. Male, thirty-seven years old."

"I'm not a toymaker, by the way," replied T.C. "I'm Director of Transport."

"Ooo! Fancy!" the unnamed elf replied with his eyes bulging out.

T.C. went on the attack. "What are you doing here?" he asked. "Why aren't you making toys? Why do you bother serving Santa's greatest nemesis?"

Krampus finally joined the conversation by throwing a dried sausage across the table, smacking T.C. in the face. "I'm done," Krampus said, sliding out of the chair. "You two have ruined my meal." He marched to the hallway, then stopped and swung around to face his guest. "Without further ado," Krampus said with a flourish in his tone and movement, "it's time to visit the dollhouse." Krampus grinned devilishly at T.C.

"I really don't think that's a good idea, Your Excellency," said the elf.

"Who cares what you think?" Krampus snapped back.

"Well, you do, for one," replied the elf. "You ask me questions all the time. Why would you ask me questions if you didn't care about my thoughts?"

"Good point," said T.C.

"Then stay!" Krampus yelled. "Come with me, dog boy, let me give you the full tour, starting with our lovely dollhouse." T.C. didn't say anything. He walked dutifully behind Krampus. Before T.C. moved into the deeper shadows of the hallway, he heard a metallic object slide across the wood floor and hit his hoof. He bent down quickly and came back up with it. It was a key. The elf had slid him a key. Without looking back, T.C. slipped the key into his vest pocket and followed Krampus's heavy breathing down the curving corridors.

By the time they arrived at the dollhouse, they had taken two freight elevators, three separate spiral staircases, a small draw-bridge (which was still inside the castle), and an empty sewage drain that ran the length of a shopping mall. The journey was very quiet, and T.C. thought Krampus showed surprising athleticism through the rigor of the trek. *Perhaps this is Krampus's method of working out,* thought T.C.

The sewage pipe spat them out into a walled-off section of the backyard. To T.C. it was a cross between a courtyard and a prison yard. The fifty-foot walls were covered in moss, garland, and barbed wire. The only thing in the square space of red dirt and brown grass was a giant cage filled with girls ranging from eight to twelve years old. Krampus walked up to the cage with a look of grim inspection on his face, as if he was tending to rabbits.

"This is my masterpiece," Krampus said to T.C.

Ashen-colored fabrics hung from their limbs. The girls walked around the cage in a daze, weaving slowly like fish in a fishbowl. It was hard for T.C. to get an accurate count on how many there were with all the moving around. Eighty? Two hundred? Some were sitting, some even sleeping, but there was no talking. Each one seemed alienated from all the others, walking around in their own personal state of bewilderment. It was the saddest thing T.C. had ever seen in his entire life. He couldn't help it. He started to cry.

"I said, 'This is my masterpiece,'" repeated Krampus. He now looked at T.C. instead of the girls. "Did you hear me the first time?"

"Yes, I did," said T.C. "And I think I'd like to get closer." Krampus walked the few feet to the cell door and promptly unlocked the door. He swung it open with his face full of cheer. The girls had no reaction to the wide open door. They all moved like sleepwalkers, never quite alert or aware enough to escape their captivity. As T.C. trotted by Krampus he stopped. "Where are the boys?" Using his tail, Krampus prodded T.C. backwards, forcing him to cross the threshold into the cell. As soon as he did, Krampus abruptly slammed the cell door and locked T.C. inside.

"The boys are in the lower level," said Krampus. "But I don't like to go down there. It's too scary."

Krampus marched back to the drainpipe they had crawled out from with the clumsy urgency of a four-year-old.

"Next time you visit this cage, Krampus," said T.C., who had now moved to the very back of the cage, "don't be surprised if it's empty." Krampus decided the best way to deal with this statement was to bring up a wholly new topic.

"Tomorrow is my birthday!" Krampus announced as he crawled backward into the pipe. "There will be a party and some cake." Krampus wanted to mention one more thing, something like "and you're all invited," but he just couldn't bring himself to do it. So he closed the lid of the drainage pipe behind him and crawled back into the darkness.

Back in the dollhouse, as soon as Krampus shut the lid, T.C. noticed one girl in the very back of the cage that was unlike all the others. She was sitting cross-legged, facing the wall, blindfolded. T.C. approached her and asked, "What's your name, little girl?"

"What's your name, little girl?" she repeated.

"You were the first, weren't you?" asked T.C. "You're Nancy."

15
STARING IS RUDE

The boat was fairly crowded at this point. The boatman had picked up seven other passengers within a three-hour span, though two were dumped overboard before they arrived. The other passengers were an odd mix: a giant hamster named Boris dressed in a business suit who repeatedly voiced his concern about "making his connection." Then there was Xanadu, the out-of-work clown en route to visit his wealthy brother who made a fortune selling unicorn honey, which is derived from the animal's tears. There was the disheveled rabbit named Ester, who claimed he was the actual Easter Bunny, but no one in the boat seemed to believe him or care much. And finally there were the two Frogg brothers, attorneys-at-law. Brothers as well as lawyers, they were not, in fact, frogs, but ordinary people whose faces just looked slightly frog-like. They were fairly quiet, murmuring legalese to each other and then snickering throughout the trip. To Geronimo's estimate, there was only room on the boat for one more, maybe two.

After being explained the rules right before he hopped into the vessel, Geronimo had not said a single word the entire three hours of the journey. He had lucked out that the boatman had his back turned while Geronimo was breaking the rule of not looking back. He didn't allow himself to slip again as he watched the boatman throw overboard a leprechaun and a ballerina for breaking one of the three rules. After their abrupt departure, the boat chitchat came to a grinding halt.

Geronimo was just about to doze off when he heard the boatman whisper, "This will be our last pickup of the night. Looks like we have three. Please make room accordingly." Geronimo lifted his eyelids with great effort. He saw a green sign about thirty yards away. Too tired to wait thirty yards, he fell back asleep.

Two hours later, Geronimo opened his eyes again to the sight of a sleeping Eleanor sitting across from him. Geronimo had thrown a life jacket over his body before falling asleep, so Eleanor never saw him, until she too fell asleep. He pushed the life jacket aside and sat upright.

"Eleanor!" The sound of her name came out of his mouth like a blowgun. It was still dark outside and all the passengers had dozed off, with the exception of Murdock, Gromp, and Geronimo. Geronimo immediately recognized Murdock's face from a photo he had seen attached to a file on Santa's desk before he left. He would have tried to speak to Murdock if it were not for the odd stare the elf was giving him. It wasn't a particularly friendly stare—more competitive. This really threw Geronimo off, so he decided to look around the boat. Gromp sat beside Geronimo and across from Murdock and Eleanor to keep a close eye on his two captives.

Instead of Geronimo trying to decipher the meaning of Murdock's stare, he decided to switch up his tactics, and he turned to Gromp.

"What're you, some sort of movie star?" Geronimo asked.

"I'm a bounty hunter," said Gromp. "And I'll bounty hunt you if you're not careful. So shut it."

"Where are you headed?" asked Geronimo.

"My father's castle. If you're still on the boat when we arrive, you should come in for dinner," said Gromp, "I'm sure you'd taste delicious."

"No talking!" hushed the boatman, "that's your final warning." He sounded like a parent supervising a sleepover. "Hey, gnome, I forget your name," said Murdock inside Geronimo's head. "Hey, gnome! Are you hearing me?"

Geronimo nodded but at the wrong person. Geronimo was gawking up at Gromp as if he was the one speaking inside his head.

"How are you doing that?" Geronimo whispered to Gromp.

"Doing what?" asked Gromp.

"It's not him, you fool, it's the elf!" said Murdock telepathically. "Look at me, you dimwit!"

Geronimo decided to keep looking at Gromp instead of Murdock since he wasn't too crazy about the elf's tone.

"Okay, okay, I get it," said Murdock within Geronimo's mind. "I've come on too strong, and I shouldn't have called you a 'dimwit.'"

"Or . . ." Geronimo said, still looking up at Gromp, who was himself getting more and more unnerved by Geronimo's stare.

"Or a fool," Murdock added inside Geronimo's head.

Just as Geronimo was about to turn his gaze to Murdock, Gromp stood up with an explosive fury and bellowed, "Stop staring at me!"

Gromp screamed with such murderous rage that the boatman promptly walked over with his oar and, swinging with a tremendous backswing, walloped him in the ribs. This caused Gromp's body to catapult out of the boat and into the dark water. The boatman walked back to the helm as the boat fell silent. Everyone waited for a splash, a ripple, from the water below. But there was nothing. The boat drifted on into the night.

"Next stop, the Great Gorge!" the boatman announced.

~16~
THE BIRDS OF SORROW

Deep into the night, many hours after Krampus had left, T.C. was still trotting quietly about the perimeter of the cage in the hopes of getting an accurate count on the exact number of girls. After he removed Nancy's blindfold, she got up, and he lost track of her in the maze of bodies. He felt the key in his pocket and made his way to the front gate, where he fit the key into the keyhole and it fit snug. He turned it and with a *click*, the gate unlocked. Before opening the door, he wanted to try Nancy's name one more time.

"Nancy?" T.C. said at a stage whisper volume. "Nancy," he tried again. Nothing. His soft voice could not be heard through the girls' quiet clatter, and T.C. was not about to shout her name and wake the sleeping Krampus. He shrugged his shoulders and slowly walked through the gate. The gate made a quiet creaking sound, like a baby cricket crying for food. *"Crick-crick, crick-crick,"* went the gate. "*Crick-crick*," it went once more before it stopped, fully open.

"Crick-crick, crick-crick," said Nancy amidst the moving throng of girls.

"Nancy," T.C. said.

"Nancy," said Nancy as she weaved her way out of the moving traffic and straight outside the cell. Standing side-by-side with T.C., he noticed she had her blindfold back on. He had tossed it somewhere in the cell and she had found it.

"I don't get it," T.C. said. "Wouldn't you rather have it off, so you can see?"

Nancy repeated, "I don't get it. Wouldn't you rather have it off, so you can see?" T.C. shook his head and said, "You poor girl." He took the rag off her eyes and shoved it tight into his shirt pocket. He lowered his head to the ground and lifted her up and on to his back.

"You poor girl!" Nancy exclaimed with her eyes suddenly free and widening. The semblance of a smile stretched across her pale and solemn face.

"Hold on tight," said T.C.

"Hold on tight!" Nancy shouted with great exaltation. She felt the night breeze and the moonlight on her face. Free from the throng of girls, she could not resist shouting with joy, though T.C. knew her volume was trouble. Not more than a few seconds had passed before T.C. saw a candle flicker through an open window high up on one of the towers. *Krampus is up*, T.C. thought. They had to move now.

"Girls," T.C. shout-whispered at a medium volume. "Girls!" he repeated. They were not moving, not noticing. They were just ten feet away and kept aimlessly encircling each other. T.C. galloped back inside the cell and herded them out of the cage from the back, nudging the whole swirling blob gently toward the exit

71

until every last one of them was out. Once they were all outside of the cage, T.C. was onto the next problem. They had now scattered themselves all over the courtyard, drifting astray like quiet, confused zombies. Some girls talked to the plants while others asked the stars where their parents were. T.C. tried to convince each of the girls to follow him. He would tell them he wanted to help them find their parents, but they just wandered off as if not hearing or understanding him, asking the same question to no one in particular, again and again: "Where is my mommy?" The task of merely getting their attention proved twice as hard as trying to count them. T.C. floundered about the courtyard for about ten minutes, trying to assemble the girls and making absolutely no headway, when another light came on just beyond the courtyard walls, nearest the castle. He then heard a key turn into what must have been the door to the courtyard. In a panic, T.C. jumped behind the nearest small bush and crouched down. He heard the courtyard door creak open, and the crunch of dry grass being stepped on grew louder. The footsteps were coming right for him.

"There's no need to hide," said the elf in a library tone, standing a few feet from the bush. "I gave you the key and I'm out here to help."

T.C. scrambled up from his four-legged crouch and trotted over to the elf.

"So you are on our side," said T.C. as he leaned in toward the elf.

"Who's 'our side'?" asked the elf. The elf halted one of the roaming girls and said quietly in their ear, "Sophia, get back in the cage, please." The girl nodded her head and walked straight back toward the cage.

"Our side," replied T.C. "Santa's side. What're-what are you doing? Why are you putting them back in? I thought you were helping me?"

"I'm not doing this for Santa," said the elf. Two more girls crossed his path. "Jane, Gertrude, back to the cage, please." The two girls made a beeline back to the cage. T.C. galloped over to the three girls in an attempt to block their path and shouted, "Why are you doing this?"

The elf marched over to T.C. with a huffy look on his face.

"They only listen to instruction one at a time, and they only listen to me. I need them to all get back in the cage so we can call them to leave the courtyard one-by-one. I think you would agree that it's a much more difficult operation gathering them up while loose in the courtyard. We need to move quickly. Krampus only sleeps for a few hours at a time. He could rouse any moment." The elf turned his head and called out across the courtyard, "Julie, Ruth, and Tanya, tell the Fitzsimmons girls it's time for all of us to get back in the cage. Yes, thank you."

"Wow," said T.C. "You really have a way with them."

"Well, I've been planning this escape for years," replied the elf. The two of them made their way to the gate of the courtyard while the girls walked in calm droves back into the cage. "Listen, I want to make it clear that I don't side with Krampus, and I don't side with Santa either. I'm neutral."

"What do you have against Santa?" T.C. asked.

"Well," said the elf, "the fact that he's basically running an oligarchy with him at the top, manipulating a whole race of elves to do his bidding so he can get all the glory and honor and fame and legendary status he wants. And what does the elf get? The meaning of Christmas?"

"They get an annual salary now," said T.C. "Full medical, vision, paid vacation days galore."

"Really?" asked the elf, astonished.

"Can we please just save these girls already?" T.C. shouted.

"Yes! Yes!" the elf shouted back. "Okay, okay. So you wait here at the gate and usher them out. I will feed them to you from the cage, one-by-one. When they get to you, just line them up outside alongside the courtyard wall.

"Line them up?" asked T.C. "You think I'm going to be able to line them up? You said yourself they only listen to you."

"If you speak softly and directly into their ear you'll be fine. It's the only way to communicate with them. So review: I direct them across, they see you, and you line them up against the wall. Got it?"

"Let's do it." T.C. and the elf shook hands.

"One question," said the elf. "How're you gonna get them out of here?"

"We coordinated a drop point about a quarter mile from here. Santa's sending a luxury space chopper."

"Ugh, that's so him," said the elf, "well, good luck." The elf walked back to the cage where all the girls had returned.

T.C. watched the elf guide the first child out of the pack, whisper in her ear, and direct her to him. She walked obediently over to T.C. When she reached him, he gently directed her against the courtyard wall. As he put her in place, an idea occurred to him. "Stay very still," he told her, "and when I yell 'fire,' run as fast as you can." T.C. told the next girl that, and the next, and the one after that. He told every single girl the same message over the ten-minute process. And the girls were listening. They all stood against the wall like a large class photo ready to be taken. The elf sent the last girl over. He smiled as he looked up at Krampus's window. It was still dark and quiet. He sighed as he made his way to the courtyard's entrance.

Outside the courtyard, T.C. placed the last girl in the very front and stepped back a few feet. He resembled a conductor in front of his orchestra. But instead of conducting, he tried to get a final accurate count. He raised his finger into the night air and started from the left side of the back row. "One, two, three, four—"

"Eighty-eight!" yelled a voice from the bushes near the open gate.

"What?" shouted T.C., looking toward the bushes.

Out of the bushes sprang Krampus, wielding one of his two sabers. "You dare to pull a stunt like this on the eve of my birthday?" he shouted.

The elf was about twenty yards from the open gate when he saw Krampus and his saber held high and shining against the moonlight. The nameless elf broke into a sprint in hopes of preventing bloodshed. While running he watched as Krampus garbled some angry, incoherent words together before rushing at T.C. The centaur stood his ground twenty yards from the oncoming demon. The elf could only hear the unfolding events as T.C. was unseen on the other side of the courtyard wall. Moments later there was a loud *thump*. The elf watched Krampus's body as it soared over the wall and into the courtyard. The elf reached the exit and closed the courtyard door behind him. He grabbed a shovel propped against the castle walls and slipped the handle through the courtyard door handles.

"You kicked him, didn't you?" asked the elf.

"Oh yeah," said T.C. "Come at me with a saber and you're gonna get a one-way ticket on T.C. Airlines."

"Good work," said the elf. "You take the girls. I need to stay back to save the boys." The elf took Nancy's hand and kissed it. She looked down at him and he gave her a fatherly wink. "Be good to my girl, T.C. And Nancy, you listen to him. He will help you find your parents."

"Don't worry about the boys," said T.C., eager to get going. "Santa has a plan for a second invasion. It's very top secret so I can't say any more about it. It's called 'Operation: Geronimo.'"

"I'm not about to wait or rely on Santa. I'm gonna do this job myself and have it done before his operation even gets here."

"So you say," said T.C. "It's been great working with you." They shook hands once again.

"Despite our differences," said the elf.

"Despite our differences," repeated T.C.

The two of them suddenly heard loud, rasping breathing straight above them. They both looked up and there he was. Krampus had scaled over the wall from the inside of the courtyard. Now he was standing twenty feet directly above them. Drool dripped down from his long hanging tongue as he held his saber high overhead. Krampus wasted no time. He jumped into the air with the blade pointing down at his targets. T.C. and the elf scrambled out of Krampus's drop zone.

"Fire!" yelled T.C. The girls immediately scattered, running into the woods, around the castle, in all directions. Krampus crashed more than landed. His saber jostled from his grip and flung from his hand. Meanwhile, the elf slipped deftly into the shadows, jumping into a worm bin propped against the castle wall. During the melee, Nancy was knocked off T.C. by one of the fleeing girls. T.C. turned around to find her but she had instantly blended into the havoc. T.C. watched Krampus crawl to his saber a few feet from him. The centaur chose saving the girls over taking on Krampus, so he galloped for the woods to gather up the girls fleeing in that direction.

By the time Krampus grabbed his saber and had regained his composure, most of the girls had scattered themselves into the woods. He yelled off in the direction of the woods, "Don't you worry, dog boy, I'll eat what children I have left for Christmas dinner!" Krampus then heard a child's sniffling behind him. He turned back toward the gates of the courtyard and saw Nancy standing there. She was inches from the gate, waiting for someone to open it, crying and confused. Krampus walked over and slid the shovel out and opened the gate. "There you go, my dear, back home at last" said Krampus as he patted her on the shoulder. Krampus watched her as she walked back to the cage with her fists balled up against her eyes, choking with tears. "And why wait?" said Krampus, "I'll eat little Nancy tomorrow for breakfast—bright and early."

Krampus walked back to the secret side entrance of the castle he had come out of and pulled on the handle, but it wouldn't budge. He laughed as he felt for the key in the robe of his pocket. The laughing stopped as he continued to pat himself down with no success. "I locked myself out of my own castle," he said to himself in disbelief. "I locked myself out of my own castle," he repeated in hot tears, burying his head into his hands as he crumbled to the ground. The whimpering sounds of Nancy and Krampus sang through the desert landscape like two birds of sorrow.

~17~
BULL JAZZ

Just before seven the next morning, Santa and Rose sat by the phone, waiting for Krampus to call. Despite how enticing this plan had seemed to Santa the night before, he was now struggling to stay awake, cursing the task as well as its early hour of execution.

"This is madness," Santa said in a low and distant tone with his eyes closed. "Sheer, utter madness," he repeated while licking his dry, parched lips. He resembled a fat and tired lizard.

"He's going to call any minute," Rose replied. The sound of her voice was somewhere between gentle morning birds and wind chimes. She sat upright with nostrils flared. The steam of her tea wafted up to her eyes.

"I believe you," said Santa as he yawned. "I just won't be conscious for it, is all."

Then the phone rang. They let it ring twice before Santa answered.

"Hello," said Santa in a slightly lilted voice, trying to sound like his wife. Rose winced at the impression. "Yes, this is your brother. Happy birthday," Santa said. Santa waited a few seconds then hung up the phone, shaking his head.

"He hung up on me," Santa said. "I haven't talked to him in five hundred years and he hung up on me." Santa got up from the coffee table, exposing the onslaught of gingerbreads embroidered onto his pajamas. "I'm going back to bed," he said. "Don't feel bad, sweetie, it was worth a shot." As Santa stomped softly down the hall, the phone rang again. This time Rose picked up. "Hello," she said. Santa stopped and turned around. There was a pause before Rose continued. "I didn't mean to trick you," she said. "We're just very concerned." After a few moments Rose hung up.

"He hung up on me too."

"What did he say?"

"He said to tell Nicky he's going to eat Nancy today as part of his birthday breakfast feast and to stop meddling in his affairs."

"That just makes me want to meddle more."

"This is just one big game between the two of you," said Rose, "with all these lives at stake."

"Well, I'm trying to stop the game," said Santa.

"Are you so sure?" asked Rose. "Are you trying to stop it, or play it?"

"Maybe you've got to play it to stop it."

Rose shook her head. "Just be careful with whatever your next move is. He feels betrayed by me. He's especially vulnerable and unpredictable right now. And he's threatening to eat a child in the very, very near future, so you better cook something up fairly fast."

"I'm the vulnerable and unpredictable one right now. You should be comforting me," said Santa. "I sent out two space choppers last night. T.C. had a few losses, but he got most of the girls out of there."

"But not Nancy," said Rose.

"No, not Nancy," repeated Santa.

Silence fell over both of them. Shattering the silence was Santa's bedside phone. *Ring-ring. Ring-ring.* Santa looked at the phone with suspicion. "There's only three other people in the world that have this number." *Ring-ring. Ring-ring.* "And one of them is technically a bear." Santa picked up the phone. "Snopes?"

"Hey, Nicky" said Snopes. "Long time no talk."

"What do you want, Snopes?" asked Santa.

"Still got that tractor I bought ya?"

"What do you want, Snopes?"

"What's up with this gnome?"

"What's up with what gnome?"

"Don't play the fool with me, old man," said Snopes. "We go too far back for that poppycock." Snopes was pacing back and forth in the dungeon with a cordless phone to his ear.

"You know what's poppycock?" asked Santa. "You siding with my twisted-up brother. That's a rainbow of poppycock right there, bucket head."

"You just call me a 'bucket head'?"

"You just called me an 'old man,'" Santa said, standing up from the bed. He also started pacing back and forth in his bedroom.

"You are an old man," said Snopes, who stopped pacing and put his paw on Ned's jail cell. Snopes kept a steely glare on the sleeping gnome inside the cell.

"You're a bucket head," said Santa.

They both took a breath. Snopes waited a few beats before resetting the conversation.

"There's a sleeping gnome in my dungeon that won't get up. I want to know who sent him, why, and what of it?"

"I sent him," said Santa. "And I advise you to release him as he is under full protection of the Nicholas Doctrine, and thusly no harm should ever befall him, else the punisher will be severely punished."

"There is no such thing as a Nicholas Doctrine," replied Snopes.

"Oh, there is," said Santa. "It's just that nobody pays attention to it. But they should."

Rose, still listening in, had about enough at this point. Rolling her eyes, she got up and walked out of the room.

"If you don't tell me what you're planning," said Snopes, "I'm just going to wake him up myself, get the information, and then dispose of him."

"Maybe, just maybe, he will wake up on his own," said Santa. "Ever think of that?" Snopes shook his head and hung up.

Snopes was in the dungeon standing outside of Ned's cell. His giant white paws gripped the bars.

"When will he wake up?" asked Snopes, motioning toward the unconscious Geronimo lying on Ned's cot.

Ned was sitting cross-legged in the very back of his cell, taking as much advantage as possible of this rare visit by Snopes. "Whenever he wants to, I suppose," said Ned.

"That's a bunch of bull jazz," the bear growled. His patience drained, he flashed his white fangs at the wizard. "You did this to him, and you know how to get him out," said Snopes.

"But you don't know how to get me out," said the wizard. "Isn't that so?" Ned chuckled. Snopes let loose a blood-curdling roar.

"What an angry and desperate bear you are!" Ned shouted over the raucous.

"You listen to me, you soothsayin' stink bag," said Snopes, snarling wildly. "When we do finally find the key to this cell, we will tear you to shreds."

"That sort of talk isn't going to make me want to help you," said Ned.

At that moment, Geronimo woke up with a start. He sat up abruptly and blurted out, "I'm back!" Geronimo looked around. "Eleanor? Where's Eleanor?" Ned was in disbelief. A smirk stretched across Snopes's face.

"What're you doing here, gnome?" asked Snopes.

"How did you get back?" asked Ned.

"I've lost Eleanor . . ."

"Tell me what happened," said Ned.

"Yes," said Snopes, "tell us what happened."

"Well," said Geronimo, taking a tiny, bloody dagger from his pocket and tossing it onto the stone floor. "We made it to the gorge . . ."

~18~
NO FIRE, FREEZE POP

Shortly after jumping overboard, Geronimo recognized the wall of rock in front of him while bobbing in the choppy water as the same wall he had clung to when he first went under Ned's spell. "This is as close as we get to the Great Gorge," said the boatman. "Any closer and we risk getting sucked in."

Geronimo, Eleanor, and Murdock were the only passengers left on the boat. The boatman had thrown overboard the rest of the travelers for a variety of violations: speaking loudly, rocking the boat, and whistling, among others. The boat was now floating about hundred yards out from the mouth of the gorge, where inside swirled a furious whirlpool that foamed and spat with violent force. The boatman was turning the vessel so it was parallel to the gorge's entrance. He gave the gorge a slow flyby as he yelled out, "All right, gnome, now's your chance. You jump in here and you'll get sucked into the gorge. So, jump!"

The loud voices startled Eleanor out of her long sleep. The first thing she saw was Geronimo.

"Geronimo!" she yelled.

"Eleanor!" Geronimo replied.

"What's going on?" Eleanor pleaded.

"Well," said Geronimo," I don't have much time to talk, but I need to jump off the boat and get sucked into that whirlpool over there, I think, and then find the Eleven Mysteries, then break out of the dungeon that I'm in, even now, so I can go find Krampus and deliver him to his brother, Santa Claus."

"I suggest you go ahead and jump then," Murdock replied as he stood up from his seat. "Do you need a little push? I'd be happy to assist."

"Oh, no, thank you," said Geronimo as he stood up in order to fend off any encroachment by the elf.

"I consider passengers pushing each other horseplay," said the boatman. "I'll be doing any pushing that needs to be done, thank you."

"Take me with you," said Eleanor, "Please take me back home, Geronimo! I promise to be good! Please, Geronimo, please!"

"I don't know how to get you home, Eleanor," said Geronimo. "The smartest thing you can do is listen to this elf. Do what he says. His mission is to protect you."

"Jump off the boat now or we're leaving for good," warned the boatman. The boat was on the tail end of its flyby with the boatman threatening to steer it back toward the deep sea at any moment. "You have five seconds to jump and then I'm leaving the gorge. Five . . ."

Eleanor ran over to Geronimo. "No, Eleanor!" cried Murdock. "You have to stay with me!"

"Four . . ."

"I don't care where you're going," said Eleanor to Geronimo, "I'd rather stay with you than the elf!"

"Three . . ."

Geronimo's mind was groping madly for the right decision while Eleanor continued to plead her case. "That bossy little elf has gotten me into enough trouble as it is," she told him. "Let's just go, Geronimo! Let's jump together!"

"Two . . ." said the boatman.

Just then a hand came out of the water behind Eleanor, grabbed her shirt collar, and yanked her overboard. Geronimo immediately plunged in after her. Murdock and the boatman were left alone in the abrupt silence. Murdock looked at the boatman and then jumped in himself.

"One?" said the boatman to an empty boat.

"Then what happened?" asked Snopes, who now sat crisscross outside Ned's cell, engrossed in Geronimo's retelling of the story so far.

"Who pulled Eleanor into the water?" asked Ned, whose interest was just as piqued. "Was it Gromp? It was Gromp, wasn't it?"

"If it's not too much trouble," said Geronimo, "I wouldn't mind some ginger snaps or something similarly sweet, but not too desserty. I haven't had a decent sweet in I-don't-know-how-long, and I'm feeling a little light-headed."

"I'll grab a cookie from the jar," said Snopes, who scampered up the ladder and out of the dungeon, leaving the door above open in his haste. Geronimo stared at the moon-shaped shaft of light projected onto the stone floor. Ned turned to him and said in a conspiratorially soft whisper, "You did visit the Eleven

Mysteries, didn't you?" Geronimo nodded his head. "And so you must know," said Ned, "that this is the very moment in which you need to escape."

Again, Geronimo nodded. He stood up, walked past the bars, and scaled up the ladder and out of the dungeon. Ned sat there in the renewed quiet for a while. "Good-bye, gnome," Ned said to himself, "I'll miss your company." As a tear left his eye, he started to chuckle over his foolish emotions. "A silly old man," he muttered. The familiar stomping of bears came booming back into his world as Snopes grunted with quick purpose down the ladder.

"It's like Penn Station around here lately," said Ned.

Snopes scurried to the bars, holding a large cookie jar with one arm, and barked, "Where did he go?"

"I don't know," said Ned. "You left the hatch open. He could be halfway to China by now."

Snopes grew so infuriated with himself that he raised his half-filled, gallon-sized glass cookie jar high above his head and threw it down very close to his big, white feet. The jar smashed into bits against the stone floor, and small glass shards gouged into Snopes's bare feet, buckling his massive body to the ground. Clutching his bloody feet with his giant paws, he writhed on top of the countless bits of glass spread about the floor. Using the most of this opportunity, Ned walked up to the door of his cell, brought his hand around to the front of the keyhole, and unlocked the door with the missing key. Ned walked out of the cell and looked down at the giant, whimpering bear. "Here's your key back," he said as he dropped the key onto the bear's chest. Snopes wiggled his body in an attempt to get up and attack Ned, but the very act of wiggling caused his body to seize up in pain. "Gggrrrrr!" was all Snopes could get out through the labored puffing of his nostrils.

"I won't be needing it anymore," said Ned as he made a casual stride toward the ladder, his black shoes squeaking through the darkened room. Ned stopped again at the base of the ladder. The light from the door above shined down on him like a spotlight. "Today, I leave my imprisonment after forty-seven years."

"You had the key to your own cell for the last twenty," said Snopes. "You could've escaped at any point!"

"I needed the gnome to finish my mission," said Ned. "It's complicated and I don't expect you to understand. In fact, I prefer you not understand." And with that, Ned made his way up the ladder toward freedom. "Yeah, patch me into Freeze Pop," said Snopes, who finally managed to stagger to his feet as he leaned against the cell bars. He talked into his walkie-talkie he had strapped to his belt. "You there, Freeze Pop? We have an escaped prisoner. Set off the campus-wide alarm system! Freeze Pop, do you hear me?"

"Yeah, Freeze Pop hear you, man," said a fuzzy, squealed response on the other end.

Snopes banged his walkie in frustration. "I only got one light left on my battery indicator, Freeze Pop, so listen closely—activate the code red security alarms! We have a prison break!"

"Hey, you break me, I break your face," squealed Freeze Pop on the other end.

"What? What're you talking about? I'm trying to tell you to sound the alarms and alert the Great Eleven! There's been a dungeon break!" Snopes looked back over at the ladder. Ned had left.

"Like I said, you try to break me, I break your *face*!" Freeze Pop repeated with even more agitation and confusion in his voice.

"The wizard and the gnome have escaped!" continued Snopes. "Run to the smoking lounge and tell them that! Now! Go!" With his legs all cut up and gashed from the sprayed glass, Snopes had no way of getting up the ladder without help.

"Curse that wizard," muttered Snopes.

"You curse me, I curse your face too!" belted an enraged Freeze Pop, still replying over the walkie.

"Freeze Pop, you're fired," said Snopes.

"Please, boss, I take back all the break faces. Don't fire me. Honestly, I think I may have been mishearing you this whole time. Give me one more chance, boss, please!" Freeze Pop's words whimpered into garbled crying.

⁓19⁓

BEFORE THE UGLY STICK

Eleanor didn't make it to the Eleven Mysteries of the Universe. The pull of the tidal wave was so strong she lost grip of Geronimo's hand and spun out toward the gorge's rocky shores. The back of her head collided with a pile of rocks as the current pushed her over the pile and onto the dry, rocky shore on the other side. She lay there for the remainder of the day until her unconscious body was dragged from the light of moon and stars into a cave a few feet away.

In the morning, Eleanor climbed out of the cave, awakened by the sunlight bouncing off the cave walls. She scrambled toward the sun's warmth with her head wrapped in white bandages and her wet clothes replaced with a tunic made up of intertwining silk scarves all in various shades of blue. She sat on the rock pile and looked out over the massive gorge. She felt the bandages on her head. Her head was pounding so hard the pain alone brought her to tears. She couldn't remember why she had the bandages on.

Who put them on? How did she get here? There were so many questions it just made her want to scream. So she did.

"Shhh, keep it down, little bambina!" said a voice from the cave. Eleanor whipped around. "Who said that?" she shouted.

"This is a breeding site for giant electric turtles," said the voice, "and it's high season right now. Quickly get back inside. I promise I'll explain everything!"

"Are you the one who dressed me like a jellyfish?" Eleanor asked.

"Jellyfish?" said the voice in the cave. "We all thought you looked so nice. Besides, it was the queen that dressed you in fresh linens, bambina, so don't get haughty with me. But enough of this, you stay there and we'll come get you."

"Queen? What queen?"

"The queen of Pointless," said the voice. The sounds of chatter inside the cave intensified. Dark clouds snuck into view overhead. There was a buzz of static electricity in the air. She could feel the hairs on her arms begin to rise. Thunder clapped behind her. She turned back around to face the water. Flashes of lightening rained down upon the gorge. Dozens of giant electric turtles the size of hippos shot out of the water, spun in the air, and then torpedoed back into the hostile waves.

"You're right, this isn't safe," Eleanor said to mostly herself. She started walking backward, further away from the water's edge, when she tripped over a rock. She went flying backward with her arms waving. She closed her eyes and waited for the arrival of physical pain. But there was none.

It felt as if she had landed on a zillion balls of socks. "Hey, little bambina!" she heard the voice from the cave say from the darkness of her closed eyes. She opened her eyes and saw a guinea pig with the letter "A" shaved into his belly, standing upright on her stomach. She also noticed that outlining her horizontal body were guinea pigs that had caught her and were now marching her back inside the cave.

"A guinea pig?" asked Eleanor.

"My name is Amando," said the guinea pig. With this, Eleanor lost consciousness again. Concerned, Amando looked around at his fellow guinea pigs. "Did I come on too strong?"

"What do we do?" asked a guinea pig named Tino. "We can't leave her out here."

"You guys remember when we found that injured doe in the castle forest?" asked Amando. They rest of them all nodded, murmuring with recollection. They then gathered under each of Eleanor's limbs, grabbed an arm or a leg with their front paws, stood up on their hind legs in unison, and walked her slowly into the cave.

When Eleanor came to, she was seated around a fire with eleven guinea pigs and a camel. Sitting directly across the fire from her was the camel dressed in what looked like royal garments. The camel wore a crown of desert flowers on its head. Purple and gold scarves fell over the camel's six humps, forming a circle on her back. Eleanor was struck by the grandeur beaming from the camel's face. She seemed to be smiling broadly at Eleanor. It was a protective, motherly, endless love sort of smile. Eleanor couldn't stand it. However, she couldn't help but wonder what it would be like to ride on a camel with six humps. *Not like those clunky-looking, two-humped camels*, she thought. This was some sort of camel limousine. Regardless, she chose to avert her eyes from the animal entirely. Instead, she watched the smoke from the fire rise up and out of a hole in the cave directly above them.

"Oolong tea?" asked Amando, who sat beside her. He was trying his best to break the awkward silence. With great effort, Amando held up a cup of hot tea for Eleanor to drink. While the cup was a perfect size for Eleanor, it was humungous in Amando's tiny, guinea pig hands. Eleanor kept her eyes on the hole in the cave above them, refusing Amando's offer. However, Amando would not give up so easily. He frowned sternly and kept the cup lifted toward her as it teetered and tottered, his hands trembling.

"No need to force it on her," said the camel in a light, sweet, feminine tone. Eleanor finally looked back at the camel. She was struck by the superiority and sophistication radiating from her. Something about her smile made Eleanor miss her own mother, and that made Eleanor want to cry all over again. She was so tired of crying. She decided to just keep staring at the fire instead. Amando finally put the cup down. "It's just that we're *all* drinking oolong tea," said Amando. "It would be the polite thing to do."

"Enough of that nonsense," said the camel. "She will do what makes her comfortable." Eleanor couldn't resist any longer. She looked around the fire at each guinea pig. They were all drinking small cups of oolong tea. Even the camel had a small bowl in front of her.

"I'm sorry, Queen Fatilahh," confessed Amando, "but I really don't think she is the one."

"She is the one!" cried Giovanna, a female guinea pig seated to the left of Eleanor.

"She is!" cried Ernesta, another female guinea pig to the right of Eleanor. "She is! She is! She is" was suddenly chanted by the majority of the guinea pigs. The camel nodded with the rising cries. "I believe she is the one," she said quietly, silencing the guinea pigs all around her with her voice. "You are the one Nicky has been talking about. I feel it as sure as the blood that pumps in my heart."

"So you're a queen of guinea pigs?" asked Eleanor.

"My name is Fatilahh," said the camel, "and, no, I am no queen. My friends here just like to call me that."

"All hail, Queen Fatilahh!" shouted out another guinea pig named Frederico, with his eyes closed and hands in the air. All eleven guinea pigs raised their right arms and responded with, "All hail, Queen Fatilahh!"

"You see, I and these guinea pigs share a common bond," said Queen Fatilahh, "we are all the last of our kind."

"That's not true," said Eleanor. "There are plenty of guinea pigs where I live. Half the kids in my class have guinea pigs."

"They don't have a Capizzi guinea pig, I can tell you that much," said Amando.

"Have you heard of the Great Sicilian Guinea Pig War?" asked the guinea pig named Tino, who was wearing an eye patch made of string and cloth. Eleanor shook her head. "It was a ten-year war fought in underground tunnels all over Sicily. A fight broke out between the Capizzis and the Ferraros. It wasn't long until all the families were involved."

"And how did it start?" Amando asked. "Over a piece of mozzarella no bigger than the fingernail on your pinky," he said. Eleanor stole a look at the fingernail on her pinky.

"You are looking at the only survivors of that wretched war," said Frederico.

"We are a mixed bag," said Rosabella, who sat beside the queen. Rosabella's auburn coat turned rose-colored against the flickering firelight. "We are the last of all the great Sicilian families. We fled before . . . before . . ."

"Before what?" asked Eleanor, picking up her cup of tea and taking a sip without realizing what she was doing.

"Before they all killed each other!" shouted Sergio, one of the smaller guinea pigs in the group.

"Now, now, Sergio," said Queen Fatillahh, "no need to frighten her." The queen looked directly into Eleanor's eyes. "It is true, my dear, that we are both the last of our kind, and all of us are stuck here until King Krampus is removed from his castle. And you will help us remove him, child. Once he is removed, this land will flourish as abundantly as it did before."

"Before what?" asked Eleanor, putting her empty cup down.

"Do you need more?" whispered an excited and concerned Amando beside her. She nodded her head back to him, keeping her eyes on the queen.

"Before Krampus showed up," said Ottavio, who was bald between his ears. Looking at him, Eleanor could not tell if this was intentional on his part or if it fell out due to medical reasons. "Before that ugly stick showed up, this place was awesome—just awesome. At least that's what the queen says."

"Perhaps we should all introduce ourselves individually to Eleanor," said Queen Fatilahh, "so she's not so overwhelmed."

"I want my mom and dad!" Eleanor cried out. The word *overwhelmed* reminded Eleanor of her mother. It was a word her mother would always use when Eleanor would get anxious or upset in public. The word itself triggered all the thoughts of home: warm food at the table, a comfy couch, hugs from Dad before bed, kisses from Mom in the morning. Eleanor was done with all this fantasy business. "I'm so sick of talking animals!" she screamed. "I'm sick of *all* of this!" Eleanor let out a wail and buried her head in her hands. Her shoulders shook as she whimpered.

The queen and the guinea pigs looked on with concern and sadness. In the few moments of silence after Eleanor's final whimpers abated, the queen looked at Rosabella and said, "You start."

"Start with what?" asked Rosabella.

"Just say your name and something you like."

"Okay," said Rosabella. "My name is Rosabella and I like going for walks and smelling flowers—particularly in the morning." Eleanor looked up at Rosabella from her prison of fingers.

Smelling flowers in the morning was something Eleanor loved too, though she wouldn't dare admit it now.

Next was Nicolina. "Hi, my name is Nicolina," she said, "and I love to sew." She was blessed with the largest eyelashes Eleanor had ever seen on a rodent.

"Hi, my name is Sergio," said Sergio. "I was the one earlier who shouldn't have been talking about everybody killing each other. My favorite thing to do is probably eat mozzarella."

"My name is Sofia," Sofia said, "and I like painting rocks."

Next was Amando, and after that was Eleanor. They did not know her name yet, and she was not ready to tell them. Amando looked up at her as she sipped her tea. "My name is Amando Capizzi," he said, "and I love making tea for people." Eleanor scowled as she put the cup down. Closing his eyes and shaking his head, Amando added, "It is one of my deepest passions in life." Eleanor looked at Queen Fatilahh and gave a defiant shake of her head.

Tino started up on the other side of her. Eleanor noticed he wore a silver earring in his right ear. "I'm Tino and I like to mix it up." Tino looked up at Eleanor with big blue eyes. "That's it," he added. "I'm often asked, 'What do you mean by mixing it up?' And I always give the same answer: 'You'll see.'" Eleanor wanted to hate Tino, but it felt impossible.

"My name is Tatiana," said Tatiana, who had a mess of colors on her face. "I'm mostly into makeup and fashion. But mostly makeup."

"My name is Ernesta," said Ernesta, the skinniest of the group and covered in sand. "I like racing lizards, though no lizards here in Pointless. So I mostly just race them in my mind."

"My name is Ottavio," said the largest of all the guinea pigs in a deep, baritone voice. Facing Eleanor, he knelt down on one knee and said, "Your Excellency, you have blessed us all with your presence, and I look forward to the day you lead us in battle against the forces of darkness, so that peace and love may once again rule this land. That would be my favorite thing." Some of the guinea pigs cheered and hollered while Ottavio got out of the kneeling position and plopped his bottom back on the warm dirt. He grabbed his teacup, took a sip, and nodded at Eleanor, as if to say if that didn't win you over, nothing will.

Next was Giovanna. "My name is Giovanna." She wore wire spectacles and a white lab coat. "And I enjoy witchcraft."

"My name is Frederico," said the final guinea pig. Frederico was missing his right hind leg. Eleanor figured he had lost it in the war. "I love making new friends," he said while choking up on the word *friends*. "I'm sorry," Frederico said. He wiped tears from his eyes with the use of his tiny walking stick. "I don't know why I get so emotional over these things."

This last guinea pig proved to be too much for Eleanor's grief, anger, and frustration. So weary from the weight of these exhausting emotions, Eleanor let them burn off within her. The rest of them could sense the change that came over her. She was creeping toward acceptance of them, even if it was temporary. They turned to her, waiting, knowing, she would respond.

"My name is Eleanor," she said. "And I like smelling flowers in the morning too." Rosabella was quietly ecstatic over this news.

~20~
ᴛᴇᴘ

Sirens and red lights were going off all around Geronimo. He'd reached the doors on the opposite side of the gymnasium from the locker room, and now he was running through a lobby with large glass trophy cases adorning the walls. Two members of the Great Eleven, Cocoa and Sneed, were there, though temporarily indisposed. Both bears crumbled to the ground with their paws squeezed against their ears due to the paralyzing volume of their own alarm system. "Where's Freeze Pop? Freeze Pop!" yelled Cocoa.

"We just fired him!" yelled Sneed, who was curled up in a fetal position beside Cocoa. "He packed his things! He's long gone!"

"He ran all the security systems. He was the only one who knew how to turn the alarms off!" Cocoa shouted back.

Geronimo ran right past them, unnoticed, and turned left. Framed portraits of previous members of the Great Eleven filled the hallway wall. He turned a corner and then another. He could hear large, bounding paws and snarling grunts getting louder behind him. He saw a glowing "Exit" sign at the end of the hallway. Instead of trying to figure out how to open the exit door, Geronimo ducked inside the cracked-open door of a darkened room just to the left of the exit doors.

From inside the darkened room, he could hear thundering strides roll down the hallway corner. The bears were headed toward the room he was hiding in. They rushed past the slightly ajar door and slammed through the exit doors, assuming the gnome went outside. Geronimo could hear the sounds of things outside getting smashed. The sounding of the alarm morphed and deteriorated into silence with continual smashing sounds. *Someone must have found the motherboard for their security system and bashed it to pieces*, thought Geronimo.

Once the hallway sounded vacant enough, Geronimo, pressing both hands against the door, slowly pushed it closed. He didn't want the open door to expose his hideout. He turned back around to look at the room he was in. There was little too see, though his nose picked up a strong scent of leather, whisky, and smoke. Then he saw the rivulets of cigar smoke emanating from the far end of the room, billowing up from behind the largest leather chair he had ever seen. He wasn't alone. Geronimo was about to utilize his slide-crawl floor tactic as a last resort to get away, when the chair swiveled around. It was Fort, one of the Great Eleven. He was seated at a large oak desk, smoking a cigar and glowering down at Geronimo. Geronimo just stared back at him, out of plans.

"Come closer," Fort said. Geronimo hesitated for about three seconds before walking up to the desk and leaping upon the chair opposite Fort. From the chair, he leapt onto the desk and sat on a coaster, two feet from Fort's nose.

"You're pretty brave for a gnome," said Fort.

"Thanks," said Geronimo, "but don't call me 'pretty.'"

Fort turned a latch on the ground beside his feet and opened up a square hole in the wooden floor. "This tunnel acts as our emergency evacuation pipe," he said. "We call it the EEP. God forbid we ever need to use it. It will get you to safety, though," said Fort.

"Why are you doing this?" asked Geronimo.

"Let's just say I go way back with your employer." Fort stuck his claw out for Geronimo to shake. "Name's Fort." Geronimo shook the claw. "I'm an old friend of Nicky's."

"Geronimo. Santa's not my employer. I'm not getting paid for this."

"You're 'adventure organizer' then," said Fort.

"Though I really should be getting paid," said Geronimo, "considering everything I've gone through at this point."

They suddenly heard the exit doors slam back open.

"Get a move on, kid," said Fort.

"I still don't know how to get to Krampus's castle—"

"Where is he?" shouted Ringo, whirling into the darkened room. "Have you seen him? The gnome?" He marched into the lounge blind by the stark lack of light and banged his knee into an unseen coffee table. The force of the impact sent the polar bear hopping toward the couch on the other side of the room. "Why are all the lights off?" Ringo asked as he flipped a light switch on the wall behind him. The room was illuminated. Ringo looked over toward the desk and saw Fort's body bent over in his chair with the back of the chair facing Ringo. "What're you doing?" asked Ringo, now suspicious and getting up to look. He walked quickly over to the desk. Fort's body shot upright in his seat just as Ringo reached the desk. "Here it is! I found it!" exclaimed Fort who was holding a manila folder in his paw.

"What're you doing in here? We have prisoners on the loose! And Snopes is badly injured. He needs help getting out of the dungeon."

"I'm sorry. You're right," said Fort. He got out of his chair and walked quickly with Ringo toward the door. "That folder has been missing for weeks and it's been driving me crazy."

When the two of them reached the hallway, they ran into Dan, who stopped in mid-sprint.

"You two seen the gnome or the wizard?" wheezed Dan, sucking in big gulps of air between each word. He wore a headlamp and carried a pitchfork.

"No," said Fort. "How's Snopes?"

"We got him up the dungeon stairs and then he sped off on his own on one of the golf carts. Didn't say where he was going."

This was troubling news to Fort, but he wasn't about to blow his cover. Smiling back at Dan, he said, "Well, then, that's good news. He's doing well enough to operate a golf cart. Let's help our fearless leader and widen our search party. Alert all club members to keep an eye out." Sneed and Dan both nodded their heads and darted off in different directions.

Snopes was fifty yards out from the clubhouse, his legs and torso covered in bloody bandages as he floored the golf cart. He was moving at the cart's max speed, about five miles per hour. He was driving the cart along a yellow dotted line in the grass. Every now and then "EEP" would appear along the line.

~21~
DOUBLE RED LEVEL

Both still in their pajamas, Clarence and Santa sat cross-legged in Santa's office. Outside, the midday sun shone on the blanket of snow on the ground. Light poured through the large window on the wall behind them. Through the view of the window, one could see several reindeer practicing their takeoff and landing. An elf wearing a pilot's helmet and fluorescent vest directed the reindeers to a helipad far off in the distance.

On the rug between Santa and Clarence was a large map riddled with post-its. Each post-it had a different name written on it. The two of them stared at the map in silence.

"So—do you get it now?" asked Santa.

"Can you go over it one more time?" asked Clarence.

Santa sighed. He pointed at the corner of the map with a question mark on it. Stuck on the question mark were post-its that read, "Murdock," "Eleanor," "Gromp," "Krampus," and "Geronimo."

"This is where the party's at," said Santa. "Krampus's castle is somewhere in this area." Santa's finger encircled the question mark. "If all goes to double hockey sticks on this one, it's all gonna go down here." Santa jabbed his pudgy finger into the middle of the question mark.

"Okay," said Clarence.

"This is where things get weird," continued Santa. "Murdock confirmed Geronimo being on the boat last night somewhere around here." Santa pointed to the mystery region.

"How did you get a hold of Murdock?" asked Clarence.

"He has a space-texter," said Santa, suddenly avoiding the elf's eyes.

"You took my space-texter?" asked Clarence, stunned.

"He needed it," said Santa. He turned back to Clarence and clasped his fingers together in prayer-like fashion. "So then I get a call from Fort at the country club," continued Santa, "he tells me he just helped Geronimo escape from the compound." Santa moved his finger to the complete opposite end of the map where there was a post-it that read "PBCC."

"So you're saying Geronimo goes from the country club to this desert in the far corner of the universe, then back to the club in one night's span?" asked Clarence. "Do you know how many light years that would take?"

Clarence waited quietly for the answer. Santa waited quietly for him to guess. Awkward beats of silence passed between them in this manner, until finally Santa said, "Something like nine billion."

Clarence nodded his head, relieved that there was any answer at all.

"I can't even pull that sort of speed off," said Santa. "So the question is, can Geronimo get there," Santa pointed at the questioned marked region, "before my brother eats anymore children?"

"Forgive me if I'm speaking out of turn here," said Clarence, "but why don't you fly over there yourself? Survey the landscape. Look for a creepy castle."

"I was over there once before," said Santa, "many years ago. I had suspected that region even back then to be a perfect place for him to hide. I didn't realize how perfect it was until I flew over the dunes. All the navigational equipment in the chopper went haywire once I hit that desert. The needles danced. All the levers moved up and down without me even touching them. And the reindeers refuse to go near the desert, so they're no help. There is some bad mojo in that place."

The faint sound of a chopper grew louder as it descended onto the helipad outside through the window.

"That's T.C.," said Santa. "He's got the girls."

"Okay, two things," said Clarence, "one: how did you coordinate a chopper with T.C.? and two: how did *that* chopper get over the desert?" Clarence's finger was pointed toward the chopper.

"I'm afraid the answer to 'one' may be upsetting to you."

"Why would it be upsetting?" asked Clarence.

"I'm just saying," said Santa.

"Are you going to give me a reason to be upset?" asked Clarence.

"I borrowed your sister's space-texter, too," said Santa.

"Without asking first?" Clarence was appalled.

"Clarence," said Santa, "this is a very important mission and I didn't have time. So just take it easy. Gain some perspective. What I called you in here for is to tell you that we may be at double red level very soon." Santa sat back to let Clarence take in this news. The elf just stared blankly back at Santa.

Meanwhile, outside the window, elves had run out to the helipad to help the girls out of the chopper. Their gray, tired bodies climbed one by one down a rope ladder. T.C. had also gotten out of the chopper and was now in hot pursuit of Santa's office window.

"You didn't answer my 'two' question," said Clarence.

"How did that chopper get over the desert?" said Santa. "Barely is the answer. Look, see there?" Santa pointed toward the window at the sight of a human pilot being carried out of the chopper on a stretcher. "That's Colin, our ace space chopper pilot. He's the best there is. An hour ago, T.C. texted me that Colin started suffering from violent seizures as soon as they reached the desert. The seizures subsided upon landing and he's had a full recovery, but T.C. had to take over controls while reading the manual on how to land."

"Yeah, T.C.'s pretty great," said Clarence.

"The kid's a bona-fide hero," said Santa.

"So what's double red level mean, then?" asked Clarence.

Santa rolled his eyes. "Does anyone get my emails?" he asked. "This is why no one ever responds to my campus-wide emails. No one is even *looking* at them."

"You gave us email accounts?" asked Clarence. "Santa, you have to get down to the production floor more often. Half of us are still waiting for computers."

"Everyone wants a computer but not everyone needs a computer. That's the problem. Back to double red level. Double red level means papa bear leaves HQ. I'm out. None of my plans have worked and I have to go do it myself. That's double red level. I've never done it before because it leaves HQ highly vulnerable."

"Is there a single red level?" asked Clarence.

"Yes, but it's just called 'red level.' You don't have to say 'single.' We were currently in red level before we switched to double red level."

"When did you switch it?" asked Clarence.

"Just now, while we've been talking."

"Things are happening fast, then," said Clarence. "For what it's worth, I really think we can take care of ourselves when you leave. We can hold down the fort."

"I admire your bravery," said Santa, "but you really can't. No offense, but you're all the size of footballs."

Knock-knock. T.C. had made it to the window. The glass of the window was already fogged from his hot breath.

"Could you please open the window for T.C.?" Santa asked.

"I can't. It's too high. Despite my bravery, I'm only the size of a football, remember?" said Clarence.

"Oh don't be weird about it," said Santa. He heaved himself out of his sitting position and lumbered over to the window.

He slid the window open. "How many?" Santa asked.

"Only twenty-nine out of eighty-eight girls," said T.C. "I have no idea how many boys. I didn't even get to them."

"All right," said Santa, "good work. We'll talk later. Go take a nap."

"Yes, sir," said T.C. He trotted a few feet before turning back. "Oh yeah, one other thing. There's this elf there. He said he was going to try and get the boys out by himself."

"Anything else?" asked Santa.

"He doesn't like you," said T.C.

"That's fine," said Santa. "Some days I don't like me either. No biggie. Get some shut-eye." T.C. trotted off toward his quarters.

"What about Murdock?" asked Clarence. "What happened to Murdock?"

22
BATTLE AXE OR CROSSBOW

By midday, Pointless was baking under a high, blazing sun. Murdock tailed Gromp from about three sand dunes away, a distance of roughly forty yards. The elf had failed to locate Eleanor in the dark waters of the gorge earlier that night, though he did find Gromp's wet footprints under the moonlight and followed them onto the dunes from the rocky shore. He had been following Gromp for the last three hours now. What Murdock would do when he caught Gromp, and why he chose to follow Gromp in the first place were questions Murdock did not have answers for quite yet. Murdock hoped Gromp would lead him to Krampus's castle, where he could at least begin a rescue operation. This mission felt much more professionally satisfying for Murdock, than, say, trying to find a girl that wants nothing to do with him. Murdock was in the very process of texting Santa his latest status when a third party popped out of the sand just a few feet away.

"Where did you get that space-texter, man?" asked Sergio, one of the refugee guinea pigs.

"Shh!" said Murdock.

"Why you shush me?" asked Sergio. Sergio scampered over to Murdock to peek at what he was texting.

"Keep it down," whispered Murdock. "I'm following a very bad man. You mustn't speak so loud. You'll blow my cover."

"I'll blow your nose before I blow your cover," Sergio retorted in a harsh whisper.

"What are you talking about?" asked Murdock as he popped his head over the dune and saw Gromp trudging forward under the thick haze of the sun. His image was warped and watery like a mirage. Trying to ignore the chatty guinea pig, Murdock ran over the dune he took cover under and sprinted twenty yards in the sand, which luckily muffled the sound of his footsteps. He stopped against the next large dune and then looked around. There was no sign of the guinea pig. Murdock flipped his space-texter back out and punched at buttons.

"Lost Eleanor, going after Gromp," read Sergio, who had poked his head out of the wall of sand Murdock was leaning against. He was perched just above Murdock's shoulder with just his head exposed.

"What the heck are you talking about in this text, man?" Sergio asked.

Startled, Murdock spun around to face the guinea pig. "Are you following me?" he asked.

"Follow you?" repeated Sergio. "Don't be ridiculous. I'm Director of Look Out, a member of the queen's royal guard. This land is property of the queen. So if you are up to no good, which it appears that you are, I respectfully urge you to move off the premises."

"Listen," said Murdock, "I'm on a top secret mission by order of Santa himself. Now I'm currently following a very naughty individual. If you blow my cover, you could jeopardize the entire operation. I mean no quarrel or harm to you, good rodent, so, if you please, leave me to my business. I will be off the queen's territory shortly."

"My name's Sergio."

"Nice to meet you, Sergio," said Murdock. "My name is Murdock, Special Agent to Santa Claus. Sorry we can't chat more, but I really must be going. You understand?"

"I do," said Sergio, "and I appreciate your high-minded manners. Certainly something we don't see in the desert very often these days." He chuckled. Fascinated with the elf, he was secretly dying to hang out with him some more.

"I imagine not," said Murdock. "Now if you'll just let me pass, for I fear the pursued is extending the lead on the pursuer, if you catch my drift."

"Drift caught," said Sergio, "please proceed."

"Wonderful. And can I have your word that you won't follow me? As I said, this is a highly sensitive operation. I can't have any outsiders mucking it up."

"Yes, yes of course," vowed Sergio. He threw two furry little "scout's honor" fingers into the air. "You have my word. I won't follow you."

"Thank you," said Murdock. "Much appreciated. Good day to you then."

With that Murdock was off again, popping his head over the dune before sprinting off to the next dune. When he arrived to the next dune, his space-texter beeped. He took it out and read the screen: *Santa: text me when you get to castle. Need those coordinates. Also: still need to find Eleanor to complete your mission.* Murdock grunted with frustration. Santa beeped him once more. Murdock looked at his screen and it read, *Santa: don't care how big of a pill she is. After you find castle find her."* Murdock put his space-texter back in his pocket and peeked over the dune. Gromp had gained some ground on Murdock, but he was still visible. Murdock started moving again, running twice as fast this time.

Gasping for breath, he stopped to check Gromp's lead again. Murdock had cut the distance in half. Murdock looked around and noticed trees and the faint sound of water in the distance. *We must be reaching the end of the desert*, he thought. He suddenly wondered about his furry little friend and turned. He could see Sergio's fuzzy little ears twenty yards behind him, poking above the dunes. The guinea pig had decided to follow Murdock in the same manner that he was following Gromp. Murdock shook his head and sighed. "Never trust a guinea pig," he said to himself just before moving on.

A few miles from the mouth of the cave in the opposite direction of the castle was Eleanor and Queen Fatilahh. Eleanor rode atop the camel. A water pouch made of snake skin hung from her side. The queen moved like a dancer through the sand, nimble and light with each step of her hooves. Eleanor felt as if they were floating over water, one of the few sensations Eleanor found true joy in. A sense of peace washed over her as they glided over dune after dune. For the first time since being abducted, she was willing to accept what had happened to her. The queen could sense the change in Eleanor.

"Something new crosses your mind, child," she said to the girl. "Tell me, what is it?"

"If I help you defeat Krampus, will you help me get home?" asked Eleanor.

Queen Fatilahh slowed her pace to a stop. "I cannot make any promises, Eleanor, but I will promise that I will do everything in my power to get you home."

"That's good enough for me," said Eleanor. The queen continued on, bounding over ridges with an excitement that animals only experience when they have found their rider. Eleanor clutched onto her leather reins as the queen let loose a wild gallop.

"I'm glad to hear it, my dear," said the queen. "Now would you like to practice the battle axe or the crossbow first? They both have their advantages and their disadvantages."

Eleanor thought she was joking, until the queen inquired again. "Well, which one will it be, my child?"

Meanwhile, five miles from the queen's cave was Krampus, still in bed. It was a few minutes past eleven in the morning when his invisible shadow donkey, Thelma, licked her master's cheek to wake him up. Thelma rarely showed any affection toward Krampus, but the scene she had trotted into gave her reason for alarm. The window beside his bed was shattered, his right hand wrapped in bloody bandages. He didn't move so she licked his dry, scaly head a second time, then a third. No response. She nudged his head with her snout a few times. No response. After bristling against his sour-smelling skin, Thelma did what was natural and unstoppable, she sneezed directly into his face.

Krampus's eyes bulged open as he gasped for breath. Though Thelma only appeared as a shadow on the ground, all of her bodily fluids were as real as any other visible organism. So the sneeze was wet and sounded like a harsh honk.

"Get out of my way, dumb donkey," was all Krampus said as he rolled out of bed. Thelma complied, *clop-clopping* out of the room and off to her own devices. Krampus hobbled to the bathroom and redressed his bandages, disposing of the ones soaked with blood. He then made his way down the two freight elevators, the three separate spiral staircases, the drawbridge, and finally the empty sewage drain that led to the courtyard.

It was sunny and warm in the courtyard. Birds gathered atop the cage where only seven girls remained, singing a sad, pressing melody. Krampus swung the door of the cage open. He hated the birds, and hated that they made the top of the dollhouse their hangout. As he bent down and swung the sleeping Nancy over his shoulder, he vowed to one day eliminate the birds entirely.

Krampus traveled slowly and cautiously all the way back to the castle's main hall. When he arrived at the kitchen, he could still hear Nancy's gentle snore. Her head rested against his slimy shoulder as he walked toward a large oven in the kitchen. He opened the oven and rolled out a large steel platform. Krampus thought that maybe if he kept hot tar on top of the cage it would literally keep the birds from ever wanting to set foot there. As he laid the sleeping Nancy down onto the raised steel surface, he realized this plan would not work because he couldn't possibly keep the tar hot all the time. He slid Nancy into the cold, dark oven and closed the oven shut. He set the timer to start baking in one hour, so that his meal would still be hot by lunchtime. He decided to give the bird dilemma more thought after an early morning nap. He shuffled back to his bedroom and into his bed, which was still glittering with tiny glass shards. He fell asleep instantly, not seeming to notice.

~23~
BODY SWITCH

Geronimo felt like he'd been running for days in the EEP pipe. There seemed to be no end to the pipe. Every time he slowed down he would hear the sound of a tractor gaining on him from above ground. *It has to be one of the polar bears*, he thought. If he let the sound pass him, he was sure a polar bear would be waiting at the end of the pipe. He had to keep running to stay ahead of it.

Fortunately for Geronimo, the pipe was well lit. Overhead, bulbs hung from fixtures every ten feet. Though a gnome's navigation in the dark is exceptional, Geronimo knew that running over thirty miles per hour in complete darkness is just stupid for anyone. At the same time, he was relieved to see such optimal running conditions, and he flew down the pipe even faster. Running at top speed for too long would cause his body to involuntarily shutdown. He would crumble to the ground and fall into a deep sleep. He was confident he could get away with recharging somewhere in the woods where he could better hide. But if his body were to go kaput before he got to the end of the pipe, well, that would be a disaster.

Then he felt it starting in his legs. They felt rubbery. They flapped back and forth, their precision diminished. The shutdown had begun. He stared down the limitless row of lights in front of him, desperate for an end. He could feel his speed reduce to about fifteen miles per hour. He ran in zigzags to try and stay awake, nodding off as he did so. He shook his head and slapped himself. And then, just like that, he collapsed like a tiny bag of laundry. His body was motionless.

When Geronimo finally came to, he didn't waste any time getting going. He did a quick stretch, yawned, got on his feet, and started running. He had no idea how long he had been out, but based on his history of "speed blackouts" he would guess between ten to fifteen minutes.

About three miles of running later he spotted actual daylight. Geronimo deliberately slowed his pace. His eyes felt magnetized to the growing scenery at the end of the pipe. Lush green lawns lead to a blanket of forest. He spotted a blue barn in the far distance. Birds flew in and out of view. With each step forward, the smell of spruce got stronger. What lay beyond the pipe was so intoxicating for Geronimo that he nearly forgot about the potential dangers awaiting him. He was a mere forty feet from the opening when suddenly patchy darkness covered his precious view. He crept closer until the shape gained more definition. Suddenly, it was clear to Geronimo what he was seeing: the silhouette of a polar bear.

"Don't think I don't see you in there," said Snopes at the end of the pipe. "I can smell you even more than I can see you."

"M-my, what a big n-nose you have," said Geronimo, his voice shaking. His fear had undermined his attempt to play it cool.

"What, are you a c-c-comedian?" asked Snopes. "This is no joke, gnome. I'm going to eat you in the next thirty seconds and then I'm going to brag to your goodie-two-shoes boss that I just ate his super important gnome for his super important mission."

"You can't eat gnome."

"Oh, you're gonna watch me eat gnome," said Snopes.

"You can't eat what you can't catch," said Geronimo. His one and only plan was to run right past the polar bear, too quick for his big paws to snatch.

"Try me," said Snopes.

The gnome bolted at the big, white bear. Snopes squatted into a sumo position and waited ravenously as drool dripped from his large teeth. Geronimo leapt a few feet from the terrifying mass of white fur. He aimed for the bear's bent hind leg in hopes of springboarding off of it and somehow over the shoulder. But Snopes swiped him out of the air with ease before any of that could happen. Only his neck, shoulders, and feet were visible outside of the bear's clenched fist.

"You look surprised, gnome," said Snopes, raising his other arm and revealing a pepper shaker in his paw. "You forget a bear's life is catching fish with his bare paws." He sprinkled pepper all over the gnome.

"Goodbye, gnome," said Snopes, tossing Geronimo down his gullet. Snopes gulped, burped, and then sighed with a sad and worn-out expression on his face. He looked down at his glass-riddled feet and legs. He whimpered as he tried to fix the bandages.

"Looks like I got to the party a little late," said a voice from inside the pipe. Snopes looked. There was no one. "Who is that? I know that voice!" Snopes growled.

"You ate him, didn't you?" asked Ned. "You big oaf," he added as he stepped out of the darkness. Ned now stood outside of the pipe directly in front of Snopes. Snopes spun around and glared down at the wizard as he cocked his front paw back to swipe at him. "Enough of the wizardry, old man," said Snopes, "prepare to be reunited with your little friend!"

"You can't eat wizard," said Ned.

"Oh, don't start this again!" said Snopes.

"I'm totally serious."

Snopes swung his paw high above his head, ready to strike.

"Whoa, whoa, whoa, whoa," Ned said with his hands raised high and outstretched. "Allow me just one moment here. Then you may do what you will with me." This caught Snopes a little off guard. He kept his paw fixed high in the air.

"Thank you," said Ned, a little amazed at the power of his own persuasion. "I just wanted to congratulate you on being the victor; the victor over the gnome, over Santa Claus, and over goodness and decency on the whole. So before you kill me, eat me, sew me into a sweater, or whatever it may be, I just want to shake your hand." Ned put his hand out for the bear. Snopes grunted, suspicious and confused. He shook the wizard's hand and immediately felt sharp pains in his belly. The pain was so intense it made the bear buckle to his knees. *The wizard tricked me,* Snopes thought as his eyes closed involuntarily. When the bear opened his eyes back up, he was no longer holding Ned's hand, but Geronimo's. Geronimo appeared just as shocked at his own whereabouts, though he wasn't about to waste time trying to figure it all out now. He yanked his hand out of Snopes's grip and darted for the woods in the distance behind him. Snopes was in no condition to chase after the gnome. The pain sent him rolling on the grass and clutching his belly. The wizard was right. While gnomes may not have been poisonous, wizards were.

Geronimo had only run about ten yards when he heard a voice call from within the pipe, "Hey, man! You're dead meat out there! They'll never stop searching for you! Come back to the pipe! Follow me! It's your only way out!"

Geronimo stopped running and turned back to the pipe. Snopes was still incapacitated with pain, curled in a ball on the cool green grass and whimpering on the ground, so Geronimo knew he could make it back to the pipe without getting eaten a second time. "Okay, I believe you!" Geronimo shouted back, "I'm coming!" He ran past Snopes and back into the pipe.

What Geronimo saw back inside was a creature completely foreign from anything he'd ever seen before. The best way Geronimo could describe it would be a white fur ball, the size of a soccer ball, but with small hands and feet and big blue eyes. The mouth was tiny, pencil-thin, and slightly frowning. Currently, the fur ball was staring back at Geronimo a few feet away. They were not far from the opening of the pipe. Snopes had stopped whimpering outside, and had, in fact, stopped moving altogether. His chest ceased heaving. Geronimo was anxious to keep moving.

"Are you the one that was calling for me?" Geronimo asked.

"Totally, man." The creature stuck his hand out. "My name is Freeze Pop." Geronimo shook his hand, and the hint of a smile appeared on both their faces. They were just about the same height, which was a welcome change from the norm for both of them.

"I'm Geronimo."

"I know who you are, man," said Freeze Pop. They suddenly heard distant stomping above. The polar bears were on the move again. "You are, like, super famous," the creature added. "Now let's get moving!"

Freeze Pop scurried down the pipe back in the direction of the smoking lounge. Geronimo followed behind him, impressed by his speed. "How did I wind up here?" Geronimo asked him as they ran along. "I swear I was eaten by that bear."

"You totally were," said Freeze Pop. "But that wizard, he was looking for you, so I told him about the pipe. He said he might have to pull off the biggest trick of his wizard life. And he did. He totally did."

"What did he do?" asked Geronimo.

"He called it a 'body switch.' He switched bodies with you, man. Now he's in the bear's belly, and you're out here. Pretty cool trick, huh?"

"He gave his life to save me," said Geronimo. "How can I ever repay that?"

"He told me you would say something like that," said Freeze Pop, huffing and puffing as he ran. "And he told me to tell you how."

"How?" asked Geronimo. He stole a glimpse at Freeze Pop's tiny legs, the width of toothpicks.

"By succeeding in your mission," said Freeze Pop, "that's how you repay him." He looked over and caught Geronimo checking out his legs. "You like my legs? I like yours too."

Geronimo switched his gaze forward. "Where are we going now?" he asked.

"To the rooftop," replied Freeze Pop.

"What's on the rooftop?"

"The Chopper," Freeze Pop said as he slowed his pace. Geronimo noticed and did likewise. "We need to slow down so I can find the right panel."

"Why are you helping me in the first place?" asked Geronimo.

"I'm a disgruntled former employee," said Freeze Pop. "I was fired less than an hour ago."

"Sorry to hear that," said Geronimo. Freeze Pop came upon a hatch on the side of the pipe. Suddenly, they could hear stomping coming toward them from within the pipe.

"They're coming!" Freeze Pop opened a panel and punched in a code. Geronimo could now see their massive, furry, white bodies bounding toward them from fifty yards out. "Ugh, I forget the code," said Freeze Pop as he continued punching in different sets of numbers. The bears were gaining ground fast, just thirty yards away now. Freeze Pop closed his eyes and stopped putting in numbers.

"What're you doing?" yelled Geronimo. "Don't stop trying, we're running out of time!"

"Time is a grid. Running out of it is an illusion!" snapped Freeze Pop with his little furry finger pointing at him while flashing his tiny razor-like teeth.

"We're running out of grids then!" yelled Geronimo.

"Don't rush me when I'm so close to getting it," said Freeze Pop. The bears were closing in. They had only seconds left before they would be pounced on. "Ah ha!" yelled Freeze Pop as the code finally worked and the hatch opened. Freeze Pop and Geronimo jumped through the hole that was no bigger than a polar bear's paw. They landed in a tiny room the size of an empty cabinet. From there they climbed a ladder that lead to a smaller pipe. Below them, Geronimo saw big, white, furry paws groping around in the dark space. The opening was too small to fit anything else.

"I built this myself," said Freeze Pop. "In case I ever had to make a dramatic exit. This eventually leads to the rooftop. The bears don't know Jack Frost about this."

"I don't mean to be rude," said Geronimo, "but what are you, anyway?"

"I told you, man," said Freeze Pop, "I was an employee at the country club. Twenty years of loyal service, never missed a day."

"No, I mean, what sort of animal are you?"

"A polar bear—obviously," said Freeze Pop. Geronimo could sense Freeze Pop's growing irritation. He pressed on, anyway. "I just think you're a little small for a polar bear," said Geronimo. "And, to be honest, you lack a lot of polar bear features."

Freeze Pop stopped in his tracks and glared at Geronimo. "Hey listen, man," he said, "I don't talk about how weird you look or sound or whatever. So no need make me feel bad, right? You want to know about me, man?" Freeze Pop inched closer to Geronimo. Standing nose to nose. Freeze Pop's fuzz tickled Geronimo's face. "What do you want to know? That my father was a cotton ball and my mother was a watermelon? That my mother was a snowflake and my father was a fish bowl? Would that satisfy you?" Freeze Pop was now quivering with shame, exhaustion, and sadness. A tear swelled on his eyelid and ran down his furry, round face. "You want me to confess to being the freak that I am?" Freeze Pop sniveled through more tears.

"I promise to never ask about it again," said Geronimo, ashamed for being so insensitive. "I don't think of you as a freak. I think of you as a friend."

Freeze Pop nodded his body in forgiveness.

"I don't know what I am. There's your answer," Freeze Pop confessed, tears streaming down his white fur. "I've adopted a polar bear identity. Happy now?"

"Sounds great, very happy, yes," said Geronimo, desperate to move on.

"Forget it," said Freeze Pop as he turned his back to Geronimo and opened another panel behind which Geronimo noticed several small screens. Freeze Pop turned one of the screens on to display a black and white video of the rooftop, where a giant chopper was being guarded by a dozen polar bears.

"This is going to be tricky," Freeze Pop said with his eyes on the glowing screen.

"What is?" asked Geronimo. Freeze Pop pointed at the screen. "That was our way out of here."

24
LE BRULEE INSTITUTE

When Nancy finally woke up, her toes were very warm. She felt around her in the pitch black. She was stuck inside some sort of warm, metal grill. She started to cry. Burners a few inches above her nose suddenly ticked on with an orange glow. She let out a horrible shriek just before a blast of heat choked the air out of her, causing her to hyperventilate.

When the unnamed elf heard the shriek, he didn't run for the stairwell. He ran instead to the circuit breaker on the opposite wall of the castle basement.

In the dark, dank castle basement, there was another cage that was twice the size of the cage used for the girls in the courtyard. Mounted on the top of the basement cage was a sign that read, "The Tree House." This is where the elf heard Eleanor's scream. He had a wagon full of sandwiches and was passing out breakfast to scores of angry, confused, and pitiful misfit boys from all throughout history.

Standing on his tiptoes now, he opened the metal lid and flipped several switches. Instantly, all the power in the castle went out. The elf grabbed a candle from the wall and lit it with matches from his pocket. He crept slowly up the stairwell.

As quick as the burners had ticked on above Nancy's face, they just as quickly ticked off. She was sure she would be burned alive. Realizing now someone or something had temporarily spared her, her breath turned less spasmodic and slowed as she listened to the sudden patter of footsteps across the kitchen floor. The footsteps moved around the side of the industrial-sized oven and then she heard the sound of a cord unplugging from a wall.

"Can you push yourself out?" asked the elf. Nancy gripped the warm grill above her and tried pushing her feet against the front of the oven door. Multiple times she tried, but the door would not budge.

"I can't," said Nancy, whimpering.

"Fear not, my child," said the elf. The next thing Nancy heard was the sound of tiny jumping feet accompanied by small grunting noises. "I can't reach the handle," whispered the elf from outside. "Have a plan, though. Will fetch my wagon from downstairs and use it to reach the handle. Sit tight. Be back in a jiffy." Before she had time to respond, the elf pattered quickly out of the kitchen.

After switching the power back on, so as not to raise Krampus's suspicions, he noticed the pile of boys in the cage all fighting over the sandwiches he had haphazardly left dumped in a mound. They were barking, biting, and swinging at each other. He rushed down from the wagon and into the cage, intent on breaking up the skirmish, but he was promptly kicked in the face. His body flew across the cage and his head slammed against the steel bar, knocking him out for several hours.

The elf was still laid out cold on the basement floor when Gromp arrived at the castle. Exhausted from the desert walk,

Gromp now had to climb the stairs to the castle's tallest spire. When he finally reached the master bedroom, he stood over his father's bloodied, broken body.

"Wake up, Pops!" yelled Gromp. As his father groaned, Gromp noticed the state of his body. "You okay? You're bleeding all over!" exclaimed Gromp.

Krampus jolted upright in his bed. His eyes blinked bug-like. Krampus looked at his son and closed his eyes, revealing no emotion. "I'll be fine," he said. "Nothing a little gauze can't fix. Now what is it, son?"

"Eleanor got away," said Gromp, his eyes glued to the floor. He feared the judgment and disappointment awaiting him from his father. But his father was saying nothing in response. Gromp looked up from the floor, and now knew why his father was silent. Krampus had fallen back asleep. *Stupid narcolepsy*, thought Gromp.

"Oh, *Pops!*" Gromp yelled. Krampus woke back up with a start.

"Did you hear what I said?" asked Gromp.

"Yes, yes, yes," said Krampus. He rushed to his feet and grabbed a glass of water on his nightstand to splash on his face.

"Pops, you're sleeping on glass," said Gromp.

"I know," said Krampus, "it was a rough night. We need not go into it now." He walked to the bathroom. "I'm more worried about you, Grompy." He returned from the bathroom with scissors, tape, and a roll of gauze. He handed them to Gromp, turned his back on his son, and stripped out of his pajamas. Krampus's naked body revealed bruises and cuts from head to toe. He raised his arms and asked his son to "wrap the cuts as best you can." He looked at his son's shocked expression through his grimy mirror and added, "No need for drama."

Gromp stared at his father's back as he held the gauze, tape, and scissors. He was not sure of where to even start, though the thought of mummifying his father was suddenly highly appealing. Besides, he honestly felt that the mummy look would work for his father. He wouldn't be scaring people half to death all the time if he looked like he was running around with thin cotton pajamas on. Gromp began wrapping his father up with a fervor. He hoped he had enough gauze to wrap him head to toe.

"You worry me, Grompy, you know why?" Krampus asked. "Because you're just like your mother; and you remember what happened to her, don't you?"

Gromp nodded, jaw now tense with anger. He wrapped faster and tighter.

"That's right," Krampus said, nodding at his son in the mirror. "I killed her."

Gromp stopped wrapping. "You told me she died giving birth to me," he said.

"Technically, yes," said Krampus, "but if it wasn't for me and your mom's copulation, she wouldn't have given birth to you in the first place. Now where is Eleanor now?"

"I don't know," said Gromp, "a gnome took her."

"A gnome!" exclaimed Krampus. "A gnome took her?"

"He stabbed me after I was shoved overboard." Gromp raised his shirt to show a small strip of white tape between his ribs. "I lost grip of her hand and floated to shore." Krampus stared back at him with lifeless eyes. Having finished wrapping his entire chest, Gromp started on his father's arms. He dreaded what Krampus would say next.

"No cooking school," Krampus said, "no Southern France."

"You wouldn't," whispered Gromp. "Please, Father, give me one more chance." Krampus was silent, his face resolute.

Gromp fell to his knees in agony. His face twisted up, reddening. "Please," he howled, "just give me one more chance, Pop!"

"Keep wrapping!" said Krampus. After a moment, Gromp stood up and regained his composure. He resumed wrapping down his father's arms.

"I give you until noon tomorrow to find her and bring her to me," said his father, "or else I'm calling this Institute myself and telling them to cancel your spring semester."

"I give you my word, Father," said Gromp, "I will have her dragged by her hair to your feet before noon tomorrow."

"I'll believe it when I see it," said Krampus. "Did you turn the oven off downstairs? I was cooking some meat in there. I should be smelling it by now."

"I didn't turn the oven off," said Gromp. Having finished with his father's upper body, Gromp bent down and started on the legs.

"That elf is up to something," said Krampus.

"That should do it," said Gromp as he stood back up. Krampus looked at himself in his filthy, full-length mirror. He was covered in bandages from his neck down to his feet. He smirked, pleased with his new look.

"If you see an elf around here, Grompy," said Krampus, "kill it on the spot."

Murdock waited a few minutes after Gromp walked through the castle doors to leave his post behind the tree. Twenty yards behind him he could see Sergio also hiding behind a tree, still following him. "Stupid guinea pig," Murdock muttered to himself just before scooting to the main castle doors. Gromp had left the door cracked open, so the elf needed only to give it a slight budge to fit through. Once inside, he immediately heard the sound of a child's whimper. He followed it and wound up in a large kitchen. *The oven*, Murdock thought. He walked over to the whimpering oven and looked up at the handle, which was just a few inches out of reach above his head. He looked around the kitchen for something to stand on. There was nothing. Then he heard a creaking sound behind him and whipped around. There was Sergio opening the window and crawling inside with a sheepish smile on his face.

"Get out of here," whispered Murdock urgently.

"I hear the whimpering too. You need my help to get that girl out," said Sergio, "you can't open that oven without me." Sergio jumped from the windowsill to the ground. He scampered across the tiled floor and over to Murdock.

"Hey, Pops!" the two of them heard echoing down the stairwell.

"You promised you wouldn't follow me," Murdock said to Sergio. "You're a liar, and I don't work with liars."

"Oh, but with all due respect, Mr. Murdock," said Sergio, "I'm afraid you don't have a choice."

"How do you mean?" asked Murdock.

"Whoever you were following could walk back down the stairs at any moment," said Sergio, "and as you can see there is nothing in this kitchen for you to stand on in order to reach those handles." The guinea pig pointed at the out-of-reach oven handles. "You don't have time to go looking for a step stool, not to mention that going exploring around here could probably get you killed in any number of unknown ways."

Sergio's words struck Murdock, so he asked, "Well, then, how do you suppose we get her out?"

Sergio grinned and replied, "I jump on your head and pull the handle open with my teeth." He opened his mouth to reveal his pearly white chompers. Murdock's eyes widened. Sergio's teeth looked massive inside his mouth. He was amazed they even fit. Murdock nodded his head dumbly. "Okay," he said.

Without hesitation, Sergio leapt onto the counter and then onto Murdock's head. He stood upright on his hind feet and leaned a few inches forward. He braced himself against the oven with his front paws. His mouth aligned perfectly with the handle of the oven. Opening his jaws, he leaned forward a few inches until he touched the metal handles against his teeth. Once Murdock noticed the firm grip Sergio's teeth had on the handle, he grabbed the guinea pig's feet with his hands and slowly backed up. In turn, Sergio pushed off the sides of the oven with his front paws. The coffin-sized metal container started to slide out. Sergio grinned through his toothsome grip as his furry little body pulled away from the rest of the oven. That's when they heard a pair of footsteps coming down the staircase.

"You can't expect me to just whip you up a soufflé anytime I'm back home," said Gromp back to his dad as he descended the stairs. "I'm twenty-three, Pops," he continued, "I have my own life to live."

"My son the fancy chef and he doesn't make me squat," Krampus grumbled, two steps behind Gromp as they both spiraled downward.

"Well, maybe I'd actually become a fancy chef if I was getting trained at Le Brulee right now instead of running your errands and doing your dirty work around here."

"You don't get Le Brulee until you complete this dirty work around here," said Krampus. "That's what the deal is. That's what we agreed on."

They were about one flight from the ground floor when Gromp turned around on his step and looked at this father. "The problem, Dad," he said, "is that good always wins. You're going to lose this battle."

An icy chill seemed to frost over Krampus's features, and Gromp instantly knew he had said too much. Before another thought popped into his son's head, Krampus swung his arm out and decked Gromp across the chin. Gromp's body tumbled down the last flight of stairs. His body toppled to the ground floor as he fell facedown. He squirmed as an injured worm might, slow and rubbery. Krampus stared down at his son's body with a look of shock. It was clear from his expression that he did not mean to hit him as hard as he did.

"I'm-I'm sorry," said Krampus. "I forgot we were on a staircase."

Gromp groaned as his head turned toward the direction of the kitchen. He lifted his arm from the floor with great effort and pointed in the direction of the kitchen.

"What is it?" asked Krampus. Krampus hurried down the rest of the stairwell and turned toward the kitchen. The oven door was pulled open. He walked over to it and saw that it was empty. He felt a draft across his face and looked up at the open window. Beyond the windows and into the distant woods he saw an elf, a guinea pig, and his breakfast running into the foliage.

"Thelma!" Krampus yelled. "Thelma!"

25

THE PEANUT AND
THE SOY BEAN

Back in the North Pole, T.C. paced the floorboards of his barn in the wee, gray hours of the morning. After coming back a hero the day before with the chopper and the abducted girls, he got a call from Dr. Tinsel later that night who warned him to avoid any further physical stress on his heart. The doctor said the results could be terminal, and yet that wasn't the reason for his anxiety this morning. He trotted silently back and forth over his Afghan rug, occasionally looking out the open window. After a few minutes of this nervous behavior, Clarence appeared outside the window, wearing his standard late-December work uniform: white jumpsuit with red stripes on the shoulders.

"I'll have three cheeseburgers and a chocolate milkshake," shouted Clarence up at the window. Spotting Clarence, T.C. walked over to the door, then opened it and ushered him inside.

"You're late," said T.C.

"I had some business with Big Red. Went a little long," said Clarence. T.C. rolled his eyes, shut the door, and pulled the blinds down over his window. "He's leaving HQ, you know," the elf said. "He told me not to tell anyone. But I'm telling you anyway."

"That's what I have to talk to you about," said T.C.

"Yeah, what is this all about anyway?" asked Clarence. "I'm still on the clock over there."

"I'm going to smuggle myself onto the chopper before he leaves," said T.C. "He won't let me go back out there right now. Dr. Tinsel has forbidden me to do anything to raise my blood pressure. But I have to go."

"You shouldn't risk it," said Clarence. "Besides, we need you here. Especially with Big Red off campus."

"You should sit down," said T.C.

"What is it?" Clarence's eyes found a stool against the window. He dragged it to the center of the room and sat down.

"Santa is not going to come back from this trip." T.C. paused. "He's going to die on this mission." A tear instantly welled up and fell down the centaur's cheek, startling Clarence.

"Why would you say that?" Clarence asked with his own choked voice. Tears had started streaming down his face. "How could you say such a horrible thing with such certainty?"

"I dreamt it last night," said T.C. "I dreamt he would get in that chopper and never come back."

"So, wait a minute," said Clarence, wiping the tears from his eyes. "This was just a dream you had?" Clarence shook his head and got up from his stool. "You know what I dreamed last night?" He walked back to the door, done with his visit. "That I was a peanut butter sandwich and that Gladys, my wife, you know Gladys—"

"Yes, I've know your wife, Gladys," said T.C.

"Right, so she was a jelly sandwich," said Clarence. "And it was nice. Then I woke up and realized none of it was true. It was all a dream. Just like your dream of Santa dying. It means nothing." Clarence shrugged his shoulders at T.C. "Now if you don't mind, I must get back to the pelican vacuum cleaners." He kicked the door and it swung wide open, aided by the morning breeze.

T.C. went to the window to watch the elf's departure.

"I can see the future in my dreams!" he yelled out to Clarence. The elf looked back for a second and then walked away at an even quicker pace.

Santa sat in his office fifty yards from T.C.'s barn. He was dressed in his space suit: a one-piece silver suit with gold lightning bolts on the shoulders. His chair faced the war map on the wall behind his desk. He had a glum expression on his face as his chin rested on the space helmet in his lap. The room was quiet enough to hear the soft ticking of the grandmother clock in the corner. The names "Eleanor," Nancy," and others, with either Xs or question marks, were stuck to the map above Santa's down-cast head. The "Ned" post-it had an "X" over it, while "Eleanor," and "Geronimo" had question marks. The "Nancy" post-it had both an "X" and a question mark. Although Santa's body was facing the war map, his head seemed unwilling to look up at it anymore.

Rose crept quietly into her husband's office, fearful of disturbing the unusually eerie quiet of what should be an afternoon bustling with production. Rose looked at Santa's turned chair and then out the window at the tomb-silent Assembly Hall below. What she saw initially horrified her. All of the elves had stopped working and stood still as statues with their bodies facing the office window. With craned necks they all stared up into the office. Rose noticed there was very little expression on their faces. The whole scene was becoming unbearably creepy for her, and she had to say something.

"Nicky," she said softly. Santa's head jerked an inch toward her, still under the spell of the silence.

"Nicky!" she shouted. She received a pained sigh from him, a response that did not please Rose at all.

"You have to let me in, sweetie," she said. "I'm going to walk away if you don't start responding to me."

Nicky swiveled his chair around to face her. Rose was alarmed to see him in his space suit. He looked up at her with a guilty look on his face. It was the face of a child whose hand had been caught in the cookie jar. Yet Rose detected a look of anguish hiding underneath, as if he didn't really want the cookie to begin with.

"What's going on?" she asked.

"We're all praying," Santa responded.

"Praying? You're all praying?" Rose repeated in disbelief. "You put your space suit on when you pray?"

"Don't be so cold," said Santa.

Rose softened her tone and redirected the topic. "Why do you have your space suit on?" she asked. "And why are all the elves looking up at you in stone silence? What's going on?"

Clearing his throat first, Santa said, "I'm taking the chopper over myself. I was going to tell you in an hour."

"And the elves?" asked Rose.

"They're praying for me," said Santa with his eyes closed.

"You told them to pray for you?" Rose asked. Santa nodded back at her. Rose looked back at the elves, then back at Santa.

"Do they know," Rose began, "they don't have to be staring at you in order to pray for you?"

"No, they don't," said Santa. "I guess I didn't clarify that very well." Rose shook her head at her husband and walked over to the window. She slid back a section of the glass and yelled out over the hall, "You can get back to work now! Nicky appreciates your prayers." As she slid the window closed, all of the elves instantaneously resumed their work.

"Do you have any idea how ridiculous you are?" Rose asked with genuine curiosity.

"Of course I do," said Santa as he stood up and walked to the small window behind his desk. "It's my blessing and my torment." His gaze rested on the distant horizon outside his window.

"You're not getting in that chopper—"

"The lives of many girls and boys are at stake, Rose—"

"You didn't let me finish," said Rose. She walked over to him and took his hands in hers. "You're not going in that chopper without me."

"Oh, honey," said Santa. "You can't go. I know it sounds cliché, but it's just too dangerous. And besides, you'd hate it."

She looked up at his enormous, cherubic face. "Five hundred years ago I would've agreed with you," she said, "but we only have a couple hundred years left in us, Nicky. I'd rather die with you on some crazy mission than live my last few centuries without you."

"They have spiders there," said Santa quickly. Repelled, Rose staggered back a step from her husband, their hands disconnecting. "Desert spiders," he continued, "forest spiders. You hate spiders. I know you hate me even saying the word *spiders*."

"Please shut up about the spiders," said Rose, inching back toward him. "Besides, you're just trying to scare me off the mission. I go if you go. And that's that."

Santa let out a "humph," then put his helmet on. He stood there with his arms folded, looking out the window before he turned his gaze to her.

"We'll leave tomorrow morning," he said. "I just don't want you to die on account of me, is all." A tear came to Rose's eye as she curled her arm around his. She looked up at him and kissed the plastic of the helmet's bubble, leaving a red smooch imprint.

"Don't worry about me," said Rose. She slipped from his grasp and walked back to the office door. "Worry about your gnome friend," she added.

Santa slid the front plastic visor of his helmet up. "That's why I'm going," said Santa. "I'm afraid I've sent him on a suicide mission. I expected too much out of him."

"Where is he now?" Rose asked from the doorway.

"I don't know," said Santa, "I've lost contact. He's most likely on the run."

Geronimo and Freeze Pop were, in fact, running. The two of them were hustling up the slow ascent of submerged pipe once they noticed the video from the security camera that showed the chopper unguarded. Freeze Pop guessed that the polar bears had all gone to lunch, since they often ate three to five lunches per day. The only problem was that Geronimo and Freeze Pop had not seen the bears leave and had no idea when they'd return. Nonetheless, they now found themselves at the door to the rooftop. Freeze Pop opened the panel in the wall beside the door. He switched on the video screen and selected the rooftop camera footage. The screen still showed the unguarded space chopper.

"Still no guards," said Freeze Pop.

"They could come back any minute," said Geronimo.

"Which is why we go out now!" said Freeze Pop. With that, he hopped high enough to land on Geronimo's head, springboard off of it, and land onto the door handle. Freeze Pop's weight slowly lowered the handle as he began to slide off the slanting foothold. The door clicked open and swung gently outward. Sunshine blinded the both of them. Geronimo tiptoed onto the rooftop. He kept his body flat against the wall of the staircase. The hot gravel burned into his black, rubber shoes. Freeze Pop swung off the lowered handle of the door and landed with ease onto the rooftop gravel.

"Let's go!" he told Geronimo as he ran toward the chopper. As Geronimo followed him, the gnome noticed a white flash in the corner of his eye. *It was a trap*, Geronimo thought. He scurried back to the wall and re-splayed himself against it. He watched his new, furry, little friend get scooped up by the polar bear in the security uniform and thrown high into the air. Geronimo watched as other bears appeared from the other end of the rooftop. They had been hiding from a distance that was beyond the view of the rooftop cameras. They were all dressed in security uniforms with their backs turned away from Geronimo, dumbly admiring Freeze Pop's trajectory, captivated by the arc formed by his poof-ball body floating through the air.

Geronimo took this opportunity to run completely unseen toward the space chopper. He hopped inside of it and onto the seat. He looked over at the small army of bears to the left of him. They were still following Freeze Pop's descent as his body hurdled down toward the forest treetops. He looked back at the controls. There were keys in the ignition. He looked out in front of him— nothing but sky. *We must be twelve stories high*, Geronimo thought. Like a slow-moving sunset, Freeze Pop's body was still descending. He felt horrible about his little friend, but he knew this could be his only chance to move on with his mission.

He leapt onto the metal keys. The force of his impact turned the key and started the chopper's engine, lifting the vehicle into the air. The bears ran over to the rising chopper and clawed at the chopper's bottom rails, to no avail. Geronimo hopped back onto the pilot's seat and looked out the window below. He scoured the grounds for Freeze Pop as the chopper continued its rapid ascent. No sign of him. He was just about to veer directly into the side of a mountain when he read a sticker over a small compartment that read, "Auto-flight warp buttons." Geronimo hopped onto the console and used both hands to pop the compartment open. Inside were four buttons, each labeled with a different name using a sharpie and masking tape. None of the names were recognizable to Geronimo, except for one: Krampus. He stepped onto the big, red "Krampus" button. The pushing of the button triggered such a high rate of velocity that Geronimo was thrown back and pressed against the leather of the pilot's chair so tightly he passed out.

When he woke up, he was no longer in the air. The bottom half of the chopper was buried in sand, though the chopper itself appeared undamaged. When Geronimo crawled out of the vehicle, he was surrounded by desert. He breathed in and out the hot, dry desert air. Suddenly, the whole mission felt pretty pointless to him.

Murdock, Sergio, and Nancy were also on the run at the opposite end of Pointless from where Geronimo crashed. They raced across the edge of the forest where the tall, green foliage slowly gave way to sand. Murdock held Nancy's hand as they ran, while Sergio lead the way, bounding over the dunes in front of them. Murdock looked over his shoulder back at the castle and saw Krampus crawling out of the open window.

"They're after us!" Murdock yelled to Sergio.

"Don't worry!" Sergio yelled back at him. "I know a secret tunnel not far from here that leads to the cave."

The elf looked back over his shoulder again. Astride his shadow donkey, Thelma, Krampus moved through the air in a sitting position, weaving his way through the forest behind them. The haunting image grew bigger and bigger.

"He's catching up to us!" Murdock yelled.

"We're almost there!"

"I'll eat you all alive!" Krampus shrilled into the air from behind. Sergio hopped over a dune and clawed furiously into the sand. Murdock and Nancy followed his lead and dug with him until Murdock asked, "Why are we digging?"

"The tunnel door," said Sergio, "I could swear this was the right dune." Murdock looked around them; all the dunes looked identical to one another. "How do you know this is the right spot?" asked Murdock. The elf poked his head above the dune to look behind them. He could now hear the hoofed feet of the shadow donkey. Krampus had cut his distance in half. They had only a minute or two to find the tunnel.

"I know it's the right spot because it's the right spot," said Sergio. Murdock looked back down and saw Sergio brushing the sand off a flat, smooth, circular metal lid deep in the sand. "Here it is," said Sergio. He punched in three numbers on a keypad atop the lid, which caused a red light to buzz. "Juniper berries!" cursed Sergio, "password's been updated." Sergio punched three more numbers. Again the red light buzzed.

"Hurry it up!" yelled Murdock. He ran over to Sergio and looked down at the lid. Murdock held Nancy's hand as he waited for it to pop open. Behind them, the galloping grew louder and louder. Any moment now, Krampus could leap over the dune behind them and tear them all to shreds. Murdock had to save the girl even if it meant risking his own life, so he decided to create a diversion.

He ran up the side of the dune, toward a neighboring dune with the hopes that Krampus would follow, thereby buying Sergio more time to figure out the code and get Nancy to safety. Murdock was about halfway to the next dune when he looked over at Krampus and saw him hot on his tail. So hot that Murdock didn't even make it to the next dune. Thelma's unseen hoof kicked him in the head, sending him sailing through the air. Just before he lost consciousness, he saw Sergio open the metal lid for Nancy, follow her inside, then close the lid behind them. Like the end of a movie, the image blurred, fading to black.

Eleanor lay on her back and looked up at the stars. A vast perimeter of the queen's cave was now adorned with combat training equipment that had been constructed early that morning. There were catapults, crossbow targets, and double-bladed boomerangs strewn about the compound. Eleanor and Amando were both exhausted from training all day, but she had difficulty saying "no" to the queen, who was really her only ticket home. She started to sob under the light of three moons. The bizarre lunar visual upset her all the more in its lack of normalcy. This was the saddest she had ever felt in her entire life.

"Did I ever tell you the story about the peanut and the soy bean?" Amando asked. He had now situated himself not far from Eleanor, and the close proximity of his voice startled her. "Go away!" she pleaded to the guinea pig.

"I will," said Amando. "I promise I will, my dear, as soon as you tell me whether or not I've ever told you the story of the peanut and the soy bean."

"No," said Eleanor, "you haven't. Now go away!"

Amando looked over at Eleanor's distraught little face and suddenly pitied her. He did not want to be responsible for any further torment of the girl. He felt bad for pressing the issue and quietly got up, scampering into the darkness. After a few moments of silence, Amando's voice in the darkness began, "One-morning-the-peanut-woke-up-to-find-a-soy-bean-in-his-living-room," said Amando. "The-peanut-asked-the-soy-bean,-'Are-you-lost?'-and-the-soy-bean-said-'Soytof.'"

Eleanor laughed, less from the punch line and more from the speed in which Amando said it. *He sounds like a maniac*, she thought.

"Now go to sleep," said Amando, "we take the castle at daybreak."

And then there was nothing. She didn't hear another peep from him the rest of the night. As her laughter subsided she felt her spirit lighten. Something heavy seemed to roll off of her as she quickly fell fast asleep.

PART 2

~26~
I LOVE YOU FOREVER

Geronimo sat in the sand feeling miserable. Everything felt pointless. For one, the chopper wouldn't start back up, not that he knew how to navigate the thing in the first place. He needed to at least get to Krampus's castle, and here he was stranded in an endless desert. He didn't know much about deserts, but he did know they are unbearably hot and eventually they drive you crazy. So it was pointless to go anywhere. He was pretty satisfied with this conclusion when he heard a faint voice in the distance. "What a dumb unicorn you are," the voice said. "What a stupid, stupid unicorn."

The words jostled Geronimo out of his doldrums, freeing him from the spell of Pointless. The possibility of an actual unicorn being in his vicinity erased all negative thoughts. He had specifically asked Santa for access to a unicorn. Santa had clearly delivered, which meant that Santa knew where he was and had not given up on him. Suddenly, there was much reason for hope. He was immediately on the move, gliding over dunes in search of the unicorn and the voice ridiculing it. He followed the voice: "Just cry, you stupid animal, cry!" Every word caused the gnome to step quicker through the sand in a vigorous pursuit of justice. He finally had a visual: a man dressed in a raggedy clown suit loudly shaming an ashen-colored unicorn. The unicorn's horn atop its head was powder blue at the base, and then faded to white at the tip. The clown held a bucket beside the beast's pale blue eye as he barked insults at it.

"You're just a good-for-nothing horse with a stick coming out of your head," said the man. Geronimo recognized him as one of the other passengers on his earlier boat ride. The clown's name was Xanadu. Geronimo's first glimpse now of the invective-hurling clown resembled a surrealist painting.

Xanadu wore a faded, colorless clown suit with no wig, no fake red nose, and no white makeup. The only makeup on his face was a few streaks of red painted down his nose and black smudges rounding the bottom of his eyes. His chestnut hair looked oddly shifted, as if he had just recently been wearing a wig.

"What do you think you're doing?" asked Geronimo. Xanadu turned around to face the gnome. Almost not seeing him right away, he did a double take and then caught sight of Geronimo's glaring green eyes.

"It's none of your business," said Xanadu. "Take a hike." He turned his back on Geronimo and continued his verbal abuse on the mythic creature. "What're you gonna cry, unicorn? Is that it? Are you going to cry for me now?"

"I'm afraid you're making it my business, Xanadu," said Geronimo.

"How do you know my name?" asked Xanadu.

"You told the Frogg brothers your name on our little boat ride," said Geronimo, "I was listening."

Xanadu lowered the bucket from the unicorn's eye. "Then you know why I'm doing this," said Xanadu.

"Your brother got rich selling unicorn honey," said Geronimo, "and you're trying to do the same thing. That's my guess. I see no reason to berate the unicorns for the honey."

Geronimo walked up to Xanadu and the unicorn. Closer up, Geronimo could see that the clown had tears in his eyes, causing black streaks to run down his cheeks. It looked as if a child had drawn a spider on his face. "I need to make it cry in order to get the honey," said Xanadu. "It's the only way."

"The honey is in his tears?" Geronimo asked.

"Trace amounts," said Xanadu. "There's enough to make a fortune if I ever get out of this desert." Xanadu turned back to the sleek, gray animal. "What're you looking at, idiot?" Geronimo watched the smoky blue eye of the unicorn well up with a gold-tinged tear that dropped into Xanadu's waiting bucket with a *ploop*. That was quite enough for Geronimo.

"You can't do this anymore," he said.

"What're you talking about?" said Xanadu as he swished the bucket gently back and forth, ruminating on the depth of the liquid. "Who's gonna stop me, you?"

"We have to make some sort of deal," said Geronimo.

"No," said Xanadu, "we don't."

"I have a space chopper," said Geronimo. He pointed toward the beached spacecraft, which resembled a giant silver thimble thirty yards out. Geronimo could tell by the change in Xanadu's expression that the chopper was a game-changer. Xanadu had nearly dropped his bucket of unicorn tears at the sight of the chopper shining in the golden sand.

"Where'd you get that vehicle?" asked Xanadu. "Only polar bears and Santa Claus have choppers."

"Stole it from the polar bears," said Geronimo. "Long story. I'll trade you the chopper for the unicorn."

Xanadu looked down at him, ruminating.

"The chopper must be worth far more than the unicorn honey," added Geronimo.

"It is," said Xanadu, "much, much more." He walked slowly toward it as if pulled by a tractor beam. Geronimo walked up to the downtrodden unicorn and said, "The keys are sitting in the ignition. I'm in a bit of a rush, so if you don't mind I'm gonna scoot on out of here." Geronimo had reached the silken, white tail of the gray beast and climbed up it as if it were a rope in gym class. By the time he got to the top of the unicorn's rump, Xanadu was standing right in front of him beside the animal.

"How do I know I can trust you?" asked Xanadu. "How do I know that ship is even in working condition? I can't let you take the unicorn until I know for certain that vehicle works."

Geronimo stood up on top of the animal's rump and clumsily walked along its spine toward Xanadu and sat on the unicorn's mane. He gestured toward the chopper.

"Just look at it from here," said Geronimo, "there's not a flaw to be found."

"I'm too far away to tell," said Xanadu as he turned his head back toward the ship in the distance and away from Geronimo and the unicorn. Geronimo took this moment to grab the mane of the unicorn and whisper in the animal's ear, "*Go!*" The unicorn did nothing. Xanadu turned back to Geronimo.

"What're you doing?" asked Xanadu. "Get off that thing!" he shouted as he raised his arm to smack the gnome off of the horse. With his arm swinging through the air, Geronimo tried one more thing. He whispered in the animal's ear the words, "I love you forever." With this they were off. Making contact with nothing, Xanadu's outstretched arm spun his body like a top. By the time

Xanadu stood up and rubbed the kicked-up sand from his eyes, the gnome and the unicorn were barely in sight.

Xanadu turned around and ran toward the chopper. *The keys are sitting in the ignition*, Geronimo told him. He opened the door of the chopper and walked over to the pilot's chair. There was no key in the ignition. He looked around the seats, on dashboards, and inside compartments. There was no key anywhere. *The keys are sitting in the ignition*, rang hatefully through Xanadu's head as he walked back out of the vehicle and onto the scorching sand. He tilted his head up against the hot sun and shouted, "You're a rotten liar, gnome!"

Geronimo fought through heavy turbulence atop the mythical beast. Bouncing wildly up and down, he held onto the unicorn's whipping mane for dear life. Underneath the back of his green shirt was the key to the chopper. The size of the key took up the length of his back, creating the sensation of a metal brace. He gritted his teeth from the pain as his body rocked up and down, over and over. Part of him was starting to regret asking Santa for a unicorn. Another part of him still felt that even this experience was pretty awesome. Regardless, he had no idea where he was headed, or where the castle was in the first place. He had no way of knowing the unicorn was actually taking him in the opposite direction of the castle.

A half-mile from the space chopper marched Queen Fatilahh and her army of eleven guinea pigs, Eleanor among them. The queen's

145

army was headed toward the castle, the destination Geronimo hoped he was headed.

Suddenly, the words *You're a rotten liar, gnome!* echoed over the rust-colored desert.

"What was that?" asked Eleanor. Her upper body wobbled back and forth as she rode upon the queen. Marching in front of Eleanor were four rows of guinea pigs all walking upright. They all wore desert camo. Slung across all their backs were sacks of home-made spears, nunchucks, and various other hand-crafted weapons custom-made for their size. Eleanor noticed that Giovanna's bag had jars of dead spiders, bags of rotten food, and mysterious leather pouches.

Leading the pack were Amando and Ottavio, the two most formidable looking of all the battle-ready rodents. They were also the only two who wore shiny steel helmets. Eleanor thought the uniforms made them look more ridiculous than dangerous.

"It sounded like someone yelled, 'You're a rotten liar, gnome,'" said Eleanor. "It must be Geronimo. He's here in this desert!"

"It's the heat, darling," said the queen. "I often think I'm hearing things while traveling these long distances."

"I heard that too, Eleanor," said Rosabella and turned back to face her friend. Suddenly, it was horribly evident to Rosabella that she had talked out of turn. She had never seen Queen Fatilahh so angry.

"On second thought, I must've just been hearing things," said Rosabella.

"Yes," said Eleanor, "I must've been hearing things too." Knowing that Geronimo was somewhere out there trying to rescue her this very minute gave her newfound hope.

"I assure you, my child, we will stop for a rest soon," said the queen. Eleanor went back to not looking at the queen. She was starting to believe in the camel's words less and less. "I promise after we are through taking the castle, I will return you to your home," said the queen. "We make camp at dawn. Whose job is it to distribute the water and dried fish?" she asked.

"It's Sergio's job, Your Excellency," said Amando from the front.

"Sergio is not here," said Queen Fatilahh with a rising impatience in her voice. "Sergio left camp and is now AWOL. He decided he had more important things to do than defeat evil. So who's next in line?"

"I am," said Rosabella. "I will distribute the food and water when we make camp."

"Very well, then," responded Queen Fatilahh after a stretch of silence.

With that, the silent power of Pointless fell upon them as they trekked through the sand for a few more hours. No one said another word until the sun went red and their bodies collapsed unto the cooling sand. In the dimming light, the queen lowered her hind legs into the autumn-drenched dunes. The sleeping Eleanor slid down the camel's side and onto the soft sand. It wasn't until Rosabella ran over to Eleanor, listened for a moment, and yelled, "She's not breathing!" that the silence was finally broken.

~27~
STOP THAT HORSE!

Finally, after traveling half the day inside a secret tunnel underneath the sand, Sergio and Nancy emerged to the sight of an empty cave. "They left without us," said Sergio in disbelief. "Come, little girl, follow me." He ran toward the backside of the cave. Nancy followed him and watched the guinea pig open up what looked like a toy chest against the rock wall of the cave. He opened the chest and jumped inside, disappearing from view. Nancy listened as Sergio rummaged around inside. There was fumbling and tumbling with an occasional *bonk*, followed by a cursing grunt. It saddened Nancy that a guinea pig could be so foul-mouthed. This sadness gave her hope, for it was possible proof that she was beginning to break out of the dark place where she locked her spirit away on the night of her abduction hundreds of years ago. Her sadness was now mixed with anger, which made her feel even more alive. These emotions rose in her chest as her senses picked up the sound of hooves in the distance.

"Stop that horse!" yelled Sergio from inside the chest. Nancy turned toward the moving billow of sand coming right for them. "Throw your arms wide!" the guinea pig yelled from inside the chest. "Do some jumping jacks! If we steal their horse we can catch up to the others." Nancy put her arms out wide, raised her arms slowly above her head, and then did three twirls. She felt like a beam of light had turned on inside of her. She had just started dance lessons the week before her abduction, which was now a few centuries ago. A smile stretched across her face.

When Sergio climbed out of the box, he was in full military gear. Desert camo, a bag of rocks slung across his back, a slingshot hung loosely from his neck, along with his own personal cherry on top: custom-sized infrared goggles, which enabled him to see through potential sandstorms. The goggles were large, metal, and bulky, and when you looked directly at them, they would flash a red light at you. He was convinced it was too dangerous *not* to be wearing them at all times. Sergio turned his head toward the sound of the galloping and saw the gray unicorn in the distance, bolting right for the spinning Nancy. Sergio lumbered up to Nancy. "Nice job stopping the horse, soldier," he told her. He then nodded to her, code for her to stop. But she was still spinning. "At ease," he said. With this, she slowly came to a stop. He handed her a bottled water from his bag of rocks and she gulped it down. Sergio took the bottle back and put it in his bag. His hand came out holding a stone. The guinea pig stood between Nancy and the oncoming unicorn. Sergio turned his back on Nancy and stood up on his haunches. He took the sling off of his thick, furry neck and stretched the band of the sling shot all the way back with the stone loaded between his tiny pink fingers. He turned his head, which caused his goggles to shift crookedly out of place. "Just let me do the talking," he told her. He shook his head in order to wobble the goggles back into place. "And you're gonna have to be my eyes since I can't move my head very well. So keep a good look out!" Nancy stood behind Sergio as the dust ball before them grew bigger and bigger.

Ten feet in front of the rock-wielding guinea pig, the unicorn slowed to a stop. Initially, the animal appeared to have no rider. Sergio slowly lowered his slingshot, seeing no threat in a tired, sad-looking unicorn. Nancy walked toward the wall of the cave, where a jug of water sat in the shade. She grabbed the jug and brought it over to the unicorn. The unicorn plunged it's nuzzle into the cool water, eagerly drinking. The unicorn gazed gratefully into Nancy's eyes. Nancy smiled back at the unicorn, her smile so big it felt like she had grown wings on her face.

Sergio noticed the quiet friendship blooming in front of him. He was not a fan. "Don't get too attached," Sergio told Nancy. "These guys aren't built for the desert. Or friendships." He grabbed one of the unicorn's back legs and wiggled it back and forth. The unicorn lifted the leg Sergio was examining and kicked him hard, sending the guinea pig flying into the air and crashing into the sand several feet away. "See what I mean?" Sergio yelled as he sat up, feeling around his head for his goggles. "My goggles!" he cried. "Where are my sand goggles?"

"Oh these things?" said Geronimo. He sat cross-legged atop the unicorn, facing the animal's backside. The sand-coated goggles lay across the unicorn's back in front of Geronimo.

Sergio frowned at the sight of the gnome tickling the goggles with his feet and marched over to him. He took a heavy stone out of his side satchel, and reared it back into his slingshot. "Drop the goggles," said Sergio, "or . . . or . . ." Fortunately for Geronimo, Sergio could not get a clear shot from his forty-five-degree angle into the glare of the sun. He kept bobbing his head about as if there was some angle where the sun wouldn't block his target. There wasn't. So the guinea pig turned his slingshot into the direction of the unicorn's head. "Drop the goggles or the unicorn gets it in the eye."

"No!" yelled Geronimo.

"Please, stop!" yelled Nancy. Geronimo and Sergio both looked at her. Sergio was so startled to hear the sound of Nancy's voice for the first time that he pointed the slingshot back at Geronimo and shouted, "You made her talk! She hates talking!" With that, Sergio released the band and sent the rock hurling toward the gnome's forehead. Geronimo was knocked off the horse like a pool ball flying off the table. Out cold, Geronimo landed eight feet from the beast with his head buried in the sand. The rest of his body stood upright, straight as an arrow into the air. Sergio ran up to the unicorn and immediately began the process of scaling his way up the animal.

Nancy ran over to Geronimo's half-buried body. She plucked him out of the sand much like one would pluck a vegetable from the ground. She then cradled him like a baby and walked toward the unicorn. Sergio was atop the horse fitting his sand goggles back on when he turned to look at Nancy.

"Oh no," protested Sergio, "don't you dare try to bring that thing on here." The unicorn lowered her backside as Nancy approached. This caused Sergio to slide completely off the animal with his sand goggles once again flying off his face. Nancy mounted the unicorn with ease. The animal raised its rump and lofted Nancy five feet above the ground.

"All right!" said Sergio. He shook the sand from his fur and straightened his armor. He fit his sand goggles back on his head. "He can come as long as he stays unconscious." He walked over to the unicorn and patted the animal's hind leg. "Okay, do that lowering thing that you did for her." The unicorn did not respond. "C'mon!" he cried, waving his tiny hands. No response. Sergio blinked his eyes with slow and deliberate irritation. He shook his head as he started climbing up the animal's tail. "Nothing like a little favoritism to start off our adventure," Sergio said as he struggled through the unicorn's white locks. When he got to the top, he scurried around Nancy and sat down in front of her. "I hope you're ready for battle, little lady." He adjusted his goggles for a final time and wrapped a tuft of the unicorn's white mane around his fist. Nancy grabbed a tuft as well. "Mush!" yelled Sergio, "mush!" The unicorn was not moving. "Go! Go! Partire! Vamanos!" The animal remained motionless. "How do you get this thing to move? Ugh, we're gonna be so late for battle!" he lamented.

"Maybe we should ask the unicorn its name," said Nancy in a soft and gentle tone.

"Would you just be quiet? I can't hear myself think!" yelled Sergio before turning to the unicorn. With all the charm of a wet sock, he said, "What's your name? Go."

"Let me try," said Nancy. She leaned over and whispered in the unicorn's ear, "What would you like to be called, my love?"

With that, the unicorn reared its head toward the sky, raised its front legs into the air, and whinnied with joyous abandon as it darted off into the direction of the castle.

28
"FORTY-NINE!"

The dank air and poor lighting of the castle basement proved excellent sleeping conditions for the unnamed elf. He slept on his back with a sandwich bag across his face. The thin plastic would flap into his mouth with each inhale.

"Good evening, lads," said Krampus. The elf's eyes popped open to the sound of his voice. Careful not to move, the elf closed his eyes just as a rush of feet ran over him, kicking and rolling him to the back of the cage. The boys had stampeded over him en route to the front. The back of the cage turned out to be a fortunate spot, however, since the boys not only had their backs to the elf, but they also blocked Krampus's view of him. The elf listened quietly, not moving a muscle.

"I'm glad you're all able to gather on such short notice," said Krampus. He waited with a slight smirk on his face for a laugh that never came. In fact, all of their faces revealed a striking lack of emotion, though they were not completely void of facial expression. Each boy had the same slight grimace that creased down the left corner of their mouths. Krampus could not help but be impressed by the uniformity in their faces, and clothes. They all wore the same grimy, tattered pajamas—dust-colored linen pants with dust-colored tank tops. They resembled leftover children from an abandoned orphanage. They stood compact, equidistant to each other, with no individuality to be seen. Krampus took all this in and beamed over them with a sinister glee. "I assume you've all been reading my monthly newsletters," he said as he noticed a five-foot mound of his newsletters leaning precariously against the side of the cage. "Over the past year I have written much of war being near." He paced the width of the cage and shouted in their faces, "War is near! War is near! War is near! That has been the headline of every newsletter for the past eleven months!" He ran over to the pile and picked the first off the pile, waving the cover at them. The battle cry "War Is Near!" ran across the front page. He continued, "And now, my boys, war is so near it's tomorrow. As we speak, the mutant camel queen marches with her army of cantankerous Sicilian guinea pigs toward our castle in the hope of kicking us out of our home. Tomorrow we fight to the death to defend our castle!" The silence that followed Krampus's rally cry made him uneasy. "Repeat after me," Krampus said as he pumped his scaly arm in the air, "Roo roo rah!" To his astonishment, they all simultaneously pumped their fists in the air and yelled, "Roo roo rah!"

"Roo roo rah!" Krampus yelled again with another fist pump. He grinned with delight.

"Roo roo rah!" shouted the boys with mechanical precision.

"Roo roo rah!" said Krampus.

"Roo roo rah!" the boys repeated.

Out of breath now, Krampus's shoulders heaved up and down. He brought his hands to his knees and coughed. When his coughing spell subsided, he heard a faint voice from inside the cage.

"How do you know they'll arrive tomorrow?" said a raspy voice inside the cage.

"Who said that?" asked Krampus. He marched closer to the cage and glared into the sea of gray. The elf had moved into the middle of the pack of boys, who seemed oddly indifferent to his antics.

"What proof do you have that an invading army will arrive tomorrow?" asked the elf in his disguised voice, repositioning himself within the mesh of children to avoid Krampus's gaze. Krampus stomped around all sides of the cage but could not gain sight of the speaker.

"Reveal yourself!" Krampus shouted.

"Answer three questions," said the elf, "and I shall do as you say."

Krampus thought about this before responding. "In good faith to the other boys, I will answer your questions."

"How do you know the battle is tomorrow?" asked the elf.

"I have a super-powered telescope," said Krampus. "I've been watching their progress since they left their compound."

"Huh," said the elf, genuinely surprised by the response.

"Question number two?" asked Krampus.

"Close your eyes for five seconds," said the elf, "and then tell me what number you're thinking of." Krampus closed his eyes, and the elf slipped silently between the bars of the cage, jumped onto the upturned wagon, and flipped the generator back off.

"Forty-nine!" shouted Krampus, as he opened his eyes to pitch black. "Aahhh!" he screamed. "Was that the wrong number?"

Krampus had previously mentioned to T.C. his fear of the basement in order to strike terror into T.C.'s large half-reindeer heart. And it wasn't a lie, Krampus really was afraid of the basement.

Meanwhile, the elf had pattered up the basement staircase in less than twenty seconds, thanks to his recent experiences with the generator. The elf kept running, down the main hallway, through the front castle doors, and toward the desert moonlight.

The complete darkness left Krampus groping around for an hour before finding the staircase out of the basement.

Imprisoned in the lower dungeons of the castle after being captured by Krampus, Murdock heard the sound of the generator shut down an hour ago. He was trying his best to be patient, but he couldn't wait any longer. Hoping that Krampus was fast asleep, Murdock finally called his wife. He leaned against the damp stone wall of the castle dungeon and listened to her verbally unload through his unconfiscated space-texter. He knew that if he switched the space-texter's dial from "text" to "chat" he would risk being caught. But for Murdock, it was worth the risk. After all, all of this failing-to-protect-Eleanor/going-against-Santa's-orders/ending-up-in-a-dungeon business was really stressing him out. He needed to hear the sound of Vera's voice just to keep going.

"Oh, I don't get a call from you this *entire* time," said Vera, "and the one time you *do* call, you tell me you don't have time and make it short?" Back home in a suburb of tiny log cabins a few miles outside of HQ, Vera sat at her kitchen table feeding her two small children. Her brow was furrowed with worry and confusion as flame-red curls hung down around her cheeks.

"Vera, listen . . ." said Murdock.

"Listen to what?" Vera asked. "Do you know the kids barely remember who you are?"

"Vera, I'm calling you from a dungeon," said Murdock. "I could get caught talking to you at any moment. So I need you to calm down so I can say my piece."

For a time after that Murdock heard nothing but silence. He was so alarmed by the quiet he had to ask, "Are you still there?" Then he heard sniffling, long and drawn out.

"I'm so sorry," she said. In his mind's eye, Murdock could see the tears filling her eyes. "I just miss you so much, and now—now you're in a dungeon . . ." Her voice crumpled the word *dungeon* under the weight of her anguish.

"Don't worry, babe," hushed Murdock, trying to be quiet. "One month from now we'll all be in the Poconos, and it'll be like none of this ever happened. I promise you. Krampus is keeping me alive for a reason. I just know it. I think he has some plan for me."

"What kind of plan?" asked Vera.

"Yeah, what kind of plan?" asked Krampus, crouched in the darkness beyond the bars of Murdock's cell. A cold shudder ran down the elf's tiny spine.

"Who was that?" asked Vera, her voice trembling.

Murdock's head turned with a shudder toward the darkness beyond the bars of his cell. He saw nothing. It was what he heard that filled him with dread; the excited panting of Krampus.

"Tell her who it is," said Krampus.

"I'm going to call you back," said Murdock.

"Wait! Wait!" cried Vera on the other line.

Murdock shifted the space-texter in his hands to turn it off, but Krampus intercepted his attempt and swiped the device out of his elfin hands. "Don't worry about your little husband," said Krampus, now speaking into the space-texter. His face illuminated under the glowing screen. "If he decides to be a good little elf, I shall spare him from my breakfast menu." The sound of profound agony erupted on the other end: shrieking, dishes clattering, cabinets slamming, and then more shrieking. "So, good night, Vera" Krampus continued. "Remind the children that I see them when there bad or good. And even when they're sleeping." Softly chuckling, he switched off the space-texter.

Before Murdock could react, Krampus had folded his scaly, slimy hands over the elf's hands and squeezed them tighter against the bars. Then he raised his tail up to the elf's neck, sliding it once, twice around it. Murdock turned white as a sheet as his head was yanked forward by the coiled tail snug around his neck. Krampus shifted his own hideous countenance out of the shadows and into the light. His snout was the color of spinach. Inches from the bars, his dull, yellow eyes leered down at the elf. Despite the amount of physical intimidation being employed, his tone remained cordial. "I'm leaving tomorrow morning before this ridiculous battle begins. And I'm taking you with me since I'll need your help."

"Help with what?" Murdock asked.

"Locating HQ," said Krampus.

"Do I have a choice?"

"Well, I was hoping to keep this civil. But, honestly, you're really starting to tick me off." Krampus tightened his grip around the elf's frail, little neck.

"All right," Murdock screeched through his half-choked neck. "I'll talk to you straight," Murdock wheezed, "no more wisecracks." Krampus squeezed even harder, watching the elf's face turn from white to a milky blue seconds before releasing his grip altogether and recoiling his tail back behind his body. He released his grip on Murdock's hands, and the elf fell back on the ground, gasping for air.

Krampus withdrew back into the shadows, his voice hammering on through the dark. "I couldn't help but overhear your interest in the Poconos. As it turns out, I have an outlandish amount of frequent flyer miles under one of my pseudonyms. And without giving you any information that would incriminate me under any galactic court of law, I can say that if you help me locate HQ, I will guarantee you four tickets to the Poconos."

"Four tickets?" repeated Murdock. It occurred to the elf that this is exactly what Santa wanted, to deliver Krampus to HQ. This wasn't betrayal, this was completing the mission.

"You, Vera, Lu, and Tut," continued Krampus. "I can put you all on a plane to the Poconos like that." Krampus snapped his fingers. He put his hand out through the bars for Murdock to shake. "Shake on it," said Krampus. "You help me. I help you."

Murdock looked up into the darkness for a few moments before shaking the demon's hand. "It's a deal," said Murdock.

$\mathscr{e}\!\!\sim\!\!29\!\!\sim\!\!\mathscr{e}$
FIRSTS FOR ALL THINGS

Clarence sank into Santa's giant, cushy chair as evening fell over HQ. The third in command was racked with worried thoughts, one being the surprising lack of problems arising from Assembly Hall in the absence of the second in command. Clarence had been spending the whole day behind Big Red's desk just in case there were any questions or problems regarding toy manufacturing, machinery, and overall production. And, curiously, with just three days left before Christmas, there seemed to be no issues. Then it suddenly dawned on him. When slumped down in Santa's chair, he was impossible to see from the office doorway. From the hallway it appeared as if no one was in the office. He hopped on the desk to check for any action in the hallway. Nothing.

"Excuse me, Elder Clarence," said Bartlett, a first-year toymaker, as he craned his head into the doorframe.

"Yes, boy, what is it?" asked Clarence.

"We've had a hard time locating you," said Bartlett.

"I've been here the whole time!" said Clarence.

"Please understand, Elder Clarence," said Bartlett, "we've all walked by here throughout the day with endless repair needs. The pizza parachutes aren't descending properly, and Darla the talking parrot still only speaks Samoan for some reason. And then there's the whole ongoing pelican vacuum cleaner catastrophe. And every time we passed we saw no one here."

"What?" said Clarence. "I-I was here, you just couldn't see me." He hopped onto the desk and walked over to Santa's computer. "I'll send out a campus-wide email apologizing for the misunderstanding."

"I'm afraid there's something else you may need to attend to," said Bartlett.

"What is it?"

"There are two lawyers waiting out in the main lobby who are seeking clearance to use the time pond."

"What?" asked Clarence as he jumped off the desk and paced the nutcracker-embroidered rug. "How is this all happening tonight?"

Bartlett was unsure how to answer that. "They've been waiting for quite some time," was all he could say.

Clarence stormed up to Bartlett, wagging his finger in the air. "You know who uses the time pond, young man?" he asked. "Do you know the only person who has ever used the time pond, the only one with clearance?"

"I do, Elder Clarence," said Bartlett, "Santa Claus."

"No one," said Clarence, answering his own question. "No one else has ever brought up the time pond outside of Santa's circle."

"I guess there's a first time for everything," said Bartlett.

"Enough," said Clarence with a wave of his hand. "Bring them in. You're dismissed." Bartlett nodded and left. Clarence climbed back into the chair, then onto the desk, where he dangled his legs over the edge, swinging them as he waited for the two lawyers.

They arrived a few minutes later soaking wet. In drenched suit and ties, the two identical faces smiled wide and frog-like at the gawking Clarence. The elf was speechless. After an awkward period of silence in which the brothers were clearly waiting for Clarence to say something, one of the brothers looked at the other. The brother receiving the look nodded and then walked over to Clarence. He took a large ziplock bag out of his dripping brief-case. He unzipped the bag and gave the elf the contents. Clarence took them and unfolded the high-quality paper. The cover had an embossment with the image of a gavel with planets circling below. The letters "TGC" ran across the image. Clarence recognized the acronym as "The Galactic Court," the highest judicial court of law known in the entire galaxy. It all looked pretty official.

"Please take a seat," said Clarence, going back to reading the documents as he beelined for the big, red Santa chair behind the desk. The other lawyer walked into the room, and the two broth-ers stood in front of the couch. One took out another ziplock bag that enclosed two dry towels. They both laid their towels over the velvet green cushions before sitting down in perfect synchronicity. Meanwhile, Clarence flipped through pages of the document with a look of growing fascination on his face. He read silently, skim-ming pages here and there. Finally, he put the document down on his desk and looked at the Frogg brothers.

"So, let me get this straight," said Clarence with a look of marvel, "you two are brothers who are also lawyers, but you are not frogs. You just look like frogs. Correct?"

They nodded their heads in unison. One of them stood up and walked over to the desk. The lawyer's bony, lime-colored fingers gently tapped against one of the "sign here" lines on the bottom of the document. "Oh! Right," said Clarence. He grabbed

Santa's quill, which was the size of a sword for Clarence, and used it to forge Santa's signature on the last page of the document, thereby giving the lawyers legal clearance to use the time pond. He folded the papers back up and handed them to the already standing lawyers. The brother holding the briefcase slipped the documents back into the ziplock bag and put the bag back into his dripping wet briefcase. They both bowed at Clarence at the doorway before sauntering back down the hallway. Clarence followed them. He had never actually seen anyone use the time pond before, on account of Clarence not knowing how to swim. Santa wouldn't let him near it and would always say, "No clearance for Clarence!" An eruption of elfish laughter would always follow.

Arriving at the end of the hall, the Frogg brothers stopped and took out their documents to show Bartlett. Behind the elf was an enclosed biodome the size of a doctor's waiting room. Inside the biodome was a small, clear-blue pond about the circumference of a carousel, with plants and shrubs. Clarence watched the lawyers show their paperwork to Bartlett. Bartlett checked and rechecked the signature and then even looked to Clarence for triple approval. Clarence nodded at him, and Bartlett gave the documents back to the brothers, stepping out of their way to punch a code into a keypad on the wall. The doors opened with a *shoosh,* and the Frogg brothers looked at each other and giggled. Together they walked forward until their shiny black shoes reached the edge of the water. Bartlett punched in the code again and the glass doors closed shut. Clarence watched the brothers creep deeper and deeper into the pond until the tops of their heads disappeared. Bartlett walked over to Clarence and stood beside him. With great wonder they both looked out over the small, rippling pond.

"I can't believe you gave them clearance," said Bartlett.

"Let's just say I have a hunch they're on our side," said Clarence. "You've had a long day, Bartlett. Go to bed. I have a feeling tomorrow's going to be even longer."

Clarence patted Bartlett on the shoulder and walked back toward Santa's office. A few moments later, the elf looked back at the glass door to the biodome behind him. He looked down the other end of the hallway toward his quarters. Back and forth his head went, his body stuck between two warring impulses.

30

AMANDO'S FAKE BIRTHDAY

Everything in the chopper rattled. Santa struggled to control the wheel as the aircraft repeatedly rose and fell in the air, his arms jerking wildly as his hands clung to the wheel. His eyes darted from the blinding clouds to the pinging needles of his navigation system. Everything on the ship was going haywire.

Rose sat next to her husband, fastened in with her helmet on. One hand gripped her husband's thigh while the other flipped switches at a desperate, flurried pace on the large glowing switchboard in front of her. T.C. was behind them, sliding and staggering around on all fours. He knew they were going down. He held onto an overhead cabinet, trying to grab the parachutes inside.

"Forget it, T.C.!" shouted Santa. "Get in your chair and buckle up. Brace for impact!" T.C. clamored over to his stall, which was specifically designed for him, as the chopper heaved itself upward. Slammed to the back of the stall, he clamped his strap snug against his body. He watched Santa lean over to engage the landing gear.

After pushing the lever forward, Santa grabbed Rose's hand as the vessel made its final dive toward the ground. T.C. closed his eyes and waited for impact.

His wait was short. *Pop! Smash! Smash!* Large branches bashed through the ship's windows, shredding off the top of the chopper. Skewered by branch after branch, the chopper slowed its descent to a halt. The vessel swung back and forth like a Christmas ornament. This predicament surprised everyone. They all expected a desert landing, but they had overshot the soft sand for the tangled web of trees. An enormous branch had smashed through the front of the chopper, barely missing Santa and Rose. The giant stalk completely obstructed their view to one another.

"Rose? Rose, you okay?" asked Santa.

"Ugh," said Rose. "I think my arm's bleeding. I can't tell how bad it is." T.C. heard these words from the back of the chopper and sprang into action. His belt had kept him secure, and his stall had prevented branches from crashing anywhere near him. He could hear Santa fumbling with his own belt.

"Hold on," said Santa. Free of his belt, he bent over and immediately shrieked in pain. T.C. had never heard him yell like that before. The centaur unclipped his belt and immediately tilted the chopper like a seesaw as he lifted his weight out of the chair. Santa and Rose both gasped.

"Careful!" exclaimed both Rose and Santa. T.C. crept slowly toward the cockpit. The chopper teetered and tottered with each shifting of his weight.

"Just stay where you are, Santa," T.C. said, only a few steps out of his stall. "Let me attend to Mrs. Claus. You're obviously hurt yourself. Don't worsen your condition by trying to get up."

"You're not even supposed to be on this chopper, T.C.!" said Santa. "Dr. Tinsel gave you strict orders to rest. You could keel over due to overexcitement any minute!"

T.C. took another step toward the cockpit. The ship jerked softly forward. "Listen, Chief, all three of us have a higher than normal likelihood of keeling over. Let's not belabor our woes. Just be thankful I'm here to save the day."

"You haven't saved anything yet," said Santa. "Rose? Rose, are you still with us? Darling, say something, please."

"Yes, yes, I'm here," said Rose. "The two of you are giving me a splitting headache."

T.C. was making his slow trot toward the front of the chopper. Each step forward tilted the ship like a boat pitching in a stormy sea. Halfway from his stall to the cockpit, T.C. took his final step. The chopper was sent sliding off branches and down toward the forest floor. It tumbled downward under the cloak of night, finally splashing into a small lagoon. There was silence in the chopper as it drifted to the edge of the lagoon and stopped, wedging itself against large fallen tree trunks sticking into the water. T.C. had somehow slid back into his stall, where he gripped the steel bars on the inside of the stall walls. He was surprisingly unharmed. "Everybody okay?" he asked.

"We're fine. Why aren't we sinking?" asked Santa from the cockpit.

T.C. worked his way out the stall, this time sloshing through lagoon water. He waded waist-deep into the cockpit. "On my last flight with Colin, I read in the manual that they are designed to float," the centaur said as he stood over their chairs, finally getting a look at the pilot and copilot. They looked more angry than critically wounded. Stunned and relieved, he said, "I can't believe you made it through all that."

"I think I twisted my ankle," said Santa. "I'm gonna need to ride you outta this tuna can." Santa unfastened his belt and threw his body over T.C.'s reindeer backside. Using his arms, he sat up on T.C. and faced forward. He turned his head toward his wife. "Honey, how're you feeling? You need help getting out?"

"I can manage," she said as she unfastened her own seatbelt and stepped down from her elevated chair and into the cold, slimy lagoon water. The chilly water temperature start

led her, so she wobbled and fell against the curved wall of the circuit board.

"You all right there, babe?" asked Santa.

"I'm fine," she said. She took a few measured breaths before pushing herself upright, then took slow steps around the cockpit.

"Santa," said T.C., "I recommend we grab the emergency sleeping bags from the overhead compartments, find a nice, soft, dry spot not far from the lagoon here and rest for the night."

"Rest?" repeated Santa. "We've got sleeping bags, onboard?"

"I packed them this morning," said T.C. Rose walked over to the overhead cabinets and opened them. She grabbed sleeping bags from inside. Somehow she kept all three over her head as she sloshed back toward Santa and T.C.

Santa and T.C. trotted out of the bashed-out window frame, with Rose trailing behind them, lifting her long dress to step over jagged glass. Navigating all the rubble, they made it to soft sand, safe from the wreckage. They all looked back at their defeated vehicle as it waded harmlessly back and forth in the lagoon.

"Aren't you even a little glad I came now?" asked T.C.

"Not at all," said Santa.

Queen Fatilahh and her army of guinea pigs were encamped just five miles from where Santa, Rose, and T.C. had crashed. After providing immediate shade, water, and rest, Eleanor's breathing resumed shortly after it had stopped back in the desert. The only problem now was that she would not wake up. Rosabella secretly hoped that Eleanor wouldn't wake up until after the battle tomorrow morning, to spare her from both the gruesome act of war and getting hurt, or worse.

"Rosabella?" asked Tatiana from behind her. Startled, Rosabella jumped out of her snug position.

"Tatiana!" Rosabella hushed. "Don't sneak up like that."

"I didn't sneak up," said Tatiana as she eyed the lit wax candle in her hand. "I'm holding a candle."

"What are you still doing up?" Rosabella asked as she tiptoed around the *V* of Eleanor's arm and away from the sleeping child.

"My job was to make sure everyone was sleeping," said Tatiana. "And your eyes were open." She scribbled something on a clipboard she had awkwardly strung around her neck. Rosabella noticed Tatiana wore makeup around her eyes that bled down her furry face from the heat of the lit candle.

"Well, I have to stay awake to watch Eleanor, Tatiana," said Rosabella.

Tatiana stopped her furious writing. "Oh, right," she said.

"Do you think she'll ever wake up?" She had switched her attention to the sleeping Eleanor.

"Oh, she'll wake up!" said Amando from the shadows.

"Amando!" Tatiana yelled reproachfully. "You're supposed to be asleep!" Amando stepped into the candlelight. Standing on his hind legs, he appeared upright, though not quite still. In one hand he held a thimble that sloshed a gold-colored liquid from its rim. Rosabella and Tatiana both looked at each other and then raised themselves to standing position. Of the three of them, Amando was the only one having trouble standing still. He also had the hiccups.

"She'll wake up tomorrow morning," said Amando, "even if I have to shake the life out of her."

"What are you drinking?" asked Rosabella.

"Pumpkin juice," said Amando quickly with his eyes closed.

"Is that the pumpkin cider you were saving for your birthday?" asked Rosabella.

"No. Yes. Maybe. Today is my birthday." Amando sipped again from his thimble-turned-mug. Tatiana and Rosabella looked on equally aghast over Amando's choice of beverage. "Besides," continued Amando, "we may not live past tomorrow. And this vitally-nutritious juice would go to waste."

"It's cider," said Rosabella. "It has alcohol in it."

"Minor details," Amando said as he shook his head. His own vigorous head movement sent him crashing to the ground. His thimble rolled along the mud-caked forest floor. Amando found himself on all fours, yawning. Tatiana and Rosabella also lowered their bodies to the ground in order to remain at eye level with their drunken friend.

"What you said about Eleanor," said Tatiana, "that wasn't very nice."

"Of course, you're right," said Amando. His voice was low and sad. "Eleanor," he said with a rich bravado and eyes intensely shut, "if you can hear me, please accept my deepest apologies. I would never try to hurt you. Especially since, deep down, I'm not sure if it's even possible for me to hurt you."

"Go to sleep, Amando," said Rosabella. Amando nodded his head. "Good night, ladies," he said as he walked back into the shadows.

"We should go to bed too," said Rosabella, "We have a big battle in the morning." Tatiana nodded. They rubbed their wet noses together and retreated to their respective shadows.

31

THE FOG OF WAR

Nancy, Sergio, and the unicorn slept through the battle cries that rang across the purple morning sky. Sergio used the gnome's tummy as a pillow, while Geronimo lay face up in the sand. Though the gnome's eyes were closed, he was currently engaged in one of his self-described greatest skills: fake sleeping. Though Geronimo was never quite sure how effective fake sleeping actually was, he felt exceptionally good at it. As he was about to open his eyes and abort the tactic, the unnamed elf stumbled upon the scene through the thick early fog. Careful not to wake the rest of her party, the elf quietly patted Nancy's cheek. Stirring slowly, she opened her eyes to the sight of Krampus's personal assistant. She was horror-stricken at the sight of him. The elf could see the scream forming in her face. He had to use both hands to cover her mouth. "Shhh," he whispered. "I'm on your side." Nancy balked on the scream, shaking her head, hot with disagreement.

"I'm not like Krampus," said the elf. "Please, believe me when I say I would never hurt you." Nancy slowed her breath and relaxed her jaw. "You promise not to scream when I remove my hands?" Nancy nodded and the elf removed his hands.

"What's your name?" Nancy asked.

"I don't remember," said the elf. "I had a bad fall many years ago. I lost large chunks of my memory. I can't remember where I'm from, how I wound up at the castle, or even my own name. So I'd rather not have a name at all if it's all the same to you."

"What did you fall from?" asked Nancy.

"A chandelier," said the elf. His face blushed with embarrassment as he awaited Nancy's follow-up question.

"What were you doing on a chandelier?" she asked.

"It was Krampus's castle warming party. 1963. It was a different time back then." The elf shook his head, filled with regret.

"I'd like to call you Henry," said Nancy, not caring at all about the rest of the story. She sat up slowly, careful not to wake the others.

"Please don't call me Henry," said the elf, becoming less cautious with the volume of his voice. Sergio's body twitched. The sound of war grew louder in the distance. "I can't promise I'll answer to it."

"Henry!" yelled Geronimo. Henry turned toward the voice. He had to arch his neck to see the gnome. Geronimo was mounted atop the now wide-awake unicorn. Once he realized Henry was one of the good guys, Geronimo soundlessly rolled his body from under Sergio's head and made for the four-legged animal.

"Enough chatter," Geronimo said in a raspy whisper. His eyes darted over at the rustling Sergio. "You and the girl climb on this thing if you want to be saved from that maniac guinea pig." Nancy ran over to the unicorn, more than happy to get back on. Henry didn't move, choosing instead to fire questions at the gnome. "Where is your spaceship? Or did you take the boatman?"

"I did both," said Geronimo. He braided the unicorn's mane into a makeshift seatbelt. "Chopper's back that way," Geronimo motioned with his thumbs. "But it's all locked up till I get back. It's being guarded by an ornery clown. You can wait if you want and we might be able to give you a lift out of here. No promises, of course. But right now I have to go capture Krampus and save my friend, so . . ."

Henry nodded. "Understood. Go!"

"I *don't* understand!" squealed Sergio, outraged. The rubber band of his sling shot stretched back, sick and crustily. Geronimo, Nancy, and Henry had all forgotten to check in on him. The guinea pig fired the rock before Geronimo could blink. Still in recovery from the first blow to the head, Geronimo knew he could not sustain another so soon. Instead of blinking, he turned his head and winced, waiting for impact. All he heard was a muffled *thud*. He turned and saw Henry with his right arm fully extended holding the rock in his hand. Henry hurled the rock back at the jaw-dropped Sergio, who caught the ball in his stunned mouth and pitched back into the sand. Henry nodded at Geronimo.

"I owe you one," said the gnome.

"Just get me far away from here," said Henry.

"That chopper out yonder disembarks when I get back," said Geronimo. "We'll give you a lift." He nodded at Henry and then turned back to the unicorn. "Go! Go!" he shouted. The unicorn did not respond. "I forget how you get this thing started," the gnome muttered. Nancy sat right behind Geronimo and held tufts of the mane in her fists. She leaned over and whispered, "I love you," into the unicorn's ear. The unicorn whinnied and raised its front legs into the air.

"Don't love me yet," said Geronimo, who thought Nancy's remark was directed to him. Geronimo gritted his teeth as the animal lunged back down to earth. "Love me after I save youuuu!" he shouted as they galloped off. Henry listened to the "youuuu" echo over the dunes. He turned his back from it and walked in the direction of the chopper.

Ottavio and Amando lay flat in the tall grass. Their shiny brown eyes flashed between the green blades. They were forty yards out from the half-open castle doors. The rest of the guinea pig battalion were aligned in a V-formation behind their two generals. Ottavio turned his head to look behind him. He squinted into the harsh morning sunlight.

"It is time," Ottavio said. "The sun is rising in the trees behind us. The boys will be sleepy after just getting up, and blinded by the sun."

"Agreed," said Amando, "though I don't like the front gates being already half open. It's too easy, could be a trap."

"Nonsense," said Ottavio. "It's just a case of laziness on their part."

"Doesn't feel right," said Amando.

"Signal the flanks, Amando," ordered Ottavio. "It is time. The sun at our backs gives us our greatest advantage. But that advantage is fleeting. Signal now!" Amando kept his eyes on the half-open castle doors as he raised his spear from the ground and twirled it twice in the air. The rest of the battalion nodded their heads behind them. All eleven guinea pigs simultaneously rose.

Eleanor had woken up from her coma earlier that morning and was now waiting with Queen Fatilahh at the edge of the forest.

She and the queen were ten feet from the battle-ready rodents. Eleanor watched the guinea pigs jump in unison out of the grass and charge the half-open castle doors.

"I know I'm cutting you a break, little missy," Queen Fati-lahh said to Eleanor, "by permitting your absence from battle. But I assure you that if I fail to claim this castle as mine, I'll see to it you never get home." The camel's tone had slowly shifted over the past few days from gentle and mothering to cruel and threatening. Yet it wasn't the queen's words that caused Eleanor to suddenly gasp with dread. It was the throng of bloodthirsty boys that poured out of the half-open castle doors at that very moment. The dirt-smeared, angry-faced kids wielded rocks and sharp sticks. The lunatic children had flooded out of the doors, kicking and screaming.

"Oh, no," said Eleanor with tears in her eyes. She covered her eyes and crouched into the grass, rocking gently against the soft blades as she let out a low whimper.

The squeals were deafening, harsh and high-pitched. Eleanor had her eyes shut, so she didn't see what happened, but when she dared open her eyes again, she saw Ottavio and Amando's bodies piled lifelessly on top of each other near the front gates. Trickles of blood trailed from small holes in their chests. The biggest and bravest of the guinea pigs had been slain with disturbing speed. Rosabella, Frederico, Tino, Tatiana, Ernesta, Nicolina, Sofia, and Giovanna all looked at one another. They all knew they would not win in a fair fight and would have to change tactics.

Giovanna was the first to step up to the stampede roll-ing toward them. She grabbed the three small pouches, all tied together with one string, from her combat belt. She raised herself on her hind legs and lifted the bags high above her head. Giovanna waited until the boy army was just a few feet from her until she hurled all three bags to the ground. The other guinea pigs shielded their eyes as booming clouds of smoke exploded out of the ground where the pouches landed. The boys started to stumble around in the thick clouds, coughing, weaving, and bumping into each other. Giovanna couldn't escape the heavy fog either. While her witchcraft was meant to disorient the enemy, it was also meant to be thrown much farther than she had thrown it. But she didn't want to miss and she had to use them all at once, knowing it was their only chance of survival.

"Charge!" yelled Ernesta, holding her war-painted spear high above her head. Her spear was painted in the image of a lizard, the animal she was so fond of pretending to chase. She was the fastest rodent in the battalion, and without hesitation, she scurried into the blinding cloud, stabbing her spear in all directions. Inspired by their comrade's courage, the remaining six guinea pigs charged the cloud. Sofia swung rags loaded with her painted rocks. Nicolina had created a crossbow from her sewing needles. Tatiana, Tino, and Frederico all rushed in wielding long sticks with rusty baby forks fixed atop each one.

"It is time to be brave, Eleanor!" yelled Queen Fatilahh from the edge of the forest. Eleanor and the queen could see nothing of the battle. The cloud's magic was too strong for visibility, but not strong enough to smother the sound of the horror. The shrieks of rodents and children radiated from the battle haze. "Jump on top and grab the axe out of my combat skirt," said the queen. Eleanor used the foothold coming off the saddle to mount the camel queen. "As soon as we gain sight of Krampus, we charge. Understood?" Eleanor noticed the combat skirt the queen wore had the dual purpose of weapon storage—every ruffle of the skirt was actually a pocket that held some heavy, dangerous-looking weapon. She looked at the pocket closest to her, conveniently labeled "axe." She used both hands to lift the weapon out of its pocket.

"Good girl," the queen said. "And now we wait for Krampus."

Watching from the castle's tallest spire, Krampus grinned through a grimy window. From his vantage point, he watched the cloud get bigger. It was an enormous puffball of murderous confusion. It made Krampus giddy with delight.

Murdock was trapped in a birdcage at the other end of the room. He could stand without hitting the wire-laced ceiling of the cage, though the door was padlocked with a thick chain roped around the base. The room they were in was unlike any other room in the castle. It was cone-shaped, for one, since they were in the actual hollowed out castle spire. The walls and floor were steel. Switchboards filled with buttons, levers, and glowing screens wrapped around the circular wall. And then it dawned on the elf.

"This is your escape pod, isn't it?" asked Murdock.

"Correct!" Krampus said with the vigor of a game show host. His eyes remained glued to the window.

"What're you waiting for?" asked Murdock.

"I just want to see his fat face," said Krampus, rubbing his dry, scaly hands together. "I want to see his big, fat 'uh-oh' face as I take off into the air."

"Who's 'uh-oh' face?"

"My brother's!" snapped Krampus, finally turning to his captive. Krampus stomped across the metal floor and kicked the birdcage. Murdock was able to grab the bars of the cage in time to brace himself for the toppling and rolling across the floor.

"Enough questions!" said Krampus. He busied himself by checking gauges and pressing various buttons on the wrap-around wall console. Murdock was silent after that. Finally, his eyes darted back and forth as he stewed over a thought. "Oh my," muttered

Murdock to himself, surprised by his revelation. "You're doing all this because you have a gripe against your brother."

Krampus had pulled a lever halfway down when he stopped, frozen by Murdock's remark. He turned his head toward Murdock, who was sitting up in the tilted over cage.

"I get it now," said Murdock.

"You get nothing!" said Krampus. He stormed over to the cage once again. This time he picked it up, brought it to his face, and spat into it, leaving Murdock drenched in gooey saliva. Murdock coughed and sputtered as Krampus grabbed him from the cage, opened a small freezer installed into one of the consoles, and put him inside, closing the door.

Dr. Tinsel had been right. There was something wrong with T.C.'s heart, and he could feel it shutter and veer off-rhythm as he lumbered through the smoky wood. The full girth of Santa pressed down on his reindeer spine. Tomorrow was Christmas Day. He was carrying Big Red at his maximum weight. T.C.'s vision went blurry for moments at a time. He couldn't decide whether or not to tell Santa and Rose about his current symptoms. For the time being he went with "not."

Rose used two slim and sturdy branches as walking sticks. She had a bag of frozen corn she found in the chopper freezer wrapped around her arm. Rose and T.C. wobbled forward in unison as Santa sniffed the oncoming mist. He looked confused and disoriented as thin waves of smoke rolled over them. "Do you smell that?" he asked. Rose and T.C. trudged forward in silence, too tired to respond. "Lavendar rocks," said Santa, answering his own question. "This smoke is witchcraft." He coughed and started waving his hands.

"How can you be so sure?" asked Rose.

"I gave the camel queen the recipe for this chemical reaction years ago to aid in their struggle against my brother," said Santa. "It's actually less witchcraft and more just basic science. But I sold it to her as witchcraft."

"The camel queen?" asked Rose. "What camel queen? Why don't I know these things? You never talk to me about work anymore." The mist grew thicker as they crept forward.

"You're with me now, aren't you?" said Santa. "It doesn't get more intimate than this."

"Still," said Rose, "would've been nice to have known before the fruitcake hit the fan."

They had finally made it through the clearing and were now gawking at the front drawbridge of the castle where the massacre had started. Rose's jaw fell open. Her complexion turned ash gray. The boys were gone. They had followed the moving mist through the forest. All that was left was the strewn bodies of the guinea pigs across the tall, neglected grass. Rose shut her eyes and turned her head away. Santa's immense presence seemed to shrink in size. He bowed his head. T.C silently, solemnly, counted the bodies: seven guinea pigs. Suddenly, they heard a deafening sound from high atop the castle. The cone-shaped top of the tallest spire rocketed off the rest of the castle and shot into the sky. Santa, Rose, and T.C. all turned their heads upward, their faces dumb with helplessness.

"Is that him?" Rose said.

"Most likely," said Santa.

T.C. spotted a shovel leaning beside the stone wall of the courtyard. "There's a shovel over there," he said. "We should bury the bodies before we leave."

"I'm worried about our time," said Santa. T.C. looked up at his boss, appalled at the thought of leaving the dead animals exposed to the elements.

Santa tried to reason with him. "You know where he's headed, don't you? Straight to HQ. He's waited for this moment practically his whole life, for me to leave so he can jump in the time pond and terrorize Earth. We have to get there before he does."

"You two go on then," said T.C. "I'm helping with cleanup here."

"We don't have time, T.C.," said Santa. "If that was my brother taking off into the sky, then every second counts. HQ has never been more vulnerable, and now the big, bad wolf is about to pay a visit."

"I've made my decision. I'm not leaving these bodies out here to rot in the sun. My mother died like this, torn apart by a giant grizzly and left to bake in the summer heat."

"Forgive me," said Santa.

"I had no idea," said Rose.

"It's all right. But I'm not backing down. Go on without me."

Santa turned his head and saw Eleanor and the queen step out of the forest twenty yards away.

"Eleanor!" Santa cried with newfound joy. "You're here! You're alive!" The sound of Santa's voice had an invigorating effect on Eleanor's weakened spirit. Of all the fantastical characters she had met since the abduction, this was the first one who appeared to actually have her best interest in mind. She could hear it in his voice. With watery eyes and a soaring heart she ran to him. *This is it*, she thought. *I'm going home.* The queen had suddenly become disinterested in Eleanor's actions with Santa's arrival on the scene. The camel continued her casual, no-rush pace toward his party. She looked neither pleased nor displeased at the current developments.

With the help of his wife, Santa climbed off T.C. to receive the onrushing Eleanor. Rose eased him onto the ground as Santa's legs could no longer hold his massive weight. Kneeling on the grass, however, he was able to balance himself upright. He opened his arms just in time for Eleanor to crash into them.

"Please take me home. Take me home!" cried Eleanor over Santa's shoulder.

"Of course, sweetheart," said Santa. "Now that we have you, we're going back immediately. I'm so glad you're okay." Santa pulled away from Eleanor just enough to look her in the eye. "Any news of Geronimo or Murdock?" he asked. Rose dug through a travel bag that they had hitched to the other side of T.C.'s saddle.

Eleanor shook her head. "I don't know. I don't know what happened to them. Please just take me *home*!" she begged. Santa nodded. Rose rushed up to Eleanor with a bottled water and bag of airplane pretzels she had grabbed from the chopper.

"You must be famished, poor child," said Rose as she took her toward a cool spot back under the shady trees. Santa used the footrests of T.C.'s saddle to hoist himself back on his feet, leaning some of his weight onto T.C. to appear upright to the approaching camel queen. T.C. knew that if he were to move even an inch or two, Santa would likely go crashing to the ground. The only body part the centaur moved was his head. He turned it to the queen while folding his arms, slow and quiet. The queen stopped a foot in front of Santa. She bucked her head up and gave out a light snort.

"Thank you for keeping her safe," said Santa.

"I was waiting for Krampus to show up," said the queen. "I wasn't about to waste my time on those boys." The queen glanced at Eleanor. "She got lucky in the end. He never showed."

"All the same," said Santa.

The queen looked toward the tree line where Rose tended to Eleanor. "But she's not out of the woods yet," she said. "They're not safe here." At first Santa thought the queen was only taking advantage of the play on words when he also looked over at his wife and Eleanor at the tree line. All around Rose and Eleanor emerged spots of pink flesh through the foliage. The boys had returned, and they were slowly encircling the two of them. Rose and Eleanor were recuperating on a large rock. Eleanor was leaning into Rose with her eyes closed, beyond exhausted. Rose sang soft Turkish lullabies to Eleanor, singing with her eyes closed, rocking gently side to side. Together they drifted under this delightful spell until they heard Santa's urgent words: "Run, Rose, run!"

Hearing the desperation in her husband's voice, Rose bolted upright with her arm still around Eleanor. "Run, child, run!" she instructed Eleanor. They broke into a run toward Santa and the queen. A moment or two passed before the battalion of boys shot out of the foliage all at once. They wielded chains, axes, and machetes as they raced toward Rose and Eleanor. The boys didn't care who they were attacking anymore. Everything that moved was their enemy. They had been caged for too long.

T.C. abandoned his role as support for Santa and charged toward Rose and Eleanor. Santa toppled to the ground. Meanwhile, the boys were quickly gaining ground on the girls, and T.C. knew he was not going to make it in time.

Santa climbed onto the queen's saddle as they helplessly watched the unfolding events. It was all happening too fast. A wave of unbridled, adolescent rage was going to devour the woman he loved and the child he had plotted to rescue. Their rusty street weapons were swinging mere inches from their intended prey when an arresting, pulsating sound washed over the clearing from the other end of the tree line.

The sound of the unicorn was barely audible, yet the sonic force was powerful enough to stop everyone in their tracks. Even the murderous boys jolted to a standstill and turned their heads just in time to watch the unicorn jump out of the woods and into the clearing straight for the melee at the castle's front gates. Nancy rode with her body crouched against the animal. She held fistfuls of gray mane. Her aerodynamic form resembled that of a professional jockey. Above her, Geronimo stood atop the unicorn's head, holding the animal's horn for balance. He looked like the figurehead of a pirate ship crashing through stormy waters.

As the gnome approached the paused action, he realized he would have to say something that was just as amazing as his entrance. One wrong word could lead to bloodshed.

"We found King Krampus," said Geronimo, facing the boys. All the boys looked at each other with looks of confusion. They were all searching for signs of confirmation, but there was none to be found. The gnome used this fortunate bit of timing to wink in the direction of Eleanor, Rose, Santa, and T.C. "He said to meet him in the boneyard and that he was extremely proud of all of you. He's waiting with individual trophies to hand out to each and every one of you." Geronimo watched the expressions of the boys move from skepticism to glowing assurance that they had made their adopted father proud. News of Krampus waiting for them in a place they were never allowed to go filled the boys with gratitude.

The boys dropped their weapons with one collective *klunk*. Together, they walked like tired, quiet soldiers past the unicorn and through Santa's party without so much as eye contact. They walked around the side of the castle and vanished from sight.

"Where are they going?" asked Geronimo, astounded by the effect of his words.

"To the boneyard where you sent them, dingo bat," said T.C. "You guys don't have much time."

"There's an actual boneyard?" asked Geronimo.

T.C. ignored the gnome's question and turned his attention to the queen. "Your Royal Highness, do you mind giving my boss a lift to his spaceship?" The queen shook her head.

"I'm not leaving you to fend off those boys by yourself, T.C.," said Santa. "You're coming with us."

"I told you where I stand, Santa," said T.C. "I'm burying these bodies first. I'll meet up with you later, but if this is goodbye, then so be it."

"Thank you for your service, Tony Gibbons Curtis," said Santa.

"You're welcome," said T.C. "Now shut up and get out of here."

"I was just making up that there was a boneyard," said Geronimo, still baffled he guessed right.

"Geronimo, just shut up for two seconds," said Santa. "We all get that you're amazing, but right now we have to move forward and past it. Rose." Santa turned to his wife, who was still clutching Eleanor in a state of mild shock over the recent developments. Eleanor was also statue-still, with her eyes locked on Geronimo. Her head was buzzing with a hundred different thoughts and emotions.

"Rose, dear," Santa continued in his most polite tone, "you and Eleanor jump on the back of this great queen of the desert and we can get going."

"Jump on the back?" Rose repeated in utter disbelief.

The queen lowered her head down between Rose's legs. The First Lady of Christmas retained her stately posture during the unglamorous activity of sliding down the queen's thin, scruffy mane as she raised her long neck. She bumped gently against her husband as she reached bottom. Rose bent down and opened her arms toward Eleanor. "Reach up for me, sweetie," Rose grabbed her and, with the help of Eleanor's scaling feet, lifted her atop the camel and plopped her in front.

"Are you good, Eleanor?" Santa asked.

"Better than I was," said Eleanor.

"Okay, I'll take that," said Santa. He turned to Geronimo and asked, "How's Nancy?" Geronimo looked down at the bent and motionless Nancy. "Nancy!" he shouted. Geronimo could see Nancy's rib cage expand and protract, but she would not respond. "She's just sleeping. It's been a long day."

"Get down there and secure her," said Santa. "Let's ride out!" With that, the queen trotted toward the trees with Rose and Santa riding aloft. Geronimo slid down the unicorn's mane and grabbed tufts of the mane halfway down the neck so as not to crash into the sleeping Nancy below.

"We love you very much," Geronimo whispered into the unicorn's left ear. The unicorn whinnied and headed for the woods, quickly catching up with the queen.

"By the way, Santa," said Geronimo, "thanks for delivering on the unicorn."

"That wasn't me," said Santa. "I don't know where that thing came from." Geronimo looked up at the animal's gray twitching ears as it bounded through the crunch of dried leaves under hoof. Within him grew a deeper sense of appreciation for the mysterious beast.

By the time T.C. had clopped over to the shovel, Santa's party had vanished into the brush. It was alarming for T.C. to lose sight of them so quickly. In the distance he could hear the faint, oncoming roar of children, deceived and furious.

~32~
SIGNING OFF
ON GIBBERISH

Eleanor's parents, Richie and Susan, sat on their front porch deep into the night. All the other houses on their street were completely dark inside. The two of them stared at the fully decorated Christmas tree propped upside down in their yard waste. Their faces were slack and beaten from heavy waves of grief that pounded them week after week. Their eyes were bloodshot from lack of sleep.

"The money we wasted," said Susan in a distraught, faraway voice. Her bedraggled eyes rested on the flashing, silver ornament that poked out of the crooked lid of the garbage.

"I thought it would help," replied Richie, not looking at his wife. "I was wrong." He let his head loll back against the orange canvas of his camping chair. The stars looked huge to him. *Christmas*, he thought as he blinked, *Eve*. He blinked again. *Christmas* (blink), *Eve* (blink). He kept his gaze on the stars while blinking and thinking *Christmas Eve* for quite some time, wishing for a miracle.

Slosh, slosh. Slosh, slosh.

"What is that sound?" asked Susan.

Christmas Eve, Christmas Eve, thought Richie. He was stuck in his own cosmic spell.

Slosh, slosh.

Slosh, slosh.

"Do you hear that?" Susan asked again.

Christmas slosh *Eve* slosh. Yes, Richie did hear it now. He finally looked over at his wife's face. Her eyes were scrunched together with alarm. They looked at each other and came to the same realization at the exact same time. Something was walking toward them from their own backyard with very wet footwear.

"We're being *approached*," Susan whispered. She leaned forward as her grip tightened around the arms of her chair.

"It's so late," Richie whispered back, silently springing to his feet. He walked to the edge of the patio where the sound was coming from while Susan rushed into the house. Richie peered into the darkness as the sloshing grew louder.

"Who's there?" he shouted. The noise stopped for a moment. The screen door opened behind him. Richie looked back at his wife who was handing him a fire poker. He took it as she clutched his shoulders. The next sound they heard was that of repressed giggling, followed by more sloshing.

Richie swung the poker over his shoulder as he crept toward the end of the patio. He was going to clock whatever emerged out of the pitch black. The giggling stopped, followed by the sound of a cleared throat.

"We mean you no harm, Mr. Abbott," said a voice from the darkness. It was calm and croaky. Two stout, roundish figures wearing fedora hats and trench coats stepped out of the shadows and onto the front steps. Short, plump, and dripping wet, the rim of their hats sat just above their eyes. They looked like kid detectives. He immediately relaxed his grip on the poker. Chalk it up to stupid teenage pranks. He looked over at Susan, who seemed to concur with his assessment. Their fear quickly morphed into anger.

"Do you realize I could have your mothers on the phone in the next two minutes?" Susan asked the strangers, leading to another eruption of muffled giggling by the intruders.

"Enough with the giggling!" Richie shouted. The two strangers immediately stopped. Across the street, a second-story bedroom light came on.

"Listen, kids," Richie began, "Halloween was two months ago. Now I'm asking you nicely to get off our property and go home. It's Christmas Eve, for crying out loud, and you're waking up the neighbors."

One of the intruders took his hat off. His head was bald and flat on top. His forehead was a wrinkled, pale green. "We apologize, Mr. and Mrs. Abbott, for our untimely arrival. We realize how absurd and terrifying this must be for you. My name is Darrell Frogg. And this is my brother Herman."

Herman bowed. After finishing his bow, he giggled to himself. Richie and Susan couldn't tell if the bow was sarcastic or not. Husband and wife held each other, mutually weirded-out at this point.

"Mr. and Mrs. Abbott, we are the Frogg Brothers, Attorneys-At-Law." Darrell seemed to think this would leave some impression on Richie and Susan. It did not. Herman leaned over and whispered something into Darrell's ear.

"Okay, okay, you were right," whispered Darrell. He turned back to the couple. "I thought you may have heard of us. Please forgive my arrogance. A nasty byproduct of our trade, I'm afraid."

Richie and Susan stared back at them, still frozen and speechless. Darrell grabbed a plastic envelope from inside his trench coat and slid it toward Richie's and Susan's feet.

"I need you to sign the bottom of this," said Darrell. Susan picked it up.

"What is this?" asked Richie. "What do you want from us?"

"The same thing you want," said Darrell, "to find your daughter and bring her abductor to justice."

"Is this some sort of sick joke?" Susan shrieked.

"I'm glad for your sake it is not, Mrs. Abbott," said Darrell. "Believe it or not, we know who took Eleanor, and we are also the only ones capable of getting her back."

Susan cupped her mouth with her hands and slid down the wall of her house. Richie ripped the plastic envelope open and took out the document inside. The language was indecipherable, symbols he had never seen before.

"This is gibberish!" he yelled. "Is this some sort of ransom note?"

"This is no ransom note," said Darrell. "It is a legal agreement, authorized by the highest court in the galaxy. In short, it gives us permission to subpoena your daughter, thereby saving her from a horrible fate."

"Subpoena her?" repeated Susan.

"I guarantee you both that if you sign it, your situation will start improving rapidly," said Darrell. Richie looked down at the pen in the tattered plastic envelope that was draped over his slipper.

"Sign it and we can help," said Darrell. "Don't and we can't. It's that simple, Mr. and Mrs. Abbott." Richie glared back at him. He bent down to pick up the pen, but it was already poised in the air, held up by Susan. Richie looked down at his wife's face and saw a sparkle of hope in her eyes for the first time in forever.

They both signed the bottom line of the final page. He placed the document back in the envelope, walked down the steps, and handed it back to Darrell. The lawyer smiled a big, froggy grin as he handed the envelope to Herman, who put it in his breast pocket. "I wouldn't throw that baby spruce away just yet, Richard Abbott," said Darrell. The lawyer put his drenched hat back on his head as he and his brother drifted back into the darkness.

"Wait a minute," yelled Richie. He ran down the three porch steps with Susan behind him. Darrell reappeared under the hazy yellow of the porch light.

"Why are you both soaking wet?" asked Richie.

"The pond in your backyard," said Darrell, "it's so incredibly wet." Herman erupted with hearty giggles. Darrell closed his eyes as he stretched his grin with deep satisfaction and spun his portly body back in the direction of the pond in the backyard. Susan looked at her husband. The soft chuckling resumed as Darrell joined his brother in the darkness of the backyard.

"When will we hear from you again?" Susan asked.

Unresponsive, the Frogg brothers seemed to ignore this final question. They waddled toward the pond at the far end of the backyard, snickering to each other the whole way. The giggling soon turned to gurgling as they vanished under the water's surface altogether.

Richie and Susan watched the shadowy figures descend into the Jacuzzi-sized, moonlit pond.

"When's the last time you've been in the pond?" asked Susan.

"I've never been in the pond. Have you?"

"I didn't think there was anything in it."

33
PLENTY OF LEVERAGES

The four of them sat in the cool sand under the shade of the beached chopper. Xanadu, Ernesta, Sophia, and the purple-eyed Sergio all waited as if at some galactic bus stop. They all wore the same pitiful expressions on their faces, knowing they had no place else to go.

"I think it looks stupid," Ernesta explained to Sergio, halting Xanadu's next thought. They all sat tightly together in order to fit in the narrow slice of shade the chopper casted.

"Do you see an actual eye patch floating around?" Sergio asked. He fully extended his tiny arms and swept them over the expanse of the desert to make his point in classic Italian fashion. "Neither do I, which is why I had to do *this*," Sergio pointed to the article in question: the right lens of his sand goggles was smudged black.

She shook her head, disgusted. "Why are you giving yourself an eye patch?"

"That elf named Henry disfigured my right eye. The damage appears to be permanent, I'm afraid." Sergio flipped his goggles up to show Ernesta a run-of-the-mill black eye, purple and swollen. "The blurriness is too distracting so I have to put it in time-out."

"You're just cutting off the whole right side of your peripheral vision," said Ernesta.

"I rarely use the right side, anyway," replied Sergio, flipping his goggles back down.

Xanadu suddenly shot up onto his feet. Startled, Ernesta and Sergio both looked up at the towering clown. He had been so quiet they'd forgotten he was there.

"Someone's coming," Xanadu muttered. Ernesta and Sergio scrambled upright and onto their hind legs. The clown took out rainbow-colored binoculars from an unseen shirt pocket and peered through them.

"Where are they?" asked Sergio.

Ernesta pointed to where she saw the two large animals coming toward them in the distance. "Off to the right," she said. Ernesta looked over at her cousin, who was wobbling his head around to try and see what they saw with the left lens of his sand goggles.

"Forget about it," said Ernesta.

"Don't tell me to forget about it!" yelled Sergio.

"All right, here's the deal," said Xanadu as he put his binoculars back into his hidden pocket. The cousins stopped their quarreling and stood at attention. "I've decided I don't need to kill the two of you. As long as I get the unicorn back, no one will get hurt, capeesh?" Their mouths gaped open while they goggled at the tall, shabby clown.

Sergio leaned toward Ernesta and whispered with forced alarm, "He speaks Italian."

"Understood," said Ernesta.

"My name is Xanadu," said the clown.

"Your name is *what?*" Sergio asked, visibly irritated.

"Xanadu," he repeated, "but don't let them know that you know my name. Make them think we're strangers just in case we need to use the leverage later."

"Hmmph," said Sergio, "too bad for your plan I didn't bring any leverages with me." Sergio grinned with wild abandon.

Xanadu pointed his finger at Ernesta. "Your job is to make sure he speaks as little as possible when they arrive."

"Are you asking me to knock him out?" Ernesta asked. "I can do that."

Two hundred yards out from the beached chopper was Santa and his company, looking through his own red-and-white binoculars. "Oh, brother," he muttered, "one of the guinea pigs just decked the other guinea pig. Things are getting ugly." His wife's shoulder suddenly slid into his view. *Uh-oh,* Santa thought. He was growing shorter already. This phenomenon always occurred a few days after Christmas Day. But today was December 24th, the morning of Christmas Eve. Santa didn't know the meaning of it, but he knew it couldn't be a good thing. He was now the same height as his wife, which was the normal state of things eleven months out of the year. The Queen turned her head toward Santa and noticed the swift and dramatic change. In the last few minutes of travel Santa morphed from six feet seven to five feet eight.

"Mr. Claus!" said the queen, "you've shrunk!"

"Nevermind that," said Santa. "It's normal. It's just happening a little early."

Geronimo finally looked over at their shrunken leader. His brow furrowed with consternation. He decided not to make a big deal of it.

"Toss me those binoculars, boss," said Geronimo. The gnome thought this sort of relaxed language would show Santa just how calm and confident he was. Contrary to Geronimo's intentions, Santa shot him a not-a-fan-of-what-you-just-said look.

"Are you feeling okay, Geronimo?" Santa asked.

"I'm fine!" Geronimo defensively shot the words out of his mouth. His face was red with embarrassment. "You're the one shrinking!"

"That wasn't a very nice thing to say," said the suddenly conscious Nancy. Everyone turned their heads to the crisp, bright sound of the six-year-old's voice.

Santa wasn't the only one transforming. Nancy hadn't been awake since they left Sergio and Henry. She had slept on the unicorn for nearly half the day. Her skin had gone from the ashy white pallor of an old photograph to a healthy, vibrant pink. Her eyes were alive and quick. Something about her nap on the unicorn had fully restored her spirit and vitality.

Not a word was said after Nancy's remark. They were all still busy ogling at her transformation as if she were an art piece in a museum.

"You're looking well," Geronimo said to Nancy.

"You should apologize to Santa," Nancy insisted of Geronimo.

"You're right. I'm sorry, Santa. I was out of line."

"We're all under a lot of pressure right now," said Santa. "Don't sweat it." He tossed Geronimo his binoculars and they landed perfectly around the unicorn's horn. Geronimo used the unicorn's mane to climb up to the head and view the left lens. The first thing Geronimo saw was Krampus's elf, Henry, sitting on top of the beached spaceship, unbeknownst to those below. Henry appeared to be staring right back at Geronimo.

"May I take a peek?" asked the queen. Geronimo raised the binoculars over his head and tossed them to Rose's outstretched hand. She caught the strap and brought the binoculars up to the camel's eyes. "Ernesta," the queen muttered. She couldn't see Sergio since he was lying in the sand. "Do we know the clown? And the elf?"

"The clown wants the unicorn," said Geronimo, "and he might try and hijack the chopper if we give him a ride. I had to trick him to get to you guys, so he's not going to be happy to see me."

"What about the elf?" the camel asked, turning to Santa.

"I didn't even see an elf," said Santa. "It could be Murdock."

"It's not. It's Henry," said Geronimo.

"Henry?" Santa, Rose, and Queen Fatilahh all asked simultaneously.

"Henry is the elf that used to work for Krampus," said Nancy.

"What?" they all exclaimed. Even Geronimo was not yet aware of this fact. Nancy immediately felt bad for saying it. "But he told me he's on our side now, and I believe him."

"He did help us escape from the slingshot-crazy guinea pig," said Geronimo.

"Well," said Queen Fatilahh, turning her head back to Santa, "what's your game plan? I'm asking because I didn't want to get involved any further. I just wanted the castle." The queen turned her head toward the spires poking out above the trees from off. She smiled dreamily over her new possession.

"I understand," said Santa. "Okay, everyone else, this is our game plan. First, don't let on that we're wise to their intentions. We play it straight up. If they're cool with us, we give them a ride to HQ. If any of them give us trouble, we don't let them on the ship. I think that's—"

"Nicky," Rose interrupted.

"What? What's wrong with that plan?"

"It's not that!" Rose said.

"What is it?" asked her husband.

"We're already here!" she said.

Santa tilted his head to see beyond his wife and the camel. They were now just a few feet from the ship and the potential passengers. Eleanor, Rose, and Santa clamored down from the camel one by one. Rose held Eleanor's hand while her other arm was entwined with her husband to keep him upright and steady. Before leaving, Queen Fatilahh looked at Ernesta and told her, "Do as you please." The queen then turned around and started toward the castle.

"Things were supposed to change," Ernesta yelled out to her queen. Queen Fatilahh stopped in her tracks. "You said once Krampus left, the desert would turn to grass, trees, and flowing streams."

The camel smiled back at the guinea pig with sadness and pity in her eyes. "Don't believe every fairy tale you hear," she said. She turned and resumed her trot back toward the castle.

After both parties watched Queen Fatilahh make her grand exit, an awkward silence passed as Xanadu and Ernesta turned to face Santa and company.

"Aloha," Santa finally said. "Raise your hand if you've been nice all year." He raised his own hand as an example. Nancy, Rose, Geronimo, and Eleanor's hands followed. Looking down at Sergio's unconscious body, Ernesta raised her hand as well. Xanadu's arms remained folded. It was painfully obvious that all Xanadu had to do was raise his hand to get a ride on the spaceship. He just could not get himself to do so.

"Okay," said Santa, finally putting his hand down. Everyone else's hands also dropped out of the sky. "Now raise your hand if you plan on being nice on the spaceship ride." His hand went back up as did everyone who had raised their hands previously. Xanadu was still holding firm. Amidst the stalwart, Sergio actually regained consciousness and, seeing almost everyone inexplicably with their hands in the air, raised his own arm in a panic.

Finally, Xanadu closed his eyes and raised his arm into the air. Santa nodded. "Welcome aboard," he said. They all put their hands back down and, without any words, arranged themselves into a single-file line.

The gnome slid the key from behind his shirt and dropped it into Santa's open palm. Santa walked through the opened hatch, and the crew quietly filed in. Once every man, elf, gnome, guinea pig, and unicorn were inside, Santa stepped inside himself and swung the door closed behind him.

"Wait!" he heard from outside. Santa opened the hatch halfway.

"Room for one more?" asked Henry.

"There's always room for an elf," said Santa.

The elf bowed. "Thank you for your mercy, oh Divine One," he said. Santa definitely detected sarcasm and his normally welcoming smile drifted off his face. Henry plastered a look of false gratitude onto his own face as he walked by Santa and across the chopper's threshold. Santa closed the hatch. A few minutes later they were in-flight and en route to HQ.

34

SITTING DEAD RED

et me outta here!" screamed Murdock from inside Krampus's icebox. Murdock had been trapped inside the small freezer for some time now. This last scream was the first one to catch Krampus's attention. It was the most desperate and bloodcurdling of them all. The sound frightened Krampus so much that he was compelled to unlock the freezer and open the lid. At first sight, he thought Murdock had escaped. He didn't see him among the empty ice cube trays and empty Reese's buttercup wrappers. He was just about to close the lid and look elsewhere when he saw a quivering ball in the corner. Krampus reached into the icebox and cradled Murdock's frosty balled-up body in his hands.

"I'm sorry you were in there for so long," Krampus said with complete sincerity. He scampered over to the birdcage and gently placed the Smurf-colored Murdock back inside. He closed and locked the cage door and then left the room. He instantly returned with a battery-powered heater the size of a shoebox. He cranked something in the back and the metal grid in front buzzed on with an orange glow. Krampus stood over the cage, hands on his hips, with a waiting-for-water-to-boil look on his face. It wasn't boiling. The little blue ball wasn't moving.

"Suffering silver bells!" cursed Krampus. He kicked the cage and it toppled to its side. Murdock bounced around and then rolled to a stop against the bars nearest the heater. His body unfurled upon impact with the warming metal. Krampus knelt down to get a closer view.

"Murdock!" Krampus shouted. "Murdock, don't die!"

The elf's clothes were now melted down to a dripping wet. His skin color improved in slow transition from blue to pink, though he still wasn't moving.

"I need you, Murdock!" pleaded Krampus. "I mean, your family needs you! Think of your children! Don't die!"

With that, Murdock's eyes fluttered. Waves of heat pelted his face.

"Poconos," muttered Murdock.

"What?" exclaimed an almost gleeful Krampus.

"You owe me Poconos."

"Of course," said Krampus. He scrambled back out of the room only to quickly return with a duffle bag. He plopped the bag down next to the cage and unzipped it.

"Here they are!" exclaimed Krampus.

He flashed Murdock four tickets to the Poconos. The airline tickets read "Astral Airlines." When Murdock saw his children's names on the tickets, Tut and Lu, he wanted to cry. Astral Airlines was the most prestigious commercial space travel out there. It was also the only known airline in the galaxy that would comfortably accommodate an elf. The prospect of stowing away on an airline like United posed too many risks of exposure to consider, whereas

Astral Airlines had its own elf section, not to mention a cloaking device that hides its presence from any man-made radar.

The emotion of joy alone worked to warm the rest of Murdock's vital organs to a functioning state. Krampus slipped the tickets into the cage between the brass bars. The tickets took up the majority of the floor space and flopped to the ground like a stiff, cardboard carpet.

"So," said Krampus, "now that I've saved your life, tell me the coordinates to HQ."

Murdock gave him a long, hard look. Finally he said, "You'll need to write this down."

"Bartlett!" Clarence yelled into the all-campus monitor from Santa's desk. He was standing on top of Santa's desk with his foot pressed down on the record button of the voice transponder. His hands were at his waist while buckets of sweat poured from his forehead. It wasn't even nine yet. Clarence caught sight of the large, empty bottle of Santa's Emergency Only Holiday Ale upside down in the trash can next to the desk. He did not remember drinking the whole bottle even though his head was doing its best to remind him.

"Bartlett!" he yelled again. Each time he yelled, rockets went off in his head. "Bartlett, where are you?"

There was no response. Finally, he took his foot off the button. His headache throbbed to such a crescendo that it felt like it was screaming. He clasped his hands against his ears and screamed along with the sound coming from his head, until he realized the sound was coming from the sky, not his head. Clarence hopped off the desk and ran to the window. He opened it and looked up into the cloudless blue, where a small metallic object was falling. The object's descent was so rapid that Clarence had no time to react before the window shattered and the room shook.

The impact of the spaceship hitting the lawn outside Santa's office caused Clarence's body to fly back across the room and slam into the door of the office. His body crumpled to the soft carpet floor. Clarence felt absolutely horrible before the explosion. Now he felt absolutely horrible and injured. Nonetheless, he would not give up. The security of HQ was entrusted to him. Giving up was not an option.

His ears rang as he crawled through the smoke in the room back to a giant hole in the wall where the window used to be. The mound of dirt created by the crashed spacecraft was twice the size of HQ. He couldn't see the spacecraft behind it. Clarence used the chair to help him hobble upright using just his left leg. His injured right leg looked like a wishbone, hanging at a forty-five-degree angle. Holding the arm of the chair in one hand, Clarence desperately looked around Santa's office for something, anything. He hobbled his way around to the front of the desk where the drawers were. He opened the middle drawer and inside was a small wooden crutch encased in glass, with "T.T." etched into the top of the crutch. The sound of panting and heavy footsteps lumbered toward him from outside.

After crawling out of the crashed spaceship, Krampus struggled up the hill of dirt while holding the birdcage entrapping Murdock. He held the cage in front of him at eye level, as if it were a lantern to light his way.

"Why haven't you let me go yet?" demanded Murdock. His hands were gripped firm around the bars as the cage swayed wildly.

"Shhh," said Krampus. "Not until I'm at the time pond. That's the deal."

"If they see me with you, they'll know I'm a traitor. My family—we'll be banished from the community."

"Nonsense," said Krampus. "Just act like a bird."

Once he reached the summit of the dirt pile, Krampus looked down at the cottage-filled neighborhoods that were still and motionless a moment ago. There was now a buzz of activity. Whole families of elves flooded out of their homes, tiptoeing toward the wreck. The sight of such a unified exodus froze Krampus in his spot.

It dawned on Murdock that this was Christmas Eve. Toymakers didn't work on Christmas Eve. In fact, most employees of any sort in HQ had the day off, leaving HQ highly vulnerable to attacks of any kind.

Looking up at the building, Murdock was now certain nothing was going to stop Krampus. They had a skeleton crew manning the entire facility. And without Santa or T.C., they might as well have rolled a red carpet out for him. Part of Murdock still hoped there was a chance he could keep his tickets while a thwarted Krampus would be sent to the Campus Rehab Center. This hope was now gone. Murdock sat cross-legged on top of the tickets with his arms folded around one of the bars.

"That's far enough!" yelled Clarence from where the bottom of the hill met the hole in the wall. He held a wooden crutch alongside his gimpy right leg and a black revolver in his right hand. Krampus was still staring at the synchronized movement of the oncoming elves when he turned his head to look at Clarence.

"Whoa!" yelled Krampus. "No need to get excited."

"Is that you, Murdock?" yelled Clarence.

Krampus turned to Murdock and waited for him to answer. Murdock did not expect this, and the silence became so awkward that Krampus finally confessed for Murdock, "Yes, it is him."

"Are you okay?" Clarence asked Murdock. "Are you hurt?"

"He's a traitor," Krampus blurted out.

"What?" yelled Clarence.

"What're you doing?" shouted Murdock. The throngs of elves heading over to the dirt hill were now in earshot. They murmured to each other as they pointed to the elf in the cage.

"He told me the coordinates to your little Munchkinland for four tickets to the Poconos," said Krampus.

"No!" yelled Vera. Murdock's wife stepped out of the mesh of startled elves.

"Vera!" Murdock yelled. His feet sprung to action. "Stay away, darling. Don't come any closer!"

To Murdock's dread, she towed four-year-old Lu and three-year-old Tut along with her. Both still in their pajamas, Tut held a dinosaur stuffy in his free hand while Lu held a candy cane in hers. Their mom dragged them halfway up the hill. Recognizing their dad's voice, both children started to cry for him.

"Don't you call my husband a traitor," Vera said. She swung around to face her baffled community.

"Please, Vera, move the children away," said Murdock, "they're not safe here!"

"It wasn't like he says," Vera said, addressing the townspeople. "He threatened to eat my husband for breakfast!" She then broke into tears, turning back to her husband. Watching his whole family cry in front of him moved Murdock to bold action. He scurried up the brass bars to Krampus's fingers and chomped into them.

"Gah!" yelled Krampus. He shook the cage in attempt to fling Murdock loose of his finger. Vera took this opportunity to pick up a chunk of rubble and hurl it at Krampus's face. It hit him square in the temple. He staggered backward a few feet, finally releasing his grip on the cage. The cage rolled down the hill toward the elves while Krampus staggered into a backward fall down the other side of the hill back toward the crash. The shiny tickets fluttered out of the cage and landed in the incline of dirt. Tut and Lu yanked their hands away from their mother's grip and ran for the pretty pieces of paper. Murdock's rolling cage ended with a crash into the side of the demolished wall, just a few feet from where Clarence stood. The collision busted the cage apart. Murdock crawled out of the bashed open door, finally free. To his horror, he looked up the hill to see Tut and Lu running for the shiny tickets near the top of the hill, with his wife running close behind them.

"Come back down!" yelled Murdock. But their father's instructions went unheeded. Tut and Lu scooped up the four tickets and slid them underneath the collar of their pajamas just before their hands were snatched up by their mother.

"Hurry!" yelled Murdock from down the hill. He could see Krampus's tangle of birch branches rise into view behind his wife. "He's right behind you!"

It was too late. First, Krampus grabbed the children and stuck them in the thicket of his branches. They held snug against the hard, ropey sticks. Krampus then snatched up the pleading Vera and marched down the hill toward Clarence and Murdock with a wretched snarl on his face. Blood trickled from a wound on his temple.

"Shoot him!" Murdock told Clarence.

"It's not a real gun," said Clarence. "It just spits out a 'Bang' sign when you pull the trigger. I was hoping he'd call my bluff."

"Are you kidding me?" asked Murdock.

"It was the nearest thing I could find," said Clarence. "Everything happened so fast!"

"Quit your quibbling," Krampus ordered. He held Vera's body horizontal in his hands. One hand held her legs while the other held the back of her head. "I'll twist your wife's head right off if you don't direct me toward the time pond in the next three seconds!" He stomped toward them with long strides. Krampus's legs moved like bony, coarse spider legs. For the community of elves, who had never seen Krampus before, it was a horror to behold.

"One!" shouted Krampus, starting to count.

"Go through his office!" Murdock shouted back. He pointed his finger at Santa's front door on the other side of the room.

"And then?" asked Krampus.

"Go right down the hallway," said Murdock. "Then make your first left."

"Pass-code?" asked Krampus.

"Eight-eight-eight-eight-one," said Clarence.

"Congratulations," said Krampus. He released Vera from his grip. She fell to the ground, though quickly got back up, unharmed. "You get your wife back." He walked by them and into Santa's office.

"My children!" yelled Murdock.

"You'll get them back after I'm in the pond," Krampus shouted as he disappeared down the hallway. Murdock was about to bolt after Krampus when Clarence grabbed his shoulder. "Take this," Clarence said, holding up his joke gun. "I'm sorry I couldn't protect you."

Murdock nodded and took the gun. "It's not your fault," he told Clarence as he took off after his children.

By the time Murdock got to the hallway, Krampus was already out of sight, but he could still hear him. He followed the sound of Krampus's grunting until the elf got to a dead end, punching in the passcode to open the biodome. Murdock sprinted down the hallway shouting, "Give them back!" He watched helplessly as the biodome opened, and Krampus walked inside and stepped lightly into the water. Murdock ran to the water's edge inside the biodome. "Okay!" said Murdock, "You're in the pond. Now give me back my children like you said you would."

Krampus ignored him as he continued his slow descent into the water. The waterline was at his shoulders when the children's whimpers turned to shrieks and the surface of the pond began to bubble. Murdock looked around for something to aid him in a rescue when he finally considered the joke gun still in his hand. He pulled the trigger and a long, metal rod flung out holding a banner that spelled "Bang!" Murdock looked back at the pond and noticed Krampus was now neck deep. The water began to swirl him around and around. Murdock realized if he could time it right, he could possibly get Tut and Lu to grab onto the rod of the gun on one of their go-arounds. As Krampus and his children swirled toward him like luggage on a carousel, Murdock timed it so that he was running alongside his ensnared children. He held the rod just over their tiny fingers. Lu quickly grabbed the metal rod with both hands while Tut, unable to grab the rod, snatched instead the "bang" banner with both hands. With the branches sinking quickly below the pond's surface, Murdock yanked the rod away from the water, dropping both his children safely onto the artificial grass. They rolled harmlessly to a stop where the turf met the biodome wall. Their father ran to them with tears of relief and joy. He got on his knees and hugged them, kissing their cheeks. He scooped both of them up and walked out of the biodome. He punched in the pass-code to close the dome in case Krampus tried to come back. He watched the glass top slowly close like a giant translucent clamshell over the dome's base.

"Look, Daddy," Tut said. He took his two tickets out and flashed them in front of his father's face.

"Two shinies," Tut bragged.

"Four shinies!" Lu corrected as she took her tickets out too. Murdock had completely forgotten about the tickets. The longer he looked at them, the angrier he suddenly became. He couldn't stop thinking of the sacrifices he was willing to make in order to get them. He was disgusted with himself. He grabbed the tickets from them and was about to rip all four tickets in half when behind him he heard, "Wait!"

It was Vera, accompanied by Clarence and the handful of townsfolk. "Don't do it," said Vera. "If you tear them, Krampus wins." Murdock thought about this for a moment. He looked at his wife, his two children, and then back at the tickets. He pictured them all rafting the same tube together, basking in the hot sun while drinking ice-cold ginger ales. He gave the tickets to his wife.

"What do we do about Krampus?" Murdock asked.

"Wait for Santa to get back," said Clarence.

"Wait?" Murdock repeated. "That's your plan, to wait?"

"For now, yes," said Clarence. "Now give me the gun back, please." Murdock handed him the gun.

"Well, how long are we supposed to wait?" asked Murdock. Clarence stared back at him, having no answer. They all stood there quietly for a few moments, not sure what to do with themselves. "This is stupid," Murdock muttered. "We can't just wait here." More silence. More waiting. "That's it," he said as he put his kids down. Released from the protection of their dad, they ran instantly to their mom. "I'm going in after him." As he started to punch "eight-eight-eight-eight-one" into the biodome interface, they all heard another shrieking sound from outside.

They looked at one another and then moved hurriedly back through Santa's office and through the giant hole in the wall.

"Hold on tight! This could get messy!" shouted Sergio from the cockpit minutes before the chopper crashed. As it turned out, Sergio was the most qualified to fly the chopper. Incidentally, Sergio and Freeze Pop actually graduated from Rodent Technical Institute together, two years before the Great Guinea Pig War.

So it was to everyone's surprise when Sergio volunteered his expertise to captain the vessel. They were all the more surprised when he dutifully started the engines and effortlessly lifted the ship off the sand. They coasted through the jet-blue sky and into blackness of space and the stars beyond. Everything was fine until Sergio realized the only thing he could not find on the giant switchboard in front of him was the button to drop the landing gear. He had no idea where it was and foolishly waited to find it until the very moment he needed to use it.

Directly behind the captain's chair, standing parallel between the cockpit and passenger area, was the unicorn. Geronimo had fashioned a seat belt from strands of her mane and was able to guide the unicorn into a skinny, narrow space between the pilot and the passengers that kept her upright during heavy turbulence.

Beyond Geronimo and the unicorn was the spaciously round passenger area. This is where Ernesta, Henry, and Xanadu struggled to stand upright while holding onto metal handles that ran in rows down the spherical steel walls.

In the back of the ship strapped to four chairs were Santa, Rose, Eleanor, and Nancy. Those were the only chairs in the otherwise sparse metallic passenger area. The ship was making a recklessly fast descent. The straps of the chairs were the only things keeping the five of them from being tipped out at such a steep angle. They all linked hands and closed their eyes, bracing for impact.

Fortunately, Sergio had some control of the vessel. He chose the frozen pond in the middle of town as his crash site, not far from Krampus's landing site. Smack dab in the middle of the village was a large roundabout that hugged the now frozen community pond. Sergio was hoping the ice would hold and they would skid across the ice, eventually slowing to a stop.

After gouging an initial chunk of ice out of the pond on impact, the chopper rose in the air a few inches and then skidded across the length of the pond, spinning wildly. Finally, it collided with an abrupt stop against a snowbank at the far end of the pond. Elves from all directions were running toward the crash site.

Once the ship had creaked to a stop, everything inside was quiet and slow moving. Behind the cockpit, Rose started unstrapping Eleanor while Santa sat still with his eyes closed.

Xanadu, Henry, and Ernesta released their grips from the metal railings of the wall, and Xanadu walked over and opened the hatch. He then turned around and leered at the unicorn. It was still tucked in the narrow corridor between the cockpit and the rest of the ship. He picked up his lidded bucket of unicorn tears and marched over to the beast.

Geronimo was still atop the unicorn. The unicorn, also unharmed, kept her balance through the landing, whipping her tail about, eager to get out of the narrow space. Geronimo noticed the tip of the unicorn's horn had been chipped off on impact and thought maybe he could save it and glue it back on later. He bowed his head to scan the floor for the tip. With his head down, he felt someone lift him up by the back of his collar, and the rest of his body was lifted upward.

"What? Hey!" yelled Geronimo.

"I'll be taking back my unicorn now," said Xanadu. With a rotten grin on his face, he released his fingers from Geronimo's collar. The gnome fell five feet from the ground and stuck the landing with just a slight bend of the knees on impact. Xanadu took a thin rope he had tied around his waist and looped it over the unicorn's neck. He walked it out of the corridor and toward the exit when he stopped, staring up at the chipped horn crowning the unicorn's head. Geronimo resumed his search for the chipped piece on the floor.

"What have you done?" exclaimed the clown. He inspected the horn closer, while behind him Geronimo spotted the chipped top. He quickly slid it into his back pocket as Xanadu turned his attention back to him. Meanwhile, Sergio had stumbled off the captain's chair and now stood beside Geronimo. With one good eye he assessed the landscape.

"This unicorn is useless now!" shouted Xanadu, his teeth clenched with fury. "Without a full horn it's worthless! The tears turn ordinary."

"Nicky!" shouted Rose from the back of the ship.

Geronimo started to scan all the moving bodies he saw, looking for Santa.

"Where's the rest of the horn?" asked Xanadu. The clown's eyes were locked on the gnome. Geronimo tried to ignore him for a second so he could finish counting.

"Nicky!" Rose shouted again from the back.

"You have it, don't you?" shouted Xanadu as he stomped toward Geronimo.

"Give it to me!" He reached his hand out to swipe at the gnome.

"Nicky, wake up!" shrieked Rose again.

Geronimo ducked under Xanadu's giant, swiping hand. He then hopped on the attacking hand itself to ride with the clown's natural backswing. Just before the other hand came whipping through to squash him, Geronimo nosedived into the air and over the clown's shoulder, landing into a sprint toward the back of the ship.

"Nicky!" Rose yelled through streaming tears.

"Get back here!" barked Xanadu as he ran after the gnome. A river of elves suddenly poured through the chopper's open hatch upon hearing the grief-soaked shrieks from Mrs. Claus. The rush of small bodies prevented Xanadu from catching Geronimo, who was instantly swallowed up in the pattering stampede of elves. It was at this point that Xanadu decided enough was enough. His bucket of tear water had tipped over during the crash, spilling whatever he had. Xanadu dropped his bucket and moved like a salmon against the stream, slipping through the open hatch and into the daylight, never to be seen again.

Geronimo slithered through the murmuring elves toward Santa's motionless body. A wound on Santa's head bled profusely as elves swarmed around him, furiously wrapping his head with gauze they found from a nearby first aid kit. The gnome saw a big, heavy steel fire extinguisher leaning across Santa's black boot that must have fallen on his head from above. Santa's massive crown rocked as Rose shook her husband's shoulders.

The sound of grief began with croaks and whimpers in the front. It slowly rolled backward, intensifying as the news spread through the community like a contagious virus.

"Where's Krampus?" Geronimo asked Rose, who was sobbing inconsolably.

"He's gone," Clarence shouted from the opening of the hatch. He was out of breath as he rested on his cane. He turned to the closest elf to him. "Daniel, alert the Emergency Care Unit. Tell them to get the stretcher." Daniel nodded and grabbed a walkie-talkie from his pocket as he departed from the crowd. Clarence turned back to Geronimo. "He went through the time pond. Where's T.C.?"

"Krampus's castle," said Geronimo.

"He told me this would happen," said Clarence, "that Santa wouldn't come back alive. He tried to warn me and I didn't believe him." Gladys walked up to her husband and hugged him. Geronimo put his hand on his shoulder and said, "It's not your fault."

"Geronimo!" Murdock shouted from outside. "How's Santa?"

"Not good."

"You know what this means?" Murdock asked the gnome.

"We all go back home and there's no Christmas this year, or ever again," Geronimo said.

"No!" yelled Murdock, nearly spitting in Geronimo's face. "Wrong answer! It means we go in that time pond and stop Krampus!"

"You and me?" Geronimo asked. "I thought you didn't like me."

"No, I think you're great," said the elf as he put his hand on the gnome's shoulder. "I was just being a jerk on the boat earlier. What do you say?"

"I say yes." Geronimo felt a potato scrap in the pockets of his shorts, leftover from the dungeon. "I owe it to a wizard friend of mine to see this through."

"I'm coming too," said Eleanor.

"And me," said Nancy.

Murdock and Geronimo both nodded, looking at them. Neither could think of reasons not to bring them back to their rightful home.

"The four of us then," said Murdock.

"How does the time pond work?" asked Geronimo.

Murdock stared back at him. "Clarence, you know how the time pond works, right?" he asked.

"I can't swim!" confessed Clarence, as if this clearly answered the question.

"No matter," said Murdock. "Let's all just take a dip and find out."

So they all took the dip and subsequently found out.

35
NO WAY SOUFFLÉ

Back at the Le Brulee Institute to finish his final term, Krampus's son, Gromp, scraped at the edge of his lemon soufflé in the big, empty, well-lit kitchen. His head was wrapped in large, white bandages just above his forehead. It was three in the morning on Christmas Eve. He watched the news from a small TV that hung from the wall. A series of Santa impersonators were being interviewed in a shopping mall. Each one described the joy that Christmas brought to people all over the world. All the forced good cheer made Gromp's stomach turn. He shook his head and pushed the porcelain saucer across the counter. The empty cup rolled off the saucer and fell onto the floor with a loud smash, spraying bits of porcelain all over the ground. *Time for bed*, he thought. With his eyes glazed over and his body almost too tired to move, he got up from his stool and walked into the pitch-black hallway, leaving the television on. His slippers shuffled off into the darkness and receded into silence.

"Krampus is coming," said a child's voice on the television. "We're all in danger."

Gromp quickly reappeared at the edge of the kitchen light, staring at the screen. Ricky, from Eleanor's neighborhood, was being interviewed. There he was at Santa's Palace, in the middle of the local mall.

Gromp noticed how spooked the child looked. Ricky kept looking down and then back up, as if he were getting information from a short and invisible source. Gromp could also see what Ricky saw since he lived in a world where elves were very real.

"I'm sorry, who's Krampus?" asked the reporter.

"Keep watch over your children tonight," said Ricky. He looked back down in the direction of his shoes. The camera would not follow since nothing appeared to be there. Ricky looked back at the reporter and warned the viewing public, "They're not safe!"

"What makes you say that, son?" asked the local reporter, now growing a tad concerned.

"The elf!" yelled Ricky. "Can't you see the elf?" He pointed down at his shoes. Finally the camera showed a creature that only Gromp, Ricky, and the handful of other children at Santa's Palace could see: it was Bartlett, the first-year toymaker from HQ.

To the rest of the viewers, there was nothing whatsoever. The reporter erupted into laughter. "Oh, you almost got me good, kid!" he said. Ricky looked up at him, dumbfounded. He kept looking up at the reporter and then down at Bartlett, who shook his head with frustration. As his laughter subsided, the reporter noticed a short man wearing an elf suit beside the empty Santa chair. "Well, there's an actual elf!" the reporter exclaimed. "Merry Christmas, kid." He playfully screwed up the hair atop Ricky's head and then motioned for his cameraman to follow him as he made his way to the bored little man in green.

Back in the Le Brulee Institute, there was more slipper shuffling down the hallway coming toward Gromp, but he didn't hear it. His mind was too stuck on the possibility of his father wreaking havoc within the world of humans. His father's unchecked, unabashed rage brought out his own. He unlocked his eyes from the TV and turned toward the coatroom near the kitchen door, where his brown trench coat hung at the end of the rack. The sleeve stuck out through the door of the closet as if calling for him.

"Gromp, Gromp," said the woman with a heavy French accent who now stood next to Gromp. It was the Grand Master Chef of the Institute, Chef Celeste Boudreaux.

"Gromp," she repeated in a stern hush. She didn't want to wake up the rest of the staff. "Are you sleepwalking again?"

"No," said Gromp. "I'm sorry for waking you."

"I heard something crash. Is everything all right?"

"Yes, I'm fine," said Gromp. "I'll clean it up before I leave." He marched over to the coat closet.

"Leave?" asked Chef Boudreaux. "Are you crazy? Tomorrow is your final exam." Gromp grabbed his trench coat and swung it over him. He then reached back into the closet to grab a broom and dustpan.

"Your lemon soufflé," the chef continued. "If you miss exam day, you have to take the entire semester over again. You know that, don't you?" Gromp continued to ignore the Grand Master Chef as he walked over to the white, shiny rubble and swept it into the dustpan. As he shook the dustpan clean above the waste bin, he looked up and said, "With all due respect, Chef Boudreaux, who in their right mind schedules final exams on Christmas Day?"

"Don't play dumb with me, young man," said Chef Boudreaux. She marched into the light of the kitchen.

"All of the students voted for the finals to be on Christmas Day," said the chef, shaking her finger at Gromp. "You yourself told me you despised Christmas and that you didn't give a hoot when the finals were."

Choosing not to respond, Gromp walked back to the coat closet to return the broom and dustpan.

"Gromp," the chef said in a pleading voice. "At the end of the day, it honestly doesn't matter to me whether you pass or fail. I'm just wondering what could be so important to make you leave now?"

Gromp checked the inside of his coat with close inspection before looking back up at Chef Boudreaux. "Because the only thing I hate more than Christmas is my father," he told her. With that, he threw his coat over his head and spun in place. After a few revolutions he vanished entirely.

36
DREAMS OF
BUTTERFLY MUSEUMS

Eleanor was the last head to dip below the surface of the time pond. The last thing she saw before her head submerged under the tepid water was Gladys running down the hallway toward the pond, her children in tow. Then just like that, a gush of water filled her vision. It felt like the moment at the end of a water slide when you crash into the pool of water at the bottom. A chaotic mess of currents tossed her body around for what felt like eternity. Finally, the water stilled and she was composed enough to pencil her body into a vertical rise. As she broke through the surface, she opened her eyes. Despite the pitch-black night, she knew she was in her own backyard. She had made it back.

Splashing above the surface of their arrival point, Geronimo initially saw nothing. In the dark of night, it was impossible to recognize anything, only swirling stars and the outlines of trees. Yet the gnome knew where he was simply by sound and smell. He knew the creaking of the crickets, their sequence and pitch. He knew the smell of wet cypress bark after a fresh rain. By the time he had reached solid ground, he knew where he was too. He felt both relieved and unnerved, for there were things moving all around him in the darkness. He heard muffled, whimpering sounds along the perimeter of the yard. He walked toward the light from the back porch. Suddenly, wiggling burlap sacks came into view. The yard was littered with them. The oversized potato sacks were tied up and highly animated. Geronimo suddenly realized what was inside the sacks: live bodies.

Before submerging, Murdock had grabbed Nancy's hand and was able to keep hold of it through their underwater somersaults. Once they bobbed to the surface, Murdock saw Geronimo and Eleanor standing on solid ground, frozen. Why weren't they moving? He didn't like it.

"Keep your body low," Murdock told Nancy as they swam to shore. "And don't say anything." They both wormed out of the water onto grass and pebbles. The elf was too small to see over the overgrown grass around the pond.

"What's happening?" he asked Nancy.

"Krampus," said Nancy. "He's on the back porch."

"You stay here," said Murdock. "Don't let him see you. If he comes toward the pond, run to the back of the yard, hop the fence, and keep on running. Got it?" Nancy nodded. Murdock scrambled to his feet. The sight before him resembled a paused video. Everyone looked startled over the presence of the other. Krampus stood under the light of the back patio with a highly active burlap sack over his shoulder. The glass door behind him was completely shattered. The tiled floor was shimmering with glass. Krampus's hand rested against the handle of the screen door as if in the act of just coming out. He first looked at Murdock and smiled, closing the screen door behind him.

"Looks like the gang's all here," he said, walking down the steps and dropping his ever-shifting burlap sack to the ground. Krampus turned his back for a moment and then turned back around, holding a hatchet.

Both Murdock and Geronimo flinched at the swift reveal of the dangerous weapon.

"Funny how people will install high-grade security systems to prevent break-ins," said Krampus. He brought the blade up to the moonlight and admired the glow of the silvery sharp edge.

While Krampus kept his eyes on the hatchet, Geronimo, Eleanor, and Murdock ran to each other. They all met up in the center of the yard. Fifty feet separated the hatchet-wielding demon from the three of them.

"Then they leave something like *this* resting against the side of the house," continued Krampus, gazing up at the stars, "for someone to use for whatever nefarious purpose."

"What's the plan?" asked the gnome to the others, out of Krampus's earshot. They huddled together ten yards from Krampus.

"Maybe I wouldn't be so evil if people didn't make it so easy," said Krampus, who now appeared to be addressing the moon.

"I didn't have time to think of one," Murdock answered Geronimo.

"I didn't even have a way to transport the bodies until I happened upon that potato truck on Clover St.," continued Krampus with his eyes still skyward. "It's as if people *want* me to do this."

Geronimo turned back to Murdock. "Well, we better think of something."

"Right," said Murdock. "Who knows how much longer he's going to go?"

"No more. That's how much," snapped Krampus. He looked straight at them as if he had been intently listening to them the entire time. "Now the horror begins," he said. He raised the hatchet high above his head and raced toward them, cackling.

Instead of passing out from sheer terror like any twelve-year-old might in such a circumstance, Eleanor went nuts, and ran toward Krampus. She had had enough. Her fear tank was empty, and she was finally home, playing on her turf. All these fantastical characters pouring into her backyard in the dead of night threatening to kill her—she was done with it. While Geronimo and Murdock watched in stunned silence, Eleanor raced toward Krampus, though slightly to the left. She knew every contour, every divot, and every lump in the grass. She had traversed the yard from every possible angle. As Krampus followed her, she dragged him as if on a string along a trajectory that lead to a hole two feet wide, two feet long, and two feet deep. She knew exactly where it was because she had made it herself two months ago. It was a butterfly museum that never quite came to fruition. Its lack of success was mainly due to Eleanor's inability to instruct or communicate with the butterflies in any way whatsoever.

Krampus's left foot hit the hole dead on. His body smacked the ground hard and fast. The hatchet escaped his grasp and flung into the air before bouncing along the grass and landing at Eleanor's feet. She picked up the hatchet and ran toward the fallen Krampus. With hot rage, she raised the hatchet high above her head as Murdock and Geronimo ran over to them. She swung the hatchet down toward his growling, supine face, but Krampus caught the handle of the hatchet in the air, his hand pressing over hers. He then grabbed her ankle and tossed her into the air. She lost her grip on the hatchet as she flew a few feet past Krampus and tumbled to the grass. Once her body came to a stop, she assessed herself for injuries. None. As soon as she stood back up, a figure from the side of the house, hidden in the shadows, grabbed her and pulled her into the darkness. "Shh. It's going to be all right," said the voice.

Meanwhile, Murdock and Geronimo stood just a few feet from Krampus. With the hatchet raised, Krampus's eyes darted from the elf to the gnome and back again. Finally, he turned to Geronimo and asked, "What're you, some kind of a gnome?"

"What're you, some kind of malnourished, half dinosaur?" replied Geronimo. Krampus laughed for a moment, causing all three to laugh. Then abruptly the hatchet-wielding madman stopped laughing and chucked the small axe at Geronimo. The gnome timed his jump perfectly, somersaulting over the spinning hatchet in midair. He landed back on his feet. The axe bounced harmlessly against the rocks near the pond. Krampus narrowed his eyes, leaped to his feet, and charged Geronimo. The gnome executed his easiest and quickest evasion when it came to any sort of attack, which was to run through the attacker's legs, clearing Krampus's legs just fine. Unfortunately for Geronimo, he did a slight miscalculation of Krampus's anatomy. The scaly, slender rope-sized tail, previously coiled and camouflaged against his back, walloped Geronimo square on the head. The blow sent the gnome rolling through the grass. Krampus spotted the gnome and raced toward him. He scooped the gnome up and raised him to his mouth.

"Sorry, no time for goodbyes," said Krampus. Geronimo dangled precariously from his left foot, pinched between Krampus's thumb and index fingers. Krampus opened his mouth, tilted his head, and closed his eyes. Suddenly, a tranquilizer dart came down from the night sky and shot deep into Krampus's right arm. His head seemed to move in slow motion as he turned toward the foreign object lodged halfway into his lean and slimy bicep. "What's happening?" Krampus asked aloud. His eyes looked lost, scared, and dreamy, just before they rolled to the back of his skull as he collapsed. Geronimo jumped out of his hand mid-fall and landed on his feet. He looked over at the house where he had last seen Eleanor. No sign of her. He turned back to Murdock, who was looking straight at the sky, searching for whoever shot the dart.

"Where did Eleanor go?" asked Geronimo.

"I didn't see," said Murdock. Geronimo looked up into the night sky. It was a clear night, yet there were no stars directly above them.

"What do you think it is?" Geronimo asked.

"I don't know," said Murdock. "But whatever it is, it must be on our side." With that said, another dart whizzed down from the black abyss high above and hit Murdock in the side of his neck. Geronimo noticed how much smaller the second dart was, as if customized for someone Murdock's size.

"Gah!" yelled Murdock. "The neck? Seriously?" He struggled violently against the attack, pivoting in circles as he grabbed at the dart to pull it out. Before being able to do so, the elf collapsed on the grass and lost consciousness.

Geronimo stared at Murdock's body, then at Krampus's body, which was now—*gone*! He turned his head to where Murdock was lying. The elf's body had now also vanished.

"Holy nutmeg," Geronimo muttered. He looked up at the black blob above him as he started a dead sprint toward the house. *They can't get me in the house*, Geronimo thought. *As long as I make it before—*

Thwup! The dart tagged him in the back. He fell forward onto the ground. Geronimo could tell the dart was in that exact spot one can never scratch when it itches, just below the shoulder blade and beside the spine. Wincing as he pushed himself off the ground, Geronimo turned his head to look up at the dart-hurling blob. The pure darkness above was replaced by stadium-sized lights that were growing larger and larger, until Geronimo's entire field of vision was swallowed up with light. *How many more times am I going pass out?* was the gnome's last thought before passing out.

Hours later, after the big black thing in the sky had left and the backyard was once again quiet and empty, the unicorn's chipped horn appeared above the surface of the time pond. It bobbed like a buoy as the rest of the unicorn slowly emerged. Once on dry land, the unicorn shook its soaked head. It turned back to the pond and thirstily drank. A swirl of wind picked up in the middle of the yard. The wind funneled into a long, skinny tornado. The unicorn picked its head up from the pond and looked over at the commotion. Nancy had fallen asleep beside the pond, but was now stirred awake. She poked her head above the large rocks that encircled the perimeter of the pond. The middle of the tornado swelled to the point of bursting. When it did, all went silent and calm again. Replacing the wind was a crouched Gromp.

Nancy ducked her head back behind the rocks. She was mad at herself for falling asleep. She was too scared to move when everyone was getting speared from the sky and then disappearing.

The crunching of the grass was getting closer. Whoever it was headed straight for the unicorn.

"Hey there," said Gromp. Nancy couldn't tell if he was addressing her or the unicorn. Her eyes were closed and her body was curled into a fetal position. "What's your name?" Gromp asked with kindness in his voice. Now Nancy knew he was talking to the unicorn. "Are you all right?" She opened her eyes and looked up. Gromp was looking down at her. A smile stretched across his face when her eyes opened.

"It's okay," Gromp said, "I'm not going to hurt you."

"I know who you are," said Nancy. "You're his son. You're going to send me back there."

"It's true I am his son," Gromp said. "But I'm not going to send you back there." He offered her his hand. "I'm going to bring you home."

She wasn't sure why, but she instantly believed him, and took his hand.

PART 3

~37~
THE TRIAL

When Geronimo came to, he was in a courtroom, perched high in the balcony. He looked out the nearest window and saw a bucolic country setting. Dirt roads and farmlands as far as the eye could see. Chickens wandered across the lawn. It all looked so charming that he almost didn't notice the five suns in the sky. He scanned the well-lit mass of mythical creatures for a familiar face.

They were nearly all there. Murdock, Clarence, and the entire elf community took up the perimeters as they sat on all the windowsills for better viewing. Ten polar bears also sat together, all wearing tan suits with the acronym "PBCC" stitched across the backs. To his relief, Geronimo also spotted a heavily bandaged T.C. in the congregation below. He stood on all fours lengthwise in the small alley between the seat and the bench in front of him. On one side of T.C. were a few shirtless boys looking around the room with lost and repentant looks on their faces. On the other side was Dr. Tinsel, whom Geronimo remembered from the initial physical he underwent upon arrival at HQ. The camel queen sat with Sergio, Sophia, and Ernesta in the back seats of the courtroom. Ernesta was in a full body cast. Drawings of lizards covered the hard white plaster. Geronimo even saw Ester and Barlow from his boat trip. Barlow sat by himself in the back corner of the room, anxiously looking at his watch while gently rocking a stroller with a sleeping infant. Ester sat across the aisle from Barlow, chatting up the figure next to him who was shrouded in a dark robe. The robed stranger kept scooting away from the desperately conversant, oversized bunny.

Finally, the gnome's attention was directed to the witness stand, where the voice of Dan Majerle boomed outward. The polar bear sat on the witness stand, wearing a purple polo shirt and holding a basketball.

"I never dealt with him directly," Dan said. "Everything went through Snopes, God rest his soul." Dan made the sign of the cross, closed his eyes, and kissed the basketball, while looking upward toward the heavens. Geronimo shook his head and focused his attention on the lawyer, who stood a few feet in front of the stand, his arms folded, saying nothing.

"Next witness!" yelled Judge Rampart, a full-grown female polar bear adorned in judge's robes, as she slammed her gavel down. Dan left the witness stand and walked back to his seat, rejoining the throng of life-forms sardined into row after row of benches.

Geronimo noticed Dan had directed all his answers at a lawyer, and that there were silent gaps between his responses, as if someone unheard was peppering him with questions.

"You're awake," said a voice directly behind him. Geronimo turned around. It was Henry. He was dressed in a white suit with a baby-blue bowtie. His hair was slicked back, though muffed up on the side.

"Henry?" Geronimo asked.

"Sorry," said Henry as he wiped a line of drool from his chin and fixed his hair. "I was supposed to watch you and I fell asleep myself."

"What's going on?" asked Geronimo.

"I couldn't help it," said Henry. "This thing is so boring. You're lucky you slept through nearly all of it."

"Where am I?" Geronimo demanded.

"How did you find me?" rasped a familiar voice from the witness stand. The unusual accent boomed through the old building. Geronimo turned back toward the witness stand and saw Freeze Pop sitting there wearing a tutu with heavy face makeup. Leaves and bramble were stuck all over his puffy, white coat, as if he had been either running through the woods or living in it for an indefinite amount of time.

"You're at Krampus's trial," whispered Henry into Geronimo's ear. "Keep your voice down."

Geronimo swiveled back around to face Henry. "How does Krampus get a trial?" said the gnome.

"He's awake!" Dan roared from his seat in the benches below. Geronimo could feel the voice shoot through the back of his head.

"Is everyone looking at me?" Geronimo asked.

Henry looked at him, then looked out the window, and then back at him. "The chickens aren't looking at you," he finally said.

Geronimo turned around. Every eye in the courtroom was on him. There at the two long tables nearest the stand where the Frogg Brothers standing at their respective tables. Krampus sat beside his defense attorney, Darrell Frogg, while at the other table was Eleanor, who sat with her prosecuting attorney, Herman Frogg. After a long and awkward silence of staring at the minuscule gnome high up in the balcony, Judge Rampart, peering through binoculars to get a better look at Geronimo, finally said, "Let's take a short recess. Bring the gnome to my chambers." The nine-foot tall, eight-hundred-pound judge got up from her ornately carved, wooden throne and lumbered through a door behind her.

"You'd better get going," Henry said, poking him from behind.

With the curtains drawn, the judge's chamber was dark and cool. The room reeked of mahogany. The leather chairs squeaked under Geronimo's feet. Judge Rampart poured herself a club soda from a bar behind her desk.

"We apologize for the dart summons. It's an unpleasant enough experience as it is, and unfortunately, we underestimated the intensity of your particular dosage." The judge slipped pickled herrings into her drink and sat down behind her desk. "To be quite honest, we weren't sure when you were going to wake up."

"I'm fine," was all Geronimo could think to say at the moment.

"Good," said the judge. "Do you know what's happening out there?"

"Not really," said Geronimo. The silence that followed his remark did not sit well with Judge Rampart. She was hoping and anticipating some interest and/or curiosity on behalf of the gnome.

"Would you like to know what we're doing?" asked the judge.

"Not really," said Geronimo. The judge's eyes widened with disbelief. *Whoops*, thought Geronimo. That was the wrong thing to say. "I mean, I'm just so tired," he corrected.

Judge Rampart looked at her watch. "You just woke up from a fourteen-hour nap," she said. "Don't tell me you're tired."

"Sure, then," said Geronimo. "Go 'head. Tell me. I'm interested."

The judge looked at him, unamused by his feigned interest. She plowed on. "The reason it matters to me that you know why we're here is because you'll be taking the stand soon."

"What?" said Geronimo, suddenly very interested.

231

"Herman Frogg called you as a witness," said the judge. "We were just waiting for you to wake up. Naturally, he'd be telling you this now, in person, if he could, but unfortunately, both lawyers are under double-blind confidentiality."

"What does that mean?" asked Geronimo.

"It means that they have the legal right to abstain from speaking. The stakes are high at this level of the judicial system. Everyone has enemies, especially the Frogg brothers. One of them says something that tips the scale toward the wrong side, and it could mean their life. So they do all their communication through telepathy. Only witnesses called to the stand hear their questions. From here on they say nothing. They speak to no one."

"Okay, fine," said Geronimo, "and Krampus is on trial for being really horrible?"

"Crimes against humanity," the judge said flatly. "That's the official charge. If convicted, he would be put him in a maximum security prison on the far edge of the universe, where he would spend eternity."

"But he's clearly guilty," said Geronimo. "Why do you need a trial?"

"Everyone deserves a fair trial, Geronimo. And believe it or not, there are a sizeable number of constituents in Krampus's camp."

There was a knock at the door. "What is it?" she asked.

The bailiff, who had the body of a human with the head of a large owl, poked his giant, feathered head into the room. "Is he ready, Your Honor?" he asked in a low, rumbling voice.

"As ready as he's gonna be," said Judge Rampart. Her eyes evaluated Geronimo before she sprung to her feet. "Let's get back to it, shall we?" She motioned with her large furry paw toward the witness stand. He nodded and walked over to the outer lip of the witness box. He stood in front of a perched microphone that was exactly his size. A thought suddenly occurred to him, and he turned his head toward the judge and asked, "Do my parents know where I—"

Slam. Slam. Slam. Judge Rampart's gavel drowned out the gnome's request. The recess had ended.

Eleanor ate a sandwich out in the hallway during the recess. She sat on a bench outside the large, marble front doors of the courtroom. To the right of Eleanor sat Murdock on the arm of the bench, nibbling on a pickle. On the other side of Eleanor sat her self-appointed lawyer, Herman Frogg. Herman had not yet uttered a single word to Eleanor since they had met earlier that morning. He spoke exclusively through telepathy. The lawyer sat bent over, scribbling notes with an earnest, somber expression. Every once in a while he'd steal a glance up at Eleanor and then quickly return to scribbling. To pass the time, Eleanor talked to Murdock to keep her feeling something close to okay.

"You never do that to someone," Murdock was in the middle of saying to her, "you have no idea how horrifying that is."

"I'm sorry," said Eleanor. Her eyes welled up. "I'm sorry I'm so mean all the time." Her lips trembled as tears glazed over her vision. The wall in front of her melted into watercolors. "I'm sorry I don't know how to stop being mean." She turned toward Murdock. "I'm just getting worse and worse." Her tortured expression seemed to beg for answers on how to fix herself. "I get it now. I don't deserve parents. I don't deserve anything!" She buried her face in her hands.

Murdock could see Eleanor had hit rock bottom. Morale was inexcusably low. Her outburst of dismay had genuinely caught him off guard.

"Eleanor," he said, "Eleanor." She kept her face in her hands. Her fingers twitched against her forehead with each heave of her chest. "Look at me, darling child."

Something ruptured inside Eleanor. The grief was torn inside her, and she looked up at Murdock. Her face was a red mess of tear-blotted hair.

"I don't know what you're talking about," said Murdock. "You're talking complete nonsense." Eleanor looked confused.

Murdock put his pickle aside and leaned in. "I'm talking about messing with my whole you-know-what phobia."

Eleanor stared back at him. She had stopped heaving, stopped crying. Murdock looked down the hallway. An assortment of odd-looking creatures dressed in business attire walked up and down. The elf conspiratorially turned his head left, right, then straight ahead at Eleanor and said, "Snakes."

"You mean the garden hose?" asked Eleanor.

"Yes!" said Murdock, happy she had responded with anything at all. "I can't believe I even said the word."

"What word?" Eleanor asked.

Murdock saw a smirk develop on the left side of Eleanor's mouth. "You *are* no good. Don't make me say it again."

"You mean that 's' word?" asked Eleanor.

"This is my whole point. There is a mass insensitivity toward this very real and very common phobia."

"Say it," said Eleanor.

"Snakes!" yelled Murdock, terrified by his own words. "Snakes! Snakes! Snakes!" When he finally stopped screaming Eleanor was laughing. He somehow broke through the tyranny raging inside of her.

"You think this is funny?" asked Murdock. "You're sick." His disgusted tone only made Eleanor laugh harder.

At that moment, Richie and Susan walked through the glass doors of the front entrance, down the hall from where Eleanor and Murdock sat. They both had a woozy, almost drugged look on their faces as they passed through the metal detectors. Neither of them could currently recall how they arrived where they were, or why they were there in the first place. But that laugh. They both knew the laugh that bounced off the walls and filled their ears with a forgotten joy, and they jolted toward her.

"I'm so sorry about this," yelled the boatman. He ran up from behind Richie and Susan and emerged between them. Turning to face them, he told them he had to go, that he could not leave his boat for too long. Richie and Susan kept walking as if they could walk right through the boatman. They knocked him to the ground as they shouldered their way past him. Then they started to run toward the sound. She was still laughing when they spotted her. They froze, their hearts arrested, their minds in shock. With her back to them, they caught the slightest glimpse of her side profile as her head bowed with laughter. She seemed to radiate with life, healthy and unscathed. She continued to laugh at Murdock's expression, who now stared back at Richie and Susan over Eleanor's shoulder. He wondered who these people were, ogling at him and Eleanor.

"Don't look now, Eleanor," said the elf. "Looks like two creeps just slithered passed security. I'll take care of it."

Eleanor turned her head around.

"Mom! Dad!" she shouted. She bounded off the bench and ran to her parents' arms. All three Abbotts were together again. They hugged, kissed, and squeezed each other, crying and laughing at the same time, delirious with relief and happiness. Incapable of speech, they spun slowly in a circle in what felt like warm, glowing light.

Murdock and Herman, who finally picked his head up from his notebook, both sat gleaming with tears in their eyes over the spectacle.

The bailiff then opened the large marble doors. "We're starting back up," said the large, squid-headed man in uniform. All the creatures from various galaxies milling about the hallway made their way back into the courtroom with the casual pace of theatergoers returning from intermission.

"Mr. and Mrs. Abbott," Richie, Susan, and Eleanor suddenly heard invading their minds. They all looked up from their family love fest to the sight of Herman Frogg's silent grin. He stood in front of them, talking inside their respective heads without opening his mouth. "I am talking to you through certain metaphysical channels of communication that only a rare few species possess. Trust me when I say that I'm giving you this information, and no one else. Do you trust me?"

Richie and Susan both nodded.

"Now by order of the Universal Court," Herman continued, "Eleanor has to stay for the rest of the trial. If she doesn't, we have no shot at convicting Krampus and putting him away for good."

Richie and Susan just stared back at Herman. Their heads didn't so much shake in disagreement as much as tremble with trauma. They had their daughter and now they wanted out. Herman could see this. He quickly changed his tactic.

"Listen, Richie and Susan, I'm just asking you to sit in this room over there for one more hour. After that we'll send your whole family home."

"Yes," said Susan. "Yes, let's do that." Richie nodded with great vigor.

"Yes, of course," said Herman inside their minds. He then led the way through the open marble doors and back into the courtroom. Richie, Susan, Eleanor, and Herman all sat back down at the prosecution's table. Richie and Susan could now see all the fantastical beings their logic-clinging brains would not allow them to see back on Earth. They could now see the gnome on the stand, the same gnome they were convinced, for years, was a figment of their daughter's imagination. Richie's and Susan's eyes danced from Judge Rampart the polar bear to Geronimo the gnome with slow and baffled faces.

Slam. Slam. Slam.

"Court is now in session," said a voice from the speakers attached to the ceilings. Herman flashed a reassuring grin at Eleanor and her parents before getting up and sidling over to the witness stand. Geronimo appeared to be listening intently to the silence. He then raised his hand in the air and said, "I promise to tell the whole truth and nothing but the truth." Geronimo put his hand down and listened to more unheard instructions. He then leaned over and said, "My name is Geronimo Nelson. I am twelve years old . . ." Geronimo waited a beat, listening to Herman's question in his head. "No, I was not hired to kill Krampus. I agreed to participate in Santa's gnome exchange program." Geronimo paused again. "How do I think the exchange is going so far? Terrible. Doing this was without a doubt my worst decision ever. I'm tired. I miss my parents. Oh, and Santa's probably dead."

The crowd gasped with shock as they all stole glances at one another.

"I hate Christmas," said Geronimo, knocking the microphone onto its side and hopping off the witness stand. This brought the whole room to an uproar.

"The nerve of that gnome!" someone shouted from the crowd.

"What blatant disrespect!" shouted another.

Geronimo marched down the aisle, walked up to the large marble doors, and pushed. Nothing. They wouldn't budge. He looked up at the windows. Not only were they occupied by unpredictable Italian guinea pigs, they were also way too high up. He was trapped.

Slam. Slam.

"Mr. Nelson," boomed the judge from her judicial throne. "We all realize you've gone through quite an ordeal. And I'm sorry things didn't work out the way you had hoped. But whether or not you like it, you're a critical piece in one of the biggest trials of the universe. I give you my word that, if you choose to cooperate, this will all be over shortly." Judge Rampart stood up and motioned toward the empty witness stand. "Please. Humor us . . ."

Tight-lipped, Geronimo sauntered back to the witness stand and jumped back onto the front lip of the podium. He picked the microphone up off its side and looked over at Herman, waiting for him to approach and continue his questioning. Instead, the lawyer leaned back in his chair and raised his skinny legs up, resting them atop the table. Herman nodded toward the defendant's table. Geronimo looked over and there was Darrell, standing with a wide grin, ready to cross-examine.

"What about Nancy's lawyer?" Geronimo asked the judge. "Why isn't he asking me more questions?"

"I guess after your little stunt he decided that the prosecution rests for the time being," said Judge Rampart. Geronimo looked back at Herman, who was now shaking his head with disapproval at the gnome. *Great*, Geronimo thought, *I've ticked off my own lawyer.*

"You may begin your cross-examination, counsel," said the Judge.

"Please tell the court the Eleven Mysteries, Mr. Nelson," Darrell Frogg telepathically inserted into Geronimo's mind.

"I don't know what you're talking about," said Geronimo. He suddenly felt ambushed. He dreaded ever having to talk about the mysteries to anyone ever, though, deep inside, he knew someone or something would start asking questions. Darrell snickered as he folded his stick-like arms and stepped lightly toward the stand.

"We all know, Geronimo," Darrell continued inside the mind of the gnome, "that you had a little visitation with the Eleven Mysteries."

"What does that have to do with Krampus?" Geronimo turned to the judge.

"Your Honor," said Darrell in both the minds of Geronimo and Judge Rampart, "earlier this morning while our gnome friend was still getting in his beauty sleep, the boatman testified that he had dropped him off at the Great Gorge for the express intent of discovering the Eleven Mysteries. The information he is withholding, your Honor, may not only solve this case, it may also solve some of the biggest riddles of our universe."

"Answer the question, Mr. Nelson," said the judge, "or I'll have to hold you in contempt of court."

"I'm sorry," said Geronimo, "I swore not to speak of the Eleven Mysteries to anyone."

"Who did you swear this to?" Herman telepathically asked as he stood up from his chair. Geronimo looked around the room, from the judge, to the lawyers, to the jury, to the throngs watching seated in bench after bench, all looking at him with ravenous looks on their faces. Krampus, Murdock, and even T.C., all had their neck's strained forward and eyes wide with anticipation. Every window was now crowded with the faces of outside onlookers. The only person that looked concerned with his actual well-being was Eleanor, who looked on with sad and helpless eyes.

"Who did you swear this to?" repeated Herman inside Geronimo's mind.

"The cherry blossoms," said Geronimo. "I swore this to the cherry blossoms."

"I don't understand," Herman said aloud. The whole courtroom released a collective gasp from the shock of finally hearing one of the lawyers speak. Herman's face turned red, clearly a slip up. Darrell glared at his brother with a disapproving look on his face.

"After I fell into the gorge," said Geronimo, "I found myself running down a trail beside a lake. Cherry blossoms lined both sides of the path. I know this sounds crazy but the cherry blossoms spoke to me while I ran. They revealed to me the Eleven Mysteries and then made me swear not to tell another soul. They told me if I revealed the mysteries to anyone, it could cause a great universal battle that would go on for eons to come. After I swore to the trees that I wouldn't tell anyone, I woke up back in the dungeon."

"That's all good and well, Mr. Nelson," said Judge Rampart. Her voice tightened as she started to lose control of the volume of her voice. "But if you don't reveal to the court what the flowers told you, I will have to detain you along with your precious humans in a holding cell for an indefinite amount of time. Unless, that is, you decide to cooperate." Geronimo heard a soft growl escape the judge's muzzle as she flashed her large white teeth at him. He looked over at Eleanor and her parents. They all had heartsick expressions on their faces. He couldn't bear causing them another moment of strife. He would tell them everything if that meant releasing him and the Abbotts.

"If I tell you everything," Geronimo said as his head nodded in the direction of the Abbotts, "they go home, safe and sound?"

"Of course," said Judge Rampart.

"Don't tell them!" yelled Eleanor.

"Don't tell 'em squat!" yelled T.C. Dr. Tinsel quickly scolded him for getting so excited.

Slam. Slam. "Quiet!" snapped the judge. Her head swiveled back to Geronimo. The gnome looked around the room, let out a sigh, and began. "The first mystery is that everything changes. The second mystery is that we are all here for a reason. The third mystery is that no one remembers what that reason is. The fourth mystery is something about pancakes, I think. Look, to be honest, I don't even remember them all."

"We have ways of making you remember," said Judge Rampart, snarling her way through the words.

"Wait a minute," replied Geronimo as he hopped on top of the microphone, ready to flee like a kitchen mouse. "I'm not the one on trial here. I'm just part of some exchange program that went horribly wrong."

"While all that may be true, the Eleven Mysteries takes precedent." The judge raised her gavel. *Slam. Slam.* "Guards!" she yelled, "take the gnome and the human family to the holding cell!"

Suddenly, eight-foot-tall, elephant-headed guards appeared out of hidden doors behind the jury in the back of the courtroom. One marched toward Eleanor and her parents while the other marched toward Geronimo.

"No!" yelled Eleanor. The Abbotts hugged each other tight. "Please stop! Don't take us!" Susan begged.

"No, please don't!" begged Richie. He turned to Herman. "You promised us you'd take us home!" Herman closed his eyes and put his hands in the air as if the whole matter was out of his hands now. At first sight of the mega-elephant guards, Geronimo's initial thought was to hurl the microphone he stood on top of at Judge Rampart's head. Though this would not have been at all constructive, it would have been deeply satisfying to Geronimo. He was in the act of picking the microphone up, in fact, when a swirling wind swelled up out of nowhere and knocked everyone in the room off of their seats. Tornado winds seemed to burst into existence in the middle of the courtroom, specifically the space between the lawyers' tables and the judge's seat. The elephant guards were blasted against the wall, unable to move against the cyclonic force of the wind. At the onset of the change in weather, both Frogg brothers pushed their respective tables onto their sides to act as shields against the furious wind.

Meanwhile, Geronimo was walking around the podium's bottom. He was slammed against the wall behind him and then he scurried to the refuge of the hollow base of the podium. He found a hole for the microphone cord, ran through, and took a peek. At that moment, the wind dissipated, abruptly and completely.

All was still when Eleanor looked over the edge of the turned-over table. There in the space between them and the judge she saw Gromp, Nancy, and the unicorn. She watched the unicorn rotate its body toward her direction. For the second time, Gromp picked out Eleanor in a crowded place. He pointed at her head poking above the pitched table and said, "*You*," just as he had done at the police station. "Come here! Quick!"

"We're getting you out of here," roared Nancy. Richie decided to trust the courtroom crashers. He grabbed Susan's hand and put his daughter's arms around his neck. Richie and Susan high-stepped over the toppled table and ran toward the unicorn.

"Guards!" shouted Judge Rampart. "More guards!" The elephant guards resumed their march toward the gnome and humans. More guards now flooded out of the secret doors behind the jury.

"Just hold on to the unicorn!" said Gromp to the Abbotts. Richie, Susan, and Eleanor each held on to a leg of the unicorn.

"Geronimo!" yelled Eleanor as she looked over at the empty witness stand. "Where did he go?"

"I'm up here," said Geronimo, who had entangled himself in the unicorn's mane. "Let's get outta here!"

"Nooo!" shouted Krampus as he hopped over the table and charged the unicorn. Gromp fussed with the inside of his coat, pushing in certain coordinates. Then the wind picked back up again. Krampus and the elephant guards, who were now just mere feet from the huddled group, were knocked back off their feet from the circling winds. Gromp, Geronimo, Eleanor, Richie, Susan, and the unicorn were in the dead calm of the eye while everything around them seemed to spin faster and faster. Eleanor's last thought before vanishing was of her arms stretching toward the ceiling like Stretch Armstrong.

Then there was nothing. No wind, no unicorn, no Gromp, no Abbotts, and no gnome. T.C. looked around the courtroom as the dust settled. He started a slow and solitary clap of approval. The sound of his satisfaction bounced obnoxiously off the big stone walls until Judge Rampart had had enough.

Slam. Slam. Slam.

"Next witness!"

38
DONKEY HUMOR

So what happened after that?" asked Penelope. "Did they find Krampus guilty or not?"

Geronimo and his parents ate along the knobby and gnarled base of the Old Oak Diner. It was a crisp, clear summer night in late July. Stars were scattered like diamonds across the dark sky.

"I told you already, Ma," said Geronimo. "I don't know yet either."

"What about Nancy?" asked Harry. "What happened to her?"

Geronimo took a small, black space-texter out of his pocket to check the small glowing screen. "Gromp brought her back home," he told his parents with his eyes fastened to the glowing screen. "We went back in time and dropped her off just a few hours after her actual abduction."

"Honey, put that thing away," his mother said. "You know how I hate those things out during dinner."

"Sorry, it's just that Murdock said he'd space-text me the verdict," said Geronimo. "They're supposed to come to a decision any minute now. It's the longest-running trial in the history of the Universal High Court." He gave his screen one last glance before pocketing his space-texter.

"Well, I'm glad it all worked out for you, Momo," said his mother.

"Mom, I asked you not to call me that in public," said Geronimo.

"But, really," said Penelope, "it's done wonders to your self-confidence."

"Actually, your mother's right," said Harold. "Ever since you've been back home, you've been a different gnome," Harold continued. "Taking the garbage out without me asking first, building a work bench, organizing a neighborhood movie night . . . you've really come out of your shell."

"Thanks, Dad," was all Geronimo could think to say. On cue, a group of gnomes Geronimo's age walked by them and one of them asked, "Hey, G, we still on for *Gnomasaurus III* tomorrow night?"

"Of course!" Geronimo yelled back, rolling his eyes toward his parents as the group walked off whooping and high-fiving each other over the news. *Bzzz, bzzz* went his pocket. Geronimo looked up at his mother, his mouth full of zucchini cake. She gave him a silent nod of permission to check it. Geronimo took the space-texter out and gazed at the glowing screen. He stopped chewing. A look of dread crept over his face.

"What is it, Geronimo?" asked Penelope.

"He was found not guilty."

"No way!" said Penelope.

Bzzz went the space-texter. Geronimo read: "Krampus testified that he's a changed man. After what happened to his brother there's no point to continuing his 'rehabilitation program,' as he called it."

"Do you think it's true, son?" asked his father. "Do you think Krampus turned a new leaf?"

Geronimo looked at his dad. "Honestly, Dad, having never really gotten to know him, I think it would be careless of me to comment."

Geronimo's parents sat back on their knobby stumps, impressed by their son's words. "Wow," said Harry, "you really have grown up."

"Maybe I just know the right things to say," said the twelve-year-old. He winked as he took a bite of his caterpillar salad.

"Like I said, kiddo," said his father as he snatched a caterpillar from his son's plate and popped it into his own mouth, "you really have grown up."

After the verdict, Krampus was escorted out of the courtroom amidst a divisive uproar. The ones who backed him and the ones who wanted him locked away jumped at each other's throats. During the melee, Krampus walked out of the building a free man, buttressed by four elephant-headed judicial guards.

Outside, Krampus walked in a straight line for a quarter of a mile until he hit a narrow, winding river. In the river was a rickety waterlogged pier where the boatman had tied his pirogue. Krampus walked down the pier and stared down at the bright, clear water that contrasted with his gnarled, bloody feet. He sat down on the pier's edge and dipped his wretched toes into the cool water. He gazed into the ripples and followed the current with his eyes as it coiled into the murky distance. The current moved toward much darker weather.

"Where to, chief?" asked the boatman.

"Black Falls," replied Krampus.

"Black Falls?" repeated the boatman. "What business do you have in Black Falls?"

"Quickly," said Krampus. He jumped into the boat and looked back in the direction he had come. There was shouting through the trees. They were coming after him. He unzipped the fanny pack around his waist and threw down a shimmering gold airline ticket onto the boat floor.

"Why are you littering on my boat?" asked the boatman.

"That's not littering, that's bribing," said Krampus. "Ever been to San Diego?"

"Round-trip?"

"Of course."

"Deal," said the boatman. He grabbed the ticket and put it in a canvas bag near the back of the boat. He shoved hard off the column he had been holding and paddled with vigor into the direction of the current. As they moved down river, Krampus looked back in time to spot the angry mob pouring out of the foliage and onto the pier.

"There's an out-of-service pier near Black Falls," said the boatman. "That's the only reason I entertain the thought of going there. I can take you as far as that pier."

"Whatever," said Krampus.

The distance traveled was entirely unknown to both parties. Neither could guess how many nights of river travel had passed. The one thing they both knew was the smell of Black Falls, and how that smell can drift for miles. The smell was sour and acrid, like wheelbarrows full of rotten oranges. Through a rolling mist they looked at each other with scrunched-up faces. Finally, the boatman swung his canvas bag around his shoulder and steered the boat toward the left side of the river where he thought he saw the pier in the near distance.

"Pier's coming up," said the boatman. "So jump if you're gonna jump. I'm tying her up there."

After not moving an inch the entire trip, Krampus pounced on the boatman. "You'll do no such thing!" he shouted and tackled him to the ground. Krampus sat on top of him and tied up his hands and knees with the efficiency of someone who has had a lifetime's worth of practice tying people up.

"You didn't think I was gonna go to Black Falls alone did you?" said Krampus. "Frankly, Mr. Boatman, I'm too scared to go by myself."

"No! Don't do this!" said the boatman. "Let me go! We had a deal!"

Krampus looked up into the creeping darkness of the water. On his left he watched pass what he assumed was the out-of-service pier. Stalks of wood stood in the rushing water mangled beyond repair. There was no pier anymore.

"Your pier's gone!" Krampus shouted over the now thunderous sound of water. "I couldn't save you if I tried."

"You can still untie me!" yelled the boatman. Krampus shook his head as he sat on the wriggling boatman. His hands were on either side of the boat as it spun and tossed every which way. The vicious current propelled them closer and closer to the three-hundred-foot drop of Black Falls.

"Murrrr!" something groaned in the hazy distance, somewhere on land. Krampus and the boatman turned their heads toward the sound.

"Murrrr," it groaned again. The mournful tone was accompanied by galloping hooves.

"Thelma!" Krampus cried out. He stood up, not caring about the boatman anymore. "It's Thelma! She's come to try and save me!" The boatman took this opportunity to rub the rope around his wrists against the knife in his canvas bag. Krampus perched his body against the side of the boat as the animal continued its sad wailing. "You are the only one that's ever really cared about me, aren't you, Thelma?" asked Krampus. As if to answer him, Thelma's hoof prints appeared in the wet sand running along the roaring river, perfectly paced with the spinning boat. "Here I come, my pet!" he shouted to her. He timed it so that he would vault himself off the boat when it was nearest the river's edge, landing squarely atop the donkey. Meanwhile, the boatman had successfully freed his hands and feet from the rope. He grabbed the paddles from inside the boat and maneuvered the boat clumsily to the water's edge in a blast of white water against rock. The boat speared out of the water as he went airborne. His body separated from the airborne vessel midair and landed on a thin strip of wet beach that ran along the river.

"Turn!" the boatman heard Krampus shout in the distance through the black mist. "Turn, you dumb beast!"

The boatman staggered upward from the ground just in time to watch Krampus go sailing over the falls astride the shadow donkey. He could hear the donkey chuckling all the way down. He turned to look up river and saw something that caused a smile to stretch over his face. There was his canvas bag hanging from a high branch of a tree on the edge of the river. Frayed out from the bag was a flash of gold from the ticket's corner, whipping in the breeze.

39

TOO MANY SUCKERS

It was late August. More lemonade stands were popping up every day. A record heat had dug its heels into the neighborhood for the last few days, so every eight- to thirteen-year-old kid had the same bright idea. *Though they don't all live on Maple Lane*, thought Ricky.

He had a wild, trickster summer smile on his face. Standing over his slapped-together establishment, he knew that to get anywhere in this town you had to take Maple Lane. His house was smack dab in the middle of the lane, on the shady side of the street even, right where one might be predisposed to pull over and stop for a cool, refreshing beverage.

And, yes, he had to make the place look nice. His eyes passed over the dual coolers, the overhead "Lemonade for the People" banner, and the American flag taped across both coolers to top it all off. He was ready for a huge day. He had noticed on his nine a.m. bike recon around the neighborhood that most other stands (the Montgomerys, the Favrets, the Suzukis) were solo operations. Not him. Not this summer.

Suddenly, Bartlett's sweat-drenched forehead popped up from under the tablecloth directly below him. He looked stressed and overworked. He flailed his arm out over the rows and rows of colored jugs they had stored under the shade of the tablecloth.

"Okay, at the moment we have four jugs of traditional lemonade, three jugs of limeade, two of orangeade, and that one jug in the back there. I have no idea what's in it, but it tastes out of this world."

"Thanks, Bart," said Ricky. "You don't have to stay down there. You can come out if you like."

"No, no, please," said Bartlett. "I love it down here. I can't stand the heat."

"Oh, okay then," said Ricky. He noticed a car slow down as it approached his stand. "I'll let you know when I need more." Ricky nodded hurriedly, trying to end the conversation. He tried lowering the cloth on Bartlett but the elf threw his thin, little arm up, having a little left to say.

"Sure," said Bartlett, "Just so you know, though, I may have a little more of that mysteryade and then conk out for a few hours."

"Okay," said Ricky as he finally dropped the cloth over Bartlett. When Ricky looked back up, a woman was waiting from inside her car. Her engine was still on and she gave him a curious stare.

"Who're you talking to, sugar pie?" she asked.

"I was skyping my grandmother," Rickey said.

The woman immediately looked ashamed over her suspicion. "Oh, how wonderful," she said.

"She lives in Kansas," said Ricky. *I have to stop*, he thought.

"What does she do in—"

"We have four different ades: lemonade, limeade, orangeade, and mysteryade."

"Thank you, my boy," said the woman as she held up a list of names to read. "I'll take two lemonades, two orangeades, and one mysteryade."

Ricky's eyebrows went up. He didn't expect such large purchases right off the back. He flipped open the cooler lids. He saw lemonade and limeade. That's all. "If you'll excuse me for one moment," said Rickey as he dropped out of frame from behind the coolers. He lifted the tablecloth up to find an already dozing Bartlett.

"Rats," cursed Ricky.

"Excuse me," said a bright and bouncy voice directly above Ricky. He dropped the cloth and looked up. There was Eleanor holding a tray filled with colorful drinks. "You said two traditional, two orange, one mystery?" Eleanor asked the lady in the car. Rickey stood up and watched the transaction with relief and amazement.

"Uh, yes, that's right," said the lady as she took the drinks in two four-pack cup holders Eleanor had given her. "Thank you, sweetheart." The lady looked into her purse and took out two twenty-dollar bills. She turned to Eleanor as she held the money toward her and said, "Thank you for the speedy service. Here's to helping along a new enterprise."

Eleanor smiled as she took the money and gave it to Ricky, who quickly stashed the twenties into his toy cash register as the lady drove off. Ricky looked back up at Eleanor. Her face shone like an angel in the sun. After being gone for twenty-six days (Ricky had marked each day on his tropical rainforest-themed calendar that hung above his bed), it was as if she came back a different person. *A way, way better person*, thought Ricky. Ricky couldn't hold it in any longer. He had to ask.

"What happened to you, Eleanor?"

Eleanor had set the glass tray on the table beside the coolers. She was arranging the drinks by color. "What do you mean?"

"How come you're so nice now?"

Eleanor looked at Ricky and suddenly wanted to cry. She had been doing so good. Scores of therapists, trauma specialists, and even hypnotists had been working with her, along with her parents, helping to try and find meaning in what they had all gone through. Over the last few summer months, the Abbotts as a whole had been making great strides toward moving on and feeling normal. Though anytime, like now, when her abduction was directly addressed she couldn't help but wince. Her insides would get all tight and scrunched. She was afraid if she tried to say something her voice would crack and she'd fall completely apart right there in front of him. So she just looked at him very still with her eyes welling up.

"Hullo there!" bellowed a voice from a stopped car. Ricky and Eleanor both turned their heads. Sitting at the driver seat of a red, top-down convertible was a short, round, bearded man wearing dark shades. He had a faint scar across his forehead.

Eleanor immediately recognized him. Her jaw dropped.

"One lemonade, please," said the man in the convertible.

"But you're—" said Eleanor.

"I'm thirsty. That's what I am."

Ricky handed him a lemonade. The man in the convertible gave Ricky a certificate. "Sorry, I don't have any bills on me," said the man, then added, "but I'm not really sorry since your parents have plenty of money." Ricky read the certificate.

"Will you accept a certificate for free karate lessons at the local dojo?" asked the man. Ricky frowned, nodding his head, and said, "Sure." He quickly folded the certificate up and slammed it away into his toy register. The man shifted the car back into drive.

"There's just one more little bit of business I have with you two before I shove off," said the man. He took a sip from the lemonade. "Mmm!" he exclaimed with lips shut. "Perfect. I believe you two have something of mine." Eleanor and Ricky both looked at each other.

"Bartlett!" the man yelled. "Bartlett I know you're under there!"

A few moments passed before Bartlett stumbled out from under the table on the street side. He yawned, stretched, and looked around, still collecting his bearings. "Do I *have* to go back?"

"Yes," said the man. "You signed a contract."

Bartlett looked at Rickey and Eleanor and waved goodbye. He then grabbed a mysteryade from the tray and climbed into the man's car.

"You be a good boy this year, Ricky," said the man. He put his car into drive. "And listen to Eleanor. She'll steer you right." He winked at Eleanor, then nodded at the both of them. Eleanor could see holographic candy canes flash off of Santa's black lenses.

"Enjoy the summer, kids," said Santa. And with that, the convertible roared off. Rickey watched the shimmering red vehicle drive the rest of the stretch down Maple Lane until it turned a corner and disappeared.

"I guess that was Bartlett's owner?" wondered Ricky. He turned back to Eleanor who was texting away on a small black space-texter. "What're you doing?" asked Rickey. "Who're you texting?"

"Someone smaller than an elf," she said.

254

Far out on the Poconos Plateau, overlooking Promised Land Lake, Murdock, Vera, Tut, and Lu found a perfect little spot: reclusive, near the water, and far from humans. Tut and Lu splashed in the water while Vera sunned on the beach, a freshly laundered floral dishrag laying between her and the hot sand. Beside her, Murdock sat in a fold-up chair meant for a toddler. With a self-concocted hazelnut daiquiri sitting in the sand within arm's reach, his smile felt as wide as the lake.

Bzzz went his phone. Murdock looked at it but didn't pick it up. He let it buzz three more times.

"Just take it," said Vera, her face buried in her folded arms.

Murdock picked it up. "I'm sorry, Murdock is unavailable right now. He is currently enjoying a well-earned vacation."

"Murdock," said Geronimo on the other line. "I just got word from Eleanor that she saw Santa."

"Yeah, he made a full recovery. Elfish medical care is no joke. Their dentistry alone is universally renowned. Can I go now?" asked Murdock.

"Sure," said Geronimo.

"See you at the reunion?" asked Murdock.

"What reunion? No thank you."

"I'm just kidding, there's no reunion. Have a fun summer, Geronimo. It was a pleasure working with you."

"Same here."

Geronimo hung the phone up on the inside wall of the hollowed out oak tree. It was late into the night as he sat on the rounded half walnut shell in the kitchen. He stared at his half-eaten cucumber sandwich. He was about to get up and head back to bed when his dad shuffled out of the shadows.

"Can't sleep either, huh?" asked his dad, taking a seat next to him on another shell. He opened a bag of peanuts that laid on the compact disc they used as a kitchen table. Harry gazed into the darkness as he munched on peanuts.

"They're better boiled," said his father.

More silence as Geronimo yawned and rubbed his eyes.

"Those Eleven Mysteries you talked about, Geronimo," his dad brought up out of nowhere, "did you really forget them?"

Geronimo looked up at his father with a wary and somewhat disappointed expression on his face. He wasn't sure how to answer.

Blrring, blrring went the phone he had hung up just moments ago. Startled, Geronimo looked at his dad.

"Go 'head, pick it up," said Harry.

Geronimo picked the phone up. "Hello?" He nodded. "Yes . . . I see . . . of course," he said, then more silent listening. Then finally, "Sure, you could put her on . . . hi . . . are you nervous? You should be. You'll never regret doing it, and you'll never want to do it again. It will be the best and worst time of your life . . . I highly recommend going through with it."

More silence. Harry stopped eating the nuts he chewed on and listened to his son's frank tone.

"Are you still there?" asked Geronimo. "Oh, good . . . are we good? Okay . . . it's late . . . no worries . . . best of luck." Geronimo hung up the phone.

"Who was that?" asked Harry.

"Some girl named Cleo, my age, lives on the east side. She wanted to know if she should sign up for the Gnome Exchange Program this coming winter," said Geronimo.

"And you think she should do it?" asked Harry.

"It's like you always say, Dad," said Geronimo with a snickering grin on his face, "there's a sucker born every month." Geronimo stood with his dad.

"Minute," said his father, "a sucker born every minute."

"That's a lot of suckers," said Geronimo.

"Would you two stop horsing around and go back to sleep!" hushed Penelope from her bed somewhere in the darkness.

"Good night, Momo," said Harry.

"Good night, Dad," said Geronimo.

With that, father and son receded into the pitch-black perimeter of the hollowed-out oak tree. Five minutes of serene silence passed. And then:

Clop, clop, clop, clop, clop, clop walked the unicorn toward their tree. Her massive head just barely fit through the carved-out aperture of the tree trunk they called a home. The big gray nostrils found the mayonnaise, dill, and cucumber. She munched away at the table, trying to be quiet.

"Great," muttered Penelope, "y'all woke up Natasha."

DISCUSSION QUESTIONS

1. What or who gives us the authority to judge others?

2. Is it possible for Krampus to transform into a source of good? His near final scene at the river was my Raskol-nikov send-up. In *Crime & Punishment,* it's clear Raskol-nikov does transform, and Krampus, in a similar natural setting, nearly also does, but not quite.

3. What would be your Eleven Mysteries?

4. Do we solve problems by adding more wood to the fire? In other words, do we fight violence with more violence? Anger with more anger? Rose calls her husband out on this point during their phone call with Krampus.

5. Early in the book, while looking in the mirror, Krampus says, "We are who we choose to be." Do you believe there is any truth to this statement? In other words, how much of who we are is determined by our environment versus our own volition?

6. If you had to choose between saving Eleanor and her parents or revealing the Eleven mysteries, which would you choose? Considering the vast importance of the Mysteries, which choice is more noble in your mind?

7. Of all the talking animals and creatures in the story, the unicorn has no speech. Why do you think that is?

ABOUT THE AUTHOR

MATT CALIRI was born and raised in the bayous of Louisiana. Since then, he has lived all across the country. He currently works with children who have behavioral challenges at the Academy for Precision Learning, a school that makes miracles happen every-day. He lives with his out-of-this-world wife, Julie, their two little jelly beans, Tavi and Mila, and his rock star step-daughter, Ella. This is his first published novel and his eighty-fifth attempt at get-ting attention.

SCAN TO VISIT

KRAMPUSNEWS.COM